PLOUGHSHARES

Winter 1995–96 · Vol. 21, No. 4

GUEST EDITORS
Tim O'Brien *&* Mark Strand

EDITOR
Don Lee

POETRY EDITOR
David Daniel

ASSISTANT EDITOR
Jodee Stanley

FOUNDING EDITOR
DeWitt Henry

FOUNDING PUBLISHER
Peter O'Malley

ADVISORY EDITORS

Russell Banks
Ann Beattie
Anne Bernays
Frank Bidart
Rosellen Brown
James Carroll
Madeline DeFrees
Rita Dove
Andre Dubus
Carolyn Forché
George Garrett
Lorrie Goldensohn
David Gullette
Marilyn Hacker
Donald Hall
Paul Hannigan
Stratis Haviaras
DeWitt Henry

Fanny Howe
Marie Howe
Justin Kaplan
Bill Knott
Maxine Kumin
Philip Levine
Thomas Lux
Gail Mazur
James Alan McPherson
Leonard Michaels
Sue Miller
Jay Neugeboren
Tim O'Brien
Joyce Peseroff
Jayne Anne Phillips
Robert Pinsky
James Randall
Alberto Alvaro Ríos

M. L. Rosenthal
Lloyd Schwartz
Jane Shore
Charles Simic
Gary Soto
Maura Stanton
Gerald Stern
Christopher Tilghman
Richard Tillinghast
Chase Twichell
Fred Viebahn
Ellen Bryant Voigt
Dan Wakefield
Derek Walcott
James Welch
Alan Williamson
Tobias Wolff
Al Young

PLOUGHSHARES, a journal of new writing, is guest-edited serially by prominent writers who explore different and personal visions, aesthetics, and literary circles. PLOUGHSHARES is published in April, August, and December at Emerson College, 100 Beacon Street, Boston, MA 02116-1596. Telephone: (617) 824-8753. Web address: www.emerson.edu/ploughshares/.

EDITORIAL ASSISTANT: Maryanne O'Hara. INTERNS: Heidi Pitlor, Julie Wolf, and Todd Cooper. FICTION READERS: Billie Lydia Porter, Michael Rainho, Robin Troy, Stephanie Booth, Loretta Chen, Barbara Lewis, Will Morton, Joseph Connolly, Kevin Supples, David Rowell, Karen Wise, John Rubins, and Anne Kriel. POETRY READERS: Mathias Regan, Bethany Daniel, Kathryn Maris, Lisa Sewell, Tom Laughlin, Renee Rooks, Mary-Margaret Mulligan, Brijit Brown, Jenny Miller, Leslie Haynes, and Mike Henry.

SUBSCRIPTIONS (ISSN 0048-4474): $19/domestic and $24/international for individuals; $22/domestic and $27/international for institutions. See last page for order form.

UPCOMING: Spring 1996, a poetry and fiction issue edited by Marilyn Hacker, will appear in April 1996. Fall 1996, a fiction issue edited by Richard Ford, will appear in August 1996. Winter 1996–97, a poetry and fiction issue edited by Ellen Bryant Voigt, will appear in December 1996.

SUBMISSIONS: Please see page 221 for detailed submission policies.

Classroom-adoption, back-issue, and bulk orders may be placed directly through *Ploughshares*. Authorization to photocopy journal pieces may be granted by contacting *Ploughshares* for permission and paying a fee of 5¢ per page, per copy. Microfilms of back issues may be obtained from University Microfilms. *Ploughshares* is also available as CD-ROM and full-text products from EBSCO, H.W. Wilson, Information Access, and UMI.

Indexed in M.L.A. Bibliography, American Humanities Index, Index of American Periodical Verse, Book Review Index. Self-index through Volume 6 available from the publisher; annual supplements appear in the fourth number of each subsequent volume. The views and opinions expressed in this journal are solely those of the authors. All rights for individual works revert to the authors upon publication.

Distributed by Bernhard DeBoer (113 E. Centre St., Nutley, NJ 07110), Fine Print Distributors (500 Pampa Dr., Austin, TX 78752), Ingram Periodicals (1226 Heil Quaker Blvd., La Vergne, TN 37086), IPD (674 Via de la Valle, Solana Beach, CA 92075), and L-S Distributors (436 North Canal St. #7, South San Francisco, CA 94080).

Printed in the United States of America on recycled paper by Edwards Brothers.

© 1995 by Emerson College

CONTENTS

Winter 1995–96

TIM O'BRIEN

Introduction

The six stories in this issue speak for themselves—forcefully, lucidly—and whatever I might say about them is irrelevant to their value as literature. The very notion of an "introduction," at least in this context, strikes me as peculiar to the brink of weird. A good story introduces itself, stakes its own artistic claims, connects itself both to the world and to literary matters. Obviously, since I selected these pieces, I am excited about their debut in *Ploughshares,* yet all I can do is urge that the coming pages be turned with care, hopefulness, and an open heart.

In a way, I am now a cheerleader. Lee K. Abbott, for example, is a writer whose work never fails to grip my heart, and "A Creature Out of Palestine," which appears here, is a story that makes me do cartwheels and yell, "Wow—read this!" It's the *wow* that matters. Not the *how.* I could elaborate, with a gun at my head, on Abbott's use of voice and irony and structure, but in the end such abstraction would amount to the unweaving of a well-made tapestry, displaying threads, destroying fabric. With good writing, I think, the most profound response is finally a sigh, or a gasp, or holy silence. As evidence, I offer the last sentence of "A Creature Out of Palestine: "He honked *adiós,* and for a time I listened to him go south, his a motor with rumble enough to make you smile, until there was only silence and me, blessed as are the dumb and well-fed, alone at my place." I have no desire to analyze such prose. Voice, sure. Irony, sure. But what about goose bumps? But what about chills and tremors? It's the woven *wow* that endures.

Similarly, in the case of "Easy Lay" by Joyce Carol Oates, I could devote enthusiastic paragraphs to issues of narrative strategy, to the author's cunning mix of reliable/unreliable narrator, but to do so would be a terrible disservice to the power and poignancy of the fiction itself. Better to yell *Bravo* at a line like this one: "Girls in my neighborhood were jealous of me the way their mothers were jealous of my mother with her blond hair, her face and figure and clothes and bronze Cougar." The pathos shines in a single vivid sentence; theme curls around physicality; reliability becomes not a just literary but a fully human problem, a chancre of the heart.

As I reread the stories by Janet Desaulniers and Gina Berriault, I feel a little dumb—that is, struck dumb, speechless—both unwilling and unable to say intelligent things. Intelligence isn't appropriate. Stomach squeezes mind. Desaulniers's "After Rosa Parks" leaves me sad and helpless, almost forlorn, almost queasy. As with Abbott's story, my eyes keep returning to the concluding sentence: "She knew she should turn around, start on dinner, but she stood a moment longer, staring out at the dark, and felt rising in her own mind the strangest and most fearsome comfort." *Fearsome comfort!* How do you analyze language like that? To what end? At what cost? Gina Berriault's "Who Is It Can Tell Me Who I Am?" has a similar effect on my intellectual appetite. I don't *want* to think. I want to feel, and keep feeling, as Berriault's prose does its lap and splash: "Further, he was a rarity for choosing to reside in what he called the broken heart of the city, or the spleen of it, the Tenderloin, and choosing not to move when the scene worsened."

I could cite equally deft, equally compelling sentences in the stories by Robert Cohen and Edward Hardy. In fact, I *will.* Cohen: "Pain, in her experience, never disappeared; it merely retreated for a while and then came back when least convenient in another form." Hardy: "Some days he was barely a let's-get-out-of-the-driveway sort of person."

But what's the point? The art in these six stories does its own internal explication, as art must, defining itself through the song of storytelling. If we like the music, we'll sometimes find ourselves humming a few bars, which is what I've done in this introduction.

MARK STRAND

Introduction

I was very casual about the way I chose poems for this issue of *Ploughshares*. I asked a few friends—those I happened to be in touch with—for recent unpublished work. I picked what I wanted. Then I went through poems that had come directly to *Ploughshares* and which the editors thought would interest me. I recall that most of the poems which I chose came to me this way.

I have no method for picking poems. I simply pick what pleases me. I am not concerned with truth, nor with conventional notions of what is beautiful. I tend to like poems that engage me—that is to say, which do not bore me. I like elaboration, but I am often taken by simplicity. Cadences move me, but flatness can also seduce. Sense, so long as it's not too familiar, is a pleasure, but so is nonsense when shrewdly exploited. Clearly, I have no set notion about what a poem ought to be.

Editing a single issue of *Ploughshares* has not allowed me to reach any conclusions about the state of American poetry. American poetry still seems to be "out there," practiced by others in many different places and under many different conditions. The number of people writing poems is vast, and their reasons for doing so are many, that much can be surmised from the stacks of submissions. Whether or not this is a healthy state of affairs I cannot say. I simply don't know. And yet, in a culture like ours, which is given to material comforts, and addicted to forms of entertainment that offer immediate gratification, it is surprising that so much poetry is written. A great many people seem to think writing poetry is worthwhile, even though it pays next to nothing and is not as widely read as it should be. This is probably because it speaks for a level of experience unaccounted for by other literary genres or by popular forms of entertainment. So, perhaps, the fact that so many are writing poetry is a sign of health.

Whatever the case, I hope that the poems I have chosen for this issue of *Ploughshares* find appreciative readers.

LEE K. ABBOTT

A Creature Out of Palestine

In those days, this was how you got to my place: Down from Ruidoso and Ski Apache, you took U.S. 70 (yes, the very route Billy the Kid, notorious bandito and youngster, hightailed horse-style to freedom in olden times) through Tularosa, past Ray's Tire and Lube and the C & C Restaurant and Lounge, into Alamogor-do ("Sunbird Capital of the World!") to the 54 cutoff where Wal-Mart Discount City meets ShowBizz Video and Big Jack's RV. Coming from the west—say, for argument's sake, you were over in Las Cruces, shaking your booty at El Patio or goofing on the *cholos* creeping their low-riders up Solano Street—you zoom through the Missile Range, past White Sands (the National Monument, bro!) and Holloman Air Force Base. Keep an eye peeled for the Taiwan Kitchen and Guy's Transmission. You spot Lester's Satellite Inn, you've gone too far.

From El Paso, which is how I got to where the going went, it's a whole other story: up 54, dead through the heart of the Ft. Bliss Military Reservation (remember, sweet pea, don't get off the road: Uncle Sam posted signs—*Danger! Peligro! Unexploded Shells*, etc.—death and destruction for the lost and lamebrain among us). About halfway up—it's eighty-three miles of scrub and chamisa and creosote and snakeweed and gnarled-up yuccas and, like set decoration from the cruel genius of Rod Serling himself, ugly mountains left and right of you across a desert flat and hostile and trackless as a nightmare—you wheeze into Oro Grande. Take a breather, *compadres*. Stop in at Dyson's Auction Barn, holler howdy or the like. If it's summer—shitfire, it's almost always summer thereabouts—pray to whatever beasts and gods you fear. Make an offering, neighbor. Write a last will and testament. Check your hoses and belts, tire pressure, your capacity for self-denial. Call your blood relations. Reconcile yourself to the wretched within you, slap on a sombrero, some sunscreen, then vamoose. Look for the Oro Grande National Forest on one side of the road. It's a single tree—a Chinese elm, maybe—as angry-looking as you would be were you lonely and windswept and ill-tended and bug-ravaged and laughed at for a lifetime.

An hour passes, you're almost at my place. You see O'Brien's Dog Ranch (imagine the hellhounds they breed out there—bald, probably, plus drooly and big as ninth-graders). Next is Alamo Transit Mix. You see Southend Road—this section of U.S. highway, two miles of blacktop and beer cans, is brought to you by the Hyper Hub Club—then Sunrise Doughnuts and the Golden Spur. Go as far as the Hi-D-Ho Drive Inn—no way am I making this up; we're talking corny here, not to mention trite, grim, imprecise, and dopey. You run in, say *Buenos Días* to the *chiquita* of the month, then oblige her to turn your ass around, amigo, because in your excitement and relief, in your fever and frenzy, you done missed my estate. *Mi rancherito. Mi casa grande.* Me, R. C. Hidey, late of this and that, white boy extraordinaire, master of disaster, former third-team All-Ohio defenseman for the Cleveland Heights Tigers hockey squad—you raced right by, podner. Didn't honk. Didn't wave. Didn't flip me the bird. And now here I wait, a half-mile south of you, standing on the two or three blades of Bermuda I tend, wearing dress sandals and my go-to-meeting Hanes T-shirt, the prime of my youth, brown as a creature out of Palestine, and utterly, unspeakably, inconceivably sore-hearted because once again, in a manner mysterious as the twentieth century itself, I have been overlooked. Ignored. *S-n-u*-double-fuck-ing-*b-e-d*.

How I came to be there in 1981 is, like the scorched geography itself, another circumstance worth a boo-hoo or two, so let's stipulate the following: Say you're a student—an *estudiante*, as it is *habla*ed in Nueva Mexico—no magna come louder to be sure, but a fifth-quarter junior Lamda Chi, eyeballing veterinary medicine, the USMC or rock 'n' roll star as career options. Say, according to the minor characters your life needs in order to be the adventure it is, that you're a "poophead" (your last girlfriend, an oily-jointed knockout named Nikki), a "slugabed" (your mother, Beverly, the Mighty Mouse of domestic engineering), or a "rounder" (your dad, Martin Hidey, Esq., attorney at law). Say you got all your fingers and toes, can snort Budweiser through your beezer, and recognize—so you think—the vast whatnot our to-and-fro has made of modern times. Suppose, moreover, that you're a standard issue ectomorph who more or less believes in life after death and the one shooter theory vis-à-vis JFK. Suppose X, suppose Y, suppose the whole damn alphabet, and when you're done with that—when a lanky, blond lefty with a birthmark like a top hat on his hairless heinie has come vividly to mind—then suppose this pile of cow flop: Comes a day, lo and verily, in the middle of English 563, Recent American Fiction, about page 68 of whatever helpful hogwash one talented typist has let spill from the yap of a dippy protagonist you've been told to root for, when you announce, in a voice like hail on a tin roof, "Christ Almighty, what am I doing here?" After that, Mister and Mrs. America, it's a stroll in high cotton. You rise, imperious as Caeser himself, leave the books behind, bid adieu to aghast Buckeyes near and far, clean out your cave at the frat house, stow the bong, and take up residence in the basement room of your old man's house on Stratford Street. Don't move for five months, fatten up like a swamp frog. Grow the beard you'd find on sixty percent of Pegleg's swabbies. Attend to the Grateful Dead. Learn the learnable via Marvel Comics and Phil Donahue. Piss into the wind. Look a gift horse in the yarbles. Wish upon a star. And then—drumroll, Ringo—say "yup" when Papa Bear, steamed as the Lord Humongous, suggests you might be better off were you, well, elsewhere. With your uncle Hal, for example. In the mountain time zone, mayhaps. The Great Southwest, in particular. The Land o' Enchantment.

Which is how this sorry specimen came to be as he was where he was when he met C-Dog Simpson and thereafter came to know, as surely as Laurel follows Hardy, shit from Shinola.

C-Dog looked like a man with three things on his mind, two of them involving money, or disease. That's what I was thinking that day he rumbled into my yard. I'd been watching *The Flintstones*, lusting unkindly for Betty Rubble, and keeping an ice pack on an eye that seemed to have turned black subsequent to a disagreement the night before at the Bear Trap, a bar I frequented Mondays and Thursdays. This must've been a Friday, I'm guessing. Late afternoon. The day like an oven on broil—another day from the less gladsome verses of the Old Testament. And me with a visitor in a vintage Chrysler Imperial. That's when I had my insight. Little did I, and so forth.

"Hey in there," he called, and I, thus beckoned and always curious about the foolish among us, moseyed forth.

He had red hair—rusty, actually. About the same rubbed-out, sun-faded color as the old Triumph sports car he was pointing to.

"This yours?" he asked, a second instance of snappy dialogue.

"Nope," I said, reasonable-like in spite of a hangover that Guinness might have wanted to hear about.

What with his posture and such, I had him made as a senior flyboy out at Holloman. Maybe that self-same sumbitch who, by dawn's early light, buzzed my acreage in his F-16. That, or a Texas-style horse owner from the Downs up at Ruidoso.

"What about this?" he said, indicating what lay around and about.

I studied what I was the sullen caretaker of: pallets of slump block, stock tanks, ATVs and brush hogs, a backhoe with a safety cage, a gooseneck hay trailer, PVC in quantity, John Deere's idea of a home-style tractor mower, a couple of generators—well, you get the picture: pre-abused manufactured items, all of which, given enough grease and greenbacks and cusswords, might in fact one day work.

"Hal's," I told him.

He nodded, doing something Dennis Hopperish with his lips.

"My uncle," I said. "He's the broker," I added, using the word I'd been told to. "I'm the help."

He was sitting in the Triumph now. Flyboy, definitely. Had that sassy cockpit manner about him. Made you want to scare up a claw hammer, mash it on his trigger finger.

"So where can I find Hal?" he asked.

In town, I told him. Did he know the Sí Señor restaurant?

"On Tenth?" he said.

It was my turn to nod now. Next to the Happy Booker, I told him. Couldn't miss it. I had a girlfriend worked there. Mona. Mona Elena Fernandez. Ummmm-doggy.

"Got the trots there once," he was saying, heaving himself out of the Triumph. "The combo plate, I believe."

He seemed to be expecting an apology, but I, nephew and dick-weed, wasn't about to deliver it.

"He's not my uncle, actually," I said. "My mother's cousin, more like it. I call him Uncle as a courtesy. He's Arab, we think. He's got a green card—"

Like a farmer in a field, he was walking in and among Uncle Hal's holdings—cast concrete cesspools (looked like teacups from Disney's Wonderland), some lawn jockeys (many absent a hand or an arm), about fifty oil drums and related debris. It was my duty, so I'd been informed my first hour on site a month before, to accompany the customer wherever. To the moon, if need be. *Guy says pole,* Hal had told me, *you vault.* So there we wandered, me and Captain Courageous.

"How's the eye?" he said.

I was tiptoeing through a spread of Delco, Mopar, and FoMoCo leftovers.

"Listen, mister," I started, "can we do this another time? I got places to be."

In addition to being snotty, this was true: My running bud-dies—Shorty, Slim, and Whitey, none of whom were—aimed to drop by in, oh, six or seven hours. We planned to make the rounds, from Boot Town to Blake's Lotaburger, hunting for the sidewinding Mescalero who'd waylaid me the evening before.

"You're a friendly fellow, ain't you?"

"Say what?" I said. That was me at my smartest back then. Amiable as a Klingon. Courteous as a cobra.

"All's I'm saying is, you catch more flies with honey than with vinegar. Get my drift?"

I looked around, innocent as the Gerber baby himself.

"I mean, snarling and back-sassing is no way to get along in this world. You see what I'm saying?"

Sixty miles thataway from my back stoop rose the Organ Mountains, good for throwing beer bottles at when you're other-wise inexpressive. Thisaway, across more miles of rock and rep-tiles big as your leg, were the Sacramentos, all purples and grays and jagged as a villain's teeth. Another thing for tourists to gawk at. But now there was nothing to point at. Just me and the jet jockey. One of us at a crossroads.

"Mister," I said, "blow it out your ass."

That's when he popped me.

Point of the chin. My head snapped back. Stars commenced. Between my ears it was Independence Day—sparklers and sputtering pinwheels and cherry bombs—and from the outer darkness a chorus was heard, voices oooey-gooey and evidently cheerless. I went down. Not felled like a tree, but more or less melted.

Became, I admit, a fair-sized puddle next to his boots.

I came to inside, on my sofa. C-Dog, my assailant, had himself arranged right next to me, a chair I'd once upon a time slept twenty hours in.

"How you feeling, boy?"

I took a second, inspecting the pulp of me. Munchkins, single-minded as savages, were inside my head with air drills, ventilating. I could be a wise-ass, I thought. Or something entirely else. Plus which, I was still seeing two of everything, including a manila file folder balanced on his knees.

"What's that?" I asked.

For an instant, he seemed as surprised as I to find paperwork near at hand and relevant.

"Randall Charles Hidey," he began, "this is your miserable life."

I pointed to the folder, about an inch thick.

"That all?"

"I see you've recovered your good humor," he said. "I like that in a citizen."

He was wearing those reading glasses you see à la Ted Kennedy, half-lenses at the tip of his nose, a dandy prop for the clucking and head-shaking and tsk-tsking that TV likes to give the earnest to do. Vice principals, for instance. Or loved ones you've busted the hearts of.

"Bad news?" I asked. Feeling had returned to my extremities. I put one of them, a leg, on the floor.

He held up a well-manicured finger. Wiggled it slyly in my direction.

"Not so fast, son," he said. "Give it a while. You've had a C-Dog respect tap, is all."

Maybe an hour passed that way—me in coffin-like repose,

Rocky Marciano licking his thumb and turning the pages before him—the outdoors ignorant of me and my predicament. I had, of course, the usual questions. For example: *Who the dickens is this guy?* And: *Cripes, what a time to be unarmed in a democracy.* This was, as my father used to say, a Sit-you-HAY-shun, but, owing to an ache in the jaw and gray matter gone suddenly soft as cooked cauliflower, I was unable to find my way out of it.

"Is it twilight," I asked once, "or just me?"

It was the aftereffect, he said. The physics of the knuckle sandwich as demonstrated by an aficionado of the sweet science.

"Middleweight," I guessed.

"Strictly amateur," he said. "Golden Gloves, Uncle Sam, AAU."

More time went by then, as only time can when you're being held hostage in your own castle, so before he told me about my father and Uncle Hal and the tanning he'd been sent to administer, I filled part of it by thinking about Mona, my Sí Señor sweet cheeks. I had it bad for that woman, I swear. Badder than bad. She was to me as carnage is to warmongers. Hell, some evenings I used to park across the street (in that well-dinged Bel Air Uncle Hal had loaned me) and just watch her through the windows, the six-pack on my lap my steadfast companions. Which is not to say, sad to say, that she returned my affections. To her, I was as I was to too many in yesteryear: a sourpuss weisenheimer, one hundred eighty-five pounds of attitude as foul as The Fuhrer's.

"You got a soda somewheres?"

C-Dog had wandered back to the kitchen, a good time for me to sit upright.

"What do you eat, boy?" he asked, coming in to join me anew. "You got nothing but beer and Ritz crackers."

"Vegetarian," I said, as large a lie as I could muster at the moment. "Buddhist. Full prajna."

"Me, too," he said. "Powerhouse Tabernacle of God in Christ. Odessa chapter."

I tell everybody nowadays—the white collars I work for at Fab 7, the duffers I play golf with at Painted Dunes—that C-Dog, once you got him to take off the aviator shades, was a semi-handsome man. Had eyes blue as marbles—the best description I could come up with in the quarter-hour we considered each other almost knee to knee, in my living room way back when.

"This is how it's gonna be," he said at last.

I'd wondered about that.

"You're getting a spanking," he said.

Imagine you're relaxing on your porch glider one splendid spring sunset, a jug of lemonade at your elbow, Wilson Pickett on the stereo, the wisteria and lilac in glorious bloom. Your wife—her name is Mona, by the way—is whipping up such edibles as are worshipped by the fatsos at *Good Housekeeping,* and your God-fearing children, Mary Beth and Randy, Jr., are in their rooms doing homework of the straight-A ilk. You got your health, Savings Bonds from work, and an automobile with thirty months left on the warranty. This is Shangri-La, folks. Home of the brave as fetched up for you by Metro, Goldwyn, and Mayer in cahoots with the poets at Burma Shave.

Then imagine an eerie sound—part whoosh, part whine—the trees here and there twisting sideways under an enormous wind, your picket fence flung plumb out of sight. Fierce light follows, whirling spots and glares from every corner of Kingdom Come. The ground quakes, geysers erupt hither and yon, and three of your neighbors' houses go blammo in a column of flame. It's a spaceship, big as a suburb, and it's landing atop your hydrangea. That's how I felt for an instant—as if R. C. Hidey had risen from idleness and was now doing hand jive with a goggle-eyed, earless Venutian midget who might vaporize North Dakota for amusement.

"Dumbfounded, ain't you?" C-Dog remarked. "Most usually are."

"No shit," I said, still my own clever self.

Whereupon he laid it out for me, the scenario. One supercilious ingrate, me. One hired gun, him. Ten solid whacks on my hindmost with a belt and, praise Jesus, maybe a change in the common catastrophe that was my character.

"A belt?" I said.

He indicated his own, a hand-tooled specimen with artful Gothic lettering.

"What's it say?" I asked.

He stood, bade me read him from loop to loop.

" 'Encouragement is oxygen to the soul,' " I read, a tissue in me beginning to quiver. "Oh, boy."

"Saw it over in Jal," he began. "An insurance company on Fir Street. Impressed me. Hope you don't think it's corny."

I know what you're thinking: *Head for the hills, tenderfoot!* But something strange had come over me, possibly a sense of right-eousness as unbidden as are visions to the crazed or eurekas to the eggheaded, so instead of bolting for the screen door, I leaned back into the couch, crossed my legs like a banker looking at his strong box. At long last, I thought, mysteries were being revealed. Me, R. C. Hidey, was going to know stuff.

"My daddy and Uncle Hal, huh?"

He tapped the folder solicitously.

"Plus your mother," he said. "Your sister, your frat brothers, couple of teachers, even Mona Fernandez. It's all in black and white."

"What teachers?"

He told me, names that went down me like stones in a well.

"Anyone else?"

He shrugged, abashed. "Well, there's Shorty, Slim, and Whitey—"

"Geez," I remarked.

He seemed saddened, too. "How true."

Funny what the mind turns to in moments dire or potent or providential. Mine turned to C-Dog's shirt—a western affair, nat-urally, with pearl snaps, line drawings of buzzards and barbed wire, plus a pattern of gold and ruby and pukey green that made you dizzy to focus upon. Just about the most ill-considered outer-wear ever seen on the unaddled adult.

"C-Dog," I said. "That's a nickname, right?"

"Navy," he told me. "Got it in the Philippines. On account of my enthusiasm."

That made sense. Given the givens, there didn't seem to be any-thing about this encounter that couldn't, in this vale or its coun-terparts, make sense. So I asked him what his real name was.

"Marion," he said. "After my mother. Middle name Gilroy, from my father."

We shared a moment then, solemn as a night in church. I could hear cars on 54 going by lickety-split, occasionally a tractor-trailer bleeping something nasty through its air horn. Outside it was all sunlight and dry heat rising in waves; inside it was semi-gloomy, a room in a haunted house, me breathing deeply but pleased my foot had stopped trembling. The last time I'd been whipped was after I'd fistfought Phil Trafton following orchestra practice in the fifth grade—laid that piss-ant out so he'd be useless for the cello for a week. My daddy swatted me, his hand swelling up afterward like a ping-pong paddle. The next night, unaffected as a felon and as merry a soul as Old King Cole, I was peeping in Marci Hightower's window and slicing the garden hoses of my neighbors. Incorrigible is what I was. Delinquent as the crinkly-eyed celebrities you see in the pictures in the post office. R. C. Hidey had been heedless, so the written record put it, mindful of little but satisfying his basest appetites.

"Ready?" C-Dog asked.

He had gloves on now—"For the grip," he'd say later; "I'm a professional"—and I remember staring at them with fascination. They seemed at once delicate and demonic, tender and terrifying, rare as angel's wings.

"Ready," I said.

You got one question, I bet: Did it hurt much?

Well, do this: Go outside to your car, open the trunk, place your index finger near the lid latch, then slam that devil hard. Don't pussyfoot. Get your weight behind it. Leap up if you have to. That's how it hurt, for in spite of his girth, C-Dog Simpson was part Hercules, part Charles Atlas—as gifted with leather-lashing as Gabriel had been with horn-honking.

"You can cry if you want," he said.

I was across his lap, boy-like, butt in the air, the only thing between me and "encouragement" a much-washed pair of BVDs. I could smell him now, Jade East or the like, a fragrance I still associate with singleness of purpose.

"Don't think so," I told him. My heart already thumping wildly, blood rushing to my lowered head, I was concentrating on his Tony Lamas, boots with sufficient sheen to see my gritted teeth in.

"Get on with it."

I heard his arm draw back.

"Suit yourself," he said.

By blow three, I was in full bawl, sucking air and sniveling. Teardrops—genuine teardrops, big as boulders—were running through my eyebrows and into my hair. He let fly, belt whistling overhead, and I braced for contact, a noise which is spelled in cartoons as "thwap!" It burned. Like sitting on a cigar the size of a baseball bat. Then a spell where I felt nothing—an "interregnum," C-Dog would say later—before pain, fierce as prairie fire, spread down my thighs. I tried thinking elsewise—of snow skiing, which I was fair at, and of ice cream, which I could eat in industrial-size quantities—but my brain, the loaf of it, was filled with words like "welt" and "blister" and "flayed."

"Nineteen sixty-seven," C-Dog said after swat five. "Did this to a youngster up in Corona."

I couldn't respond with anything but syllables with *h*'s and *f*'s throughout.

"Feisty boy," C-Dog was saying. "Took a half hour to settle his hash."

I'd found a spot on the floor to concentrate on, something that had no opinion about me or the immediate drama.

"Turned out okay," C-Dog said. "That boy is now Lieutenant Governor of Texas."

Then my fanny caught fire again. And again. And again.

"Did me a pachuco in Silver City once. He's an astronaut. You should see my scrapbook. Got me a police chief in Denver, a college dean, a couple of California movie actors. Females, too. You ever hear of Miss New Hampshire Universe 1968? Mother of five now. An eye doctor."

At this point I was overcome by a vision: C-Dog at the wheel of his Imperial, on the highways and byways. A man, clearly, with more than a line of work. He had a calling. Wrongs to right. Justice to dispense. Half Zorro, half King Arthur. In his trunk probably a full suit of armor. A shield. A lance. A terrible, swift sword.

At *número ocho*, he seemed to shift, his own breath ragged and short.

"Out"—he said, huffing—"of"—puffing—"shape."

Me, I was feeling giddy, loopy and oddly good-humored as a drunk. I was still sobbing, it appeared, but, wrong end up, mine was a world gone blue and orange, a noteworthy glow around most of my furnishings. Happily, there was less pain now. I figured my flesh was hanging off in strips, like fresh beef jerky, and C-Dog was merely exercising himself against the thin, nerveless bones of my behind. Speech hadn't yet returned, but I was suffering fewer thoughts with gibberish at the core.

Then we were done, and I had evidently moved into the last chapter of my story, the part wherein I am face-down on my couch and Marion Gilroy Simpson, flush-faced as Porky Pig, is standing over me, his special gloves out of sight, his belt once again holding up his belly.

"Here," he said.

Near as I could make out, he was offering me a jar of Crisco.

"It's vitamin E," he said. "Takes the sting out. Promotes healing."

I nodded. I may have even smiled.

"You mean I ain't dead?" I said.

He grinned himself, ten thousand of the most perfect teeth in the Northern Hemisphere.

"Slop that stuff on as needed," he said. "You'll be shipshape in no time."

That was nice to hear, and I said so, now in complete control of both the mind and meat of me.

"You hungry?" he asked.

I considered it. I was.

"Me," he was saying, "I always work up hunger on a mission. Got supplies in the car."

That was nice, too. Hell, everything was suddenly nice—the weather, my situation on earth, all the peoples of the planet, even the dinner C-Dog fixed (melted cheese, olives, tomato soup, store-bought éclairs for dessert), which, like a nurse or a friend from heaven, he served me bite-size. Anything seemed possible. Silk ties on herd bulls. Circus seals from the sky. Tyrants opening their jails. I had been, as my kids nowadays say, morphed— changed from the inside out. Wooly-minded and agog, I felt I'd emerged from a virtually sleep-like state, and now, weird as a night on Neptune, awfully strange sentiments were coming trippingly from my tongue.

"Thought I might clean up around here," I distinctly heard me say. "Paint that sign by the highway."

A good idea, C-Dog told me. Damn good.

Then it happened again—more chitchat from somebody who sounded a whole lot like me.

"Got to get a haircut, though. Maybe shave a bit more often, too."

That was the spirit, he said, then started gathering up the dishes, the proper washing of which he gave me painstaking instruction about for the next five minutes. Presently, he was back in front of me, hitching up his trousers, and for an instant I feared the bell had rung for Round Two, more whomping and wailing—more of me upended and praying for miracles. But he only shook my hand and said it was high time he hit the road, which gave me to imagine myself stranded on a wayside, thumb out, ragged as a hobo looking for help to go yonder.

"You take care, Randall Hidey," he said.

I would, I told him, and watched him aim for the door. In front of me was his—now my—folder, pages sobering to ruminate upon.

"You're not a pilot, are you?" I asked.

It was a dumb question, the answer obvious as the Pope's choice of religion, but C-Dog was sufficiently civil to address it anyhow. Not a chance, he said. He'd been a lot of things—farmer, a sewer contractor out of Big Spring, a wholesaler of Mexican artifacts, a diesel mechanic for an OTR outfit called Handy Haulers—but never a flyboy.

"Scared of heights," he said.

"What about the Triumph?" I asked. "A ruse, eh?"

He shrugged: What could he say, he said. In his business, you needed to be sly. Catch the subject off-guard.

So that's when I put it to him. About the shirt.

For a moment he looked puzzled, like a grown-up watching an infant cha-cha-cha.

"I wonder if I might buy it," I said.

To be sure, this was a seriously sappy episode, but, as I told

Mona the next day, this is how life is among the kind we are—sap, goo, every icky thing else pooh-poohed by know-it-alls.

"Buy it," he repeated, words clearly new to his vocabulary.

A keepsake, I told him. A memento. Like a postcard. Or a curio. Say you been to the Grand Canyon, or the Empire State Building, naturally you want—

"Hell," he said, "I should give it to you. No charge."

Which he did. Unbuttoned that oooohhh-worthy item and made me a present of it.

"Got ten more of them, anyway," he said. "Buy in bulk. That's my motto."

Briefly, I considered rising to watch him leave, but my butt would have no part of that plan. I lay where I was, belly down, chin on a pillow C-Dog had brought me once the athletics had ended. I lay there, I say, heard him open and close the door to his Imperial, a thwunk as good to hear as are the squeaks of delight your offspring make when they see you coming up the walk.

He didn't start her immediately, and for an instant I wondered if he'd forgotten something or had changed his mind about the shirt. Then that car turned over, chugga-chugga, and you could hear the crunch of gravel as he pulled around toward the highway. It was late evening now, many stars to bask beneath, and no evil smarty-pants out there to disturb the peace of it. He honked *adiós,* and for a time I listened to him go south, his a motor with rumble enough to make you smile, until there was only silence and me, blessed as are the dumb and well-fed, alone at my place.

That Cold Summer

At first the angel was perfectly wingless,
loitering out in the meadow below our summer place,

gazing up at the sky. A kind of Christina
without a home behind her. Whenever she was hungry,

she'd sneak into our home and steal an apple
or a peach from the walnut bowl. Once she cracked a tooth

on a porcelain grape and bled a milky light,
moaning softly while the white stuff circled her forehead

like a pie plate. Donald didn't believe it, thinking
she was just another of his crazy imaginings,

not being one to listen much to his own eyes.
Back then he mistook angel blood for a halo.

Approaching her gingerly, he looked into her pale eyes,
afraid to speak, informing me just how airy

she was, like a piece of the sky looking at herself.
She watched him like a deer caught in headlights, staring

until he touched her shoulder, and he shuddered.
Colder than snow, she was. Donald said that's why

he invited her in to warm herself. She had a long
wind inside her that fanned the flames a brilliant blue.

Personally, I didn't care for her antics,
but Donald was enchanted. Had I ever laid eyes

on a thing like that? he'd ask. As if making gales
in my home were a miracle or something. Once

I woke to find her sleeping in the silence beside me,
her legs spread wide as a crooked smile, the white

mist leaking out in a stream. The icy draft
in our bed lasted for weeks. At first I hardly noticed

the feathers slipping into cracks in the floor,
the shopping bags and the soup I kept simmering

on the stove, feathers swimming like dust in the window
light, tiny white feathers with lives of their own

like those brine shrimp they sell at drugstores
to gullible children. When the feathers

became more plentiful and blew around the rooms,
I swept them out the door, and they rose and drifted

like earthbound clouds. The angel was soon nowhere
to be seen, though her shadow spread, even grew to tower

over us. Those must have been huge wings sprouting
from her shoulders. For me, it couldn't have come

soon enough. Though the house, afterwards, was of a sudden
so familiar and empty, I often wondered how she flew.

When a Woman Loves a Man

Ethna and I were eating scones and sipping espresso at the Café Arabica when I learned of my love affair with you. Everyone has been talking about it, though it came as news to me. Good news. I had no trouble believing every word of it.

True, I have no idea what you are like in bed. Yet I need only lean back in my chair, gaze out the window and incline my thoughts towards you to remember it, as if it were yesterday, the night we spent at the Top of the Town in Chicago, staring down at the city lights.

Or was it several nights in Paris, or Venice, or Toledo, Ohio?

Perhaps that first time, you were wearing a Hawaiian shirt and those lime-green pants you barely squeeze into. It was only five o'clock in the afternoon.

How I worry about our lovemaking. I who know so little about such matters. Were my lips tender, my kisses winsome, my breasts too small? Did I, as the street musician played the harmonica outside our window, unzip my azure dress, my breasts floating away like two clouds in a brassiere, sailing out the window and into the Grand Canyon in a gondola?

Even the irises were quivering in the heat. When I touched your face, I said I had never been seduced before. Then, I bit all the buttons off your shirt, and spat them across the room like seeds. I took off your socks with my teeth.

I didn't rush you, did I?

Were you turned off by my voluminous Woolworth's underpants? What did you do with them? Perhaps you could send them back someday.

Afterwards I slipped out without even saying goodbye, wearing the jacket from your Pierre Cardin suit and your wedding band, which I tossed to Marcel, the mustachioed bellboy with hair the color of honey. He slid it on his ring finger and blew me kisses as I sashayed out into the night air.

Shivering, I turned once and tossed a handful of pebbles at your darkened window. Later I dialed your room, but no one answered. You had already vanished. And without even a trace.

How splendid to have loved you at last, though it seems I forgot to ask: when you whispered, *There is one thing I forgot to tell you,* neglecting to finish the sentence, what were you going to say?

Still Life with Motion

after Giorgio de Chirico

1.
When I became metaphysical, the artist begged my
forgiveness. A small sacrifice

2.
to rid the palette of its noise. I have traveled far on the unlikely
properties of still life,

3.
and in my bleakest postures, I have glided on the prows of
rowboats without dreaming;

4.
so I am moved, in my lunkish fashion, a dummy with a
pedestal: not a body to be proud of, but like you,

5.
it has its ghosts. I sling them over my back, bland memoranda
of interiors

6.
I leave behind, gravitating, as I do, toward the spacious

7.
colonnades where horses sleep in the shadows. Their breathing

8.
annoys me, and the sun remains in one position, that
vanishing point of familiarity.

9.

Foreground I depend on for privacy, along the steps where
gentlemen confer and conclude

10.

by taking off their hats, a gesture of the charity conclusion
offers, the betrayal. I appear as filigree,

11.

supine among the fruit. Consider this: the landscape I was
never

12.

born in, abundant with rendition and the fleshy parings of
neglect. How I adore the child

13.

running with her hoop and stick across the wide nostalgia of a
street.

An Elegy Is a Man

I have been sculpting my father's head.
I began it when he died,
when his head was most familiar,
when the priest called him a liar.

I have been sculpting my father's eye.
It had been wide and black, they say,
peerless in the art of sinking;
my father was a king.

I have been sculpting my father's breast
against a rumor that there burst
once a perturbed and brimming passion,
as if the breast were an impression,

and a shudder in the mind could translate
into something on one's palette
that unspeakable virtue of plastic.
Some have said my father was bombastic,

hence the grandiose yet winsome lean
I've applied to the curve of his spleen,
a detail for the keen observer,
one who knows my father was severe.

I have been sculpting his torrid member,
imbued it with an old-world umber,
and (here's the rescue) arranged it near a muscle,
lest it seem too large or small.

The thigh, likewise, I have been sculpting:
a girth, a mere dull thing
without its bold prerogative
to open wide and give and give...

I have been sculpting the arch of my father's foot,
that it traverse some narrow fate
which then, implacably, reforms,
the way a sea exceeds its foam.

The last stone I have shaved from his hand,
a supple folding of the palm to mind
the urge to grasp, though I will let it
hold some lovely thing, a book, a planet—
any charm of circumstance.
Emblems are effects. The body is their distance.

I have sculpted his body from memory.
There is no lament without cruelty.

Cave in the Ravine

A monster has risen out of somewhere—
its left foot clawed, gripping the earth;
the most terrible things coming out of its giant mouth—
fire, and at the same time poisonous black spears—
for the monster is not of nature
entirely.
       In front of the monster is a figure in black
that seems to be doing a dance—as we have done
from the beginning faced with such things. And
it seems to be working; what is spewed out stops
as the figure turns.
       It's hard to believe
a tiny woman could have a mouth like this;
but I know one who does. As in the fairy tale
where toads and vipers come out of the mouth
of the princess. Imagine: a woman shaped like a monster;
a monster shaped like a woman.
       And what comes out
of the mouth is powerful. Though as I step back
from the painting the fire seems to be mixed with water—
as if whatever she speaks is canceled
at the very moment she says it.
       Step back further
and it's a cave, but with a pleasant fire inside.
The figure still dances. Because of the shapes
the cave makes. The green sky. And for
the sake of the dancing.

Story

after "Farmhouse in Auvers with Two Figures"

Talk about modern. The roof as flat
as the sky, as the people. Forget Cézanne.
Just look at this. And the shape
of the roof: a fish, a car, a revolver.

And the bushes like green fire, and
the bush which seems to be growing out of the roof
and the tree in back—well, only
an indication of a tree.

The man and woman could be my friend
and her husband. A fight to the death,
someone said. Though they didn't live in a farmhouse
but an apartment in New York City.

So I thought here. With so much air to breathe.
With all the greenness. And sure enough,
the woman puts down her bundle, and turns.
And the man turns, too.

They stand there, on opposite sides of the grass
and stare at each other. I can't seem to get them
to take one step. History is too strong.
Even the kind people pass on

to each other. As the house seems to be saying something
to the next house. And it to the next house. And so on.
As stories get passed on somehow; and are fixed.
Then you can never change them.

Wind, Horse, Snow

1.

The Eskimo children balance their blackboards
on their knees and write with soft fat chalk.
A storm skitters across the frozen sea.
Smidgeons of ice have swirled into pinwheels.

2.

The painter Magritte is dabbing black paint
on his canvas. Beneath the clock he writes
"wind," beneath the door "horse."

3.

The Eskimo children have a new teacher,
from Connecticut, who wants them to learn
a poem about stopping by the woods
on a snowy evening with an intelligent horse.

4.

It is summer in the ragweed field.
Magritte says there is no picture without a frame.
When he stares from his attic window, does he see
the field, or a composition of the field?
Is it possible for me to love you
without inventing you?

5.
The Eskimo children admire the horse most.

6.
The children must pick a word to describe
the snow that batters their windows.
If it is too wet, their fathers might freeze

as they paddle home. If it is dry and powdery,
the dogs can make the run to town for food.

7.
"The word dog does not bite,"
observed William James,
who admired Magritte's horse.

8.
If my language has no future tense,
am I the same person I was as a child?

Black

My favorite God a horse the color
of my name. And when I ride him,
a heat between my legs, like tongue on ice,
friction of moon against darkness.

Over and over, the hooves, the rain,
finding the ground. Hearts, black boots
flung there in the mud behind us. And all around us,
the leaves and brambles, the spiders, wolves, the stars.

Talk

You were going to ask me why I am
here, and I'm going to tell you.
But I want you to look at the scar
on my arm, this one right here in the shape
of a mouth, though not a human one.
I like to talk about my scars, I like to talk

about all kinds of things, but there's no one to talk
to most of the time. Wherever I am
I watch, smell the air, don't sleep, I'm the one
who listens to the crazies, I listen to you
when you look out the window, talking to shapes
the snow makes in the yard, covering scars.

When you ask what that sound is I say it's cars,
can't you see them, but instead of talk
you give me a gaze, a look in the shape
of how we might look together, and I am
sinking, and trying not to, sinking toward you
down there on the floor, looking up, the One.

This is the way one gets to two, one
foot then the other, one hand on my scar,
waltzing around the kitchen with you,
the music, the music, no need to talk
of what this means to anyone, or why I am
here, the shadow on the wall a miraculous shape.

I can see in your mind a thought taking shape.
If only you could speak, you'd be the one
I came to get, to take away, but I am
sorry, I was wrong, I'll cover my scar

and leave you here, I won't try to talk
to anyone tonight, not me and not you.

Just two questions before I go: Do you
know how I got this scar? Is its shape
familiar? Come on, come on, please talk
to me, tell me you bit me, say you're the one
who left a mark on my arm, a little scar
to remember you by, I'm asking you, I'm

begging, good God, I'm pleading, you're the only one
who knows if it's a scar in the shape
of what you would say if you would talk.

Who Is It Can Tell Me Who I Am?

Alberto Perera, librarian, granted no credibility to police profiles of dangerous persons. Writers, down through the centuries, had that look of being up to no good and were often mistaken for smugglers, assassins, fugitives from justice—criminals of all sorts. But the young man invading his sanctum, hands hidden in the pockets of his badly soiled green parka, could possibly be another lunatic out to kill another librarian. Up in Sacramento, two librarians were shot dead while on duty, and, down in Los Angeles, the main library was sent up in flames by an arsonist. Perera loved life and wished to participate in it further.

"You got a minute?"

"I do not."

"Can I read you something?"

"Please don't." Recalling some emergency advice as to how to dissuade a man from a violent deed—*Engage him in conversation*—he said, "Go ahead," regretting his permission even as he gave it. Was he to hear, as the last words he'd ever hear, a denunciation of all librarians for their heinous liberalism, a damnation for all the lies, the deceptions, the swindles, the sins preserved within the thousands of books they so zealously guarded, even with their lives?

With bafflement in his grainy voice, the fellow read from a scrap of paper.

> *Greet the sun, spider. Show no rancor.*
> *Give God your thanks, O toad, that you exist.*
> *The crab has such thorns as the rose.*
> *In the mollusc are reminiscences of women.*
> *Know what you are, enigmas in forms.*
> *Leave the responsibility to the norms,*
> *Which they in turn leave to the Almighty's care.*
> *Chirp on, cricket, to the moonlight. Dance on, bear.*

The fellow granted his listener a moment to think about what he'd just heard. Then, "What do you make of it?"

"What do I make of it?"

"What I make of it," said the intruder, "is you're supposed to feel great if you're an animal. Like, if you're talking about a spider or a toad. Am I supposed to do that?"

"Do what?"

"Like, thank God because I'm me?"

"That's for you to decide. Take your time with it." Shuffling papers on his desk. "Take your time but not in here."

Watch your step with anybody playing dumb, Perera cautioned himself. They sneak up on you from behind. This fellow knew just what he was doing, pulling out a poem by Rubén Darío, reading it aloud to a librarian so proud of his Spanish ancestry he kept the name his dear mother had called him, Alberto, and there it was, his foreign name in a narrow frame on his desk for all who passed his open door to see. Maybe this fellow had been stabbed in prison by a Chicano with the name Perera, and now Perera, the librarian, a man of good will, a humanitarian, was singled out among his fellow librarians.

"What do you figure this guy's saying? Wake up every day feeling great you're you?"

"If that's what you figure he's saying, that's what he's saying. That's the best you can do with a poem."

Out in fistfuls from his parka pockets, more scraps of paper. So many, some fluttered to the floor. Cigarette packets inside out, gum wrappers, scavenged street papers of many colors that were slipped along underfoot by the winds of traffic, scraps that became transcendentally unfamiliar by the use they'd been put to: lines of poetry in a fixatedly careful, cramped handwriting.

"That spider, you take that spider." Entranced by a spider that only he could see, swinging between himself and Perera. "That spider is in its web where it belongs. Made it himself, swinging away. Sun comes out, strands all shiny, spider feels the warm sun on his back. Okay, glad he's a spider. I can see that. Same with the cricket. Makes chirpity chirp to the moon. I can accept that. That toad, too. I can see he likes the mud, they're born in mud. It's the bear I can't figure out. Would you know if bears dance in their natural state?"

"Would I know if bears dance?"

"When they're on their own?" A cough, probably incited by some highly pleasurable secret excitement from tormenting a librarian. "What I know about bears," answering himself before his cough was over, "is bears do not dance. It is not in their genetic code. I'll tell you when they dance. They dance when they got a rope around their neck. That poet slipped up there. A bear with a rope around his neck, do you see him waking up happy, hallooing the sun? Same thing."

"Same thing as what?"

No answer, only another cough, probably called up to cover his amusement over an obtuse librarian with a silk tie around his stiff neck.

"You know anything about the guy who wrote it? The bear didn't write it, that I know."

"No, the bear did not write it. Darío wrote it. A modernist, brought Spanish poetry into the modern age. Turn of the century. Born in Chile. No, Nicaragua. Myself, I like Lorca. Lorca, you know, was assassinated by Franco's *guardia civil*." Why that note? Because, if it happened to him, Alberto Perera, here and now, his death might possess a similar meaning. An enlightened heart snuffed out.

"When he says, like, Spider, greet the sun, where do you figure he was lying?" Slyly, the fellow waited.

"Was he lying?" Always the assumption that poets lie. Why else do they deliberately twist things around?

"What I mean is"—grudgingly patient—"where was he lying when the sun came up?"

"The spider, you mean?" asked Perera. "Lying in wait?"

"The poet."

"The spider was in its web. I don't know where the poet was."

"I'll tell you. The poet was lying in his own bed."

"That's a thought."

"That's not a thought. That's the truth."

"A poem can come to you wherever you are," Perera explained. "Whatever you're doing. Sleeping, eating, even looking in the fridge, or when you think you're dying. I imagine that in his case he wakes up one morning after a bad night, takes a look at the sun, and accepts who he is. He accepts the enigma of himself."

"Are you?"

"Am I what? An enigma?"

"Are you glad you wake up who you are?"

"I can say yes to that."

"You give thanks to God?"

"More or less."

"Great. I bet you wake up in your own bed. That's what I'm saying. What's-his-name wouldn't've thought up that poem if he woke up where he was lying on the sidewalk."

"Darío," said Pereda, "could very well have waked up on a sidewalk. He pursued that sort of life. Opium, absinthe. Quite possibly he was visited by that poem while lying on the sidewalk."

"Then he went back to his own bed and slept it off."

With trembling fingers the fellow gathered up his scraps from the desk. Trembling with what? With timidity, if this was a confrontation with a guardian of the virtues of every book in the place? As he bent to the floor to pick up his scraps, the crown of his head was revealed, the hair sprinkled with a scintilla of the stuff of the streets and the culture. How old was he, this fellow? Not more than thirty, maybe younger. Young, with no staying power.

By the door a coughing spell took hold of him. With his back to Perera he drew out from yet another pocket in the murky interior of the parka one of those large Palestinian scarves that Arafat wore around his head and were to be seen in the windows of used clothing stores, and brought up into it whatever he had tried to keep down. Voiceless, he left, his bare ankles slapped by the grimy cuffs of his pants.

Perera imagined him shuffling down the hall, then down the wide white marble stairs, the grandiose interior stairs, centerpiece of this eternal granite edifice. As for Darío's admonition to the spider to show no rancor, that fellow's rancor was showing all over him. Yet his voice was scratchily respectful and his fingers trembled. Anybody who inquires so relentlessly into the meaning of a poem, and presses the words of poets into the ephemerae of the streets, would surely return, borne up the marble stairs by all those uplifting thoughts in his pockets.

· · ·

Alberto Perera, a librarian if for just a few months more, shortly to be retired, went out into the cold and misty evening. A rarity, in this time when librarians' ranks were shrinking down as his own head had shrunk while bent for so many years over the invaluable minutiae of his responsibilities, including the selection of belles-lettres, of poetry, of literary fiction. The cranium shrinks no matter how much knowledge is crammed inside it. A rarity for another reason—a librarian who did not look like one, who wore a Borsalino fedora, his a classic of thirty years, a Bogart raincoat, English boots, a black silk shirt, a vintage tie.

Never as dashing as he wished to appear, however. Slight, short, and for several years now the bronze-color curls gone gray and the romantically drooping eyelids of his youth now faded flags at half-mast. Dashing, though, in the literary realm, numbering among his pen pals, most dead now: Hemingway, a letter to Perera, the youth, on the Spanish Civil War; Samuel Beckett, on critics mired up to their necks in his plays; Neruda, handwritten lines in green ink of two of his poems—what a prize! Also a note from the lovely British actress Vanessa Redgrave, with whom he'd spent an hour in London when he'd delivered to her an obscure little book of letters by Isadora Duncan, whom she'd portrayed in a film. And more, so much more. Everything kept in a bank vault and to be carried away in a black leather attaché case with double locks when he left this city for warmer climes. It was time to donate it all to an auction of literary memorabilia, on condition that the proceeds established a fund for down-and-out librarians.

Further, he was a rarity for choosing to reside in what he called the broken heart of the city, or the spleen of it, the Tenderloin, and choosing not to move when the scene worsened. Born into a family of refugees from Franco's Spain, Brooklyn their alien soil, he felt a kinship with the dispossessed everywhere in the world, this kinship deepening with the novels he'd read in his youth. Dostoyevsky's insulted and injured, Dickens's downtrodden. Eighteen years ago he'd found a fourth-floor apartment, the top, in a tentatively respectable building, a walking distance to the main library in the civic center and to the affordable restaurants on Geary Street. Soon after he moved in, the sidewalks and entrances on every block began to fill up with a surge of outcasts of all kinds. The shaven heads, the never-shaven faces, the battle-maimed, the dope-possessed, the jobless, the homeless, the immigrants, and, not far from his own corner, six-foot-tall transvestite prostitutes, and shorter ones, too, all colors. A wave, gathering momentum, swept around him now as he made his way, mornings and evenings, to and from the library. There was no city in the world that was not inundated in its time, or would be in time to come, by refugees from upheavals of all sorts.

On gray days, as this day was, he was reminded of the poor lunatics, madmen, nuisances, all who were herded out of the towns and onto the ships that carried them up and down the rivers of the Rhineland. An idea! The mayor, having deprived the homeless of their carts and their tents, would welcome an idea to rid the city of the homeless themselves. Herd them aboard one of those World War II battleships, rusting away in dry dock or muck, and send them out to sea. The thousands—whole families, loners, runaway kids—all to be dropped off in Galveston or New Orleans, under cover of a medieval night.

He ate his supper at Lefty O'Doul's, at a long table in company of other men his age and a woman who looked even older. Retired souls, he called them, come in from their residence hotels, their winter smells of naphthalene and menthol hovering over the aroma of his roast turkey with dressing. One should not be ashamed of eating a substantial meal while the hungry roamed the streets. He told himself this as he'd told himself so many times before, lifelong. He knew from youthful, saintly experiments of his own that when he fasted in sympathy, punishing himself for what he thought was plenitude, his conscience began to starve, unable to survive for very long without a body.

A brandy at the long bar, and the bartender slapping down the napkin, asking the usual. "When you going to sell me that Borsalino?" Then, "This man's a librarian," to the bulky young man in a broadly striped sweater on the stool to the left of Perera. "He's read every book in the public library. Ever been in there?"

"Never was."

"You can ask him anything," said the bartender, and the man to Perera's right did. "Do you know right off the number of dead both sides in the Civil War?"

"Whose civil war?"

Taken for a tricky intellectual, he was left alone.

A theater critic, that's what he wished to be mistaken for, passing the theaters at the right time as the ticket holders were drifting in and the lines were forming at the box office. Women's skirts and coats swinging out, swishing against him, and a woman turning to apologize, granting a close glimpse of her face to this man who appeared deserving of it. A critic, that's who he was, of the musical up there on the stage and of the audience so delightedly acceptive of the banal, lustily sung.

Past the lofty Hilton at the Tenderloin's edge, whose ultra-plush interior he had strolled through a time or two, finding gold beyond an interior decorator's wildest dreams. Its penthouse window the highest light in the Tenderloin sky, a shining blind eye. Around a corner of the hotel, and, lying up against the cyclone fence, the bundled and the unbundled to whom he gave a wide berth as he would to the dead, in fear and respect. Over the sidewalks, those slips of refuse paper he'd always noticed but not so closely as now. Alert to approaching figures, to whatever plans they had in mind for him, and warily friendly with the fraternal clusters, exchanging with them joking curses on the weather, he made his way. Until at last he stood before the mesh gate to his apartment building. A gate from sidewalk to the entrance's upper reaches, requiring a swift turn of the key before an assault. The gate, the lock, the fear—none of which had been there when he moved in.

The only man in the western world to wear a nightcap, he drew his on. Cashmere, dove color, knitted twelve years ago by his dear friend and lover Barbara, a librarian herself, a beautiful one. Syracuse, New York. Every year, off they'd go. Archaeological tours, walking tours. Three winters ago he was at her bedside, close-by in her last hours. She, too, had corresponded with writers. Hers were women—poets, memoirists—and these letters, too, were in his care. Into his plaid flannel robe, also a gift from her, the seat and the elbows worn away. He always read in this robe in his ample chair or at the kitchen table or in bed. Three books lay on the floor by his bed, among the last he'd ever consider ordering for any library. One had seduced and deceived him, the second was unbearably vain, and he was put to sleep by the third, already asleep itself, face-down on the carpet.

When he lay down the inevitable happened. At once he wondered where the poetry stalker might be, the librarian stalker with the excitable cough. Could Darío have imagined that his earnest little attempt to accept God's ways would wind up in the parka pocket of a sidewalk sleeper, trying to accept the same a hundred years later?

At his desk he was always attuned to the life of this library, as he'd been to every library where he'd spent his years, even the vaster ones with more locked doors, tonnages of archives. This morning his mind's eye was a benign sensor, following the patrons to their chosen areas. He saw them rising in the slow, creaky elevator, he saw the meandering ones and the fast ones climbing the broad marble stairs, those stairs like a solid promise to the climber of an ennobling of the self on the higher levels. The largest concentration of patrons was in the newspaper and periodical section, always and forever a refuge for men from lonely rooms and also now for those without a room, all observing the proper silence, except the man asleep, head down on the table, his glottal breathing quivering the newspaper before his face. In the past, empty chairs were always available, now every chair was occupied. And where was the young man whose pockets were filled with scraps of poetry? In the poetry section, of course, copying down what the world saw fit to honor with the printed page. *Anything in books represents the godlike and anything in myself represents the vile.* Who said that? A writer, born into grim poverty, whose name he'd recall later. If you felt vile in the midst of all these godlike volumes, what restless rage!

"Am I butting in here?"

Same parka, grimier perhaps. But look! His hair rose higher and had a reddish cast, an almost washed look from the rain. His eyes not clearer, not calmer, and in his arms four books, which he let fall onto the desk.

"This is not a checkout desk," said Perera.

"That I know. Never check out anything. No address. If you try to sneak something out, you get the guillotine. You get it in the neck."

To touch or not to touch the books. Since there was no real reason not to touch, Perera set the four books upright, his hands as bookends.

"Who have we got here? Ah, Rilke, the elegies. Good choice. And here we've got Whitman. You know how to pick them. Bishop, she's up there. And who's this? Pound? Sublime, all of them. But don't let yourself be intimidated. Nothing sacred in this place, just a lot of people whose thoughts were driving them crazy, euphoria-crazy or doom-crazy, and they had to get it out, see what *you* think about what they're thinking. That's all there is to it. Librarians in here are just to give it a semblance of order. I'm not a high priest."

"Never thought you were."

"Ah," said Perera, and the books between his hands resumed their frayed existence, their common humanity. One, he saw, had a bit of green mildew at the spine's bottom edge. It must have been left out in a misty rain or someone had read it while in the tub.

"Can I get you some coffee?" inquired the visitor.

"Strange that you should ask," said Perera. "Got my thermos here. A thirst for coffee comes over me at this hour." How closely he'd been watched! And now forced to take the plunge into familiarity, a plunge he would not have taken without further consideration if this man were the sole homeless man around. They were empowered by their numbers.

From the bottom drawer, he brought up his thermos and his porcelain cup. The plastic thermos cup held no pleasure, and he never used it. He'd use it now and not bother to guess why, and bring up also the paper bag of macaroons.

"Suppose I sit down?"

Perera nodded, and the guest sat down in the only chair, a hard chair with an unwelcoming look, a chair used until now only by Alexa Okula, head librarian, and Amy Peck, chief guard, who often described for him the assaults she had suffered that day and where in the library they had occurred.

With both hands around the cup, the guest had no trouble holding it. "This is like dessert," he said. "This is great. Got sugar and cream in it." He was shy around the macaroons. Crumbs were tripping down the parka, and when they reached the floor he covered them with his beat-up jogging shoes.

At that moment Pereda recalled the Sacramento library tragedy. When did the shooting occur? Right after a little party celebrating the library's expanded hours. And what did the assassin do then? Fled to the rooftop, where he was gunned down by the police. It was simple enough to imagine himself dead on the floor, but not so easy to imagine this fellow fleeing anywhere, hampered by the bone-cold ankles, the flappy shoes, the body's tremble at the core.

"You remember that poem?" his guest asked.

"Not verbatim," said Perera. "I did not memorize it."

"You can remember the bear, can't you, and the spider and the toad, anyway? How they're supposed to greet the sun because they are what they are?"

"That I remember," said Perera.

"What I'd like to know is, what am I?"

"You can figure you're a human being," said Perera.

"That's what I thought you'd say. What else you were going to say is, you're a human being by the sweat of your brow. Beavers, that don't take into account beavers. Beavers are dam builders. Then you take those birds who get stuff together to make a nest for the female of their choice. Other birds, too, I've seen them. Can't stop pulling up weeds or whatever stuff is around for a hundred miles, pull this out, pull that out, and off they go and back in a second. Then there's animals who dig a burrow, one hell of a long tunnel in the ground. They can't sweat, but they work. It's work, but that don't make them human."

"Work does not get to the essence. I see your point," said Perera. At a moment's notice he could not get to the essence himself, and he wished he had not used that word. It could only mean further trouble.

"Okay, take you," said the visitor. "Would you say you were human?"

"I've been led to believe that I am," said Perera.

"What you base that on," said his guest, "is you get to keep guard over this library and you got every book where it's supposed to be and in addition you got it up on a computer, what is its title, what is its number, who wrote it, and maybe you got in your head the reason why the guy wrote it. So in that way you can say you're human and maybe you're glad about it even if you don't look it. Okay, now let's say you're through work for the day and you walk home. Or you go on and have yourself a turkey or whatever they got there, roast beef, chicken and dumplings. Then you go along by that theater, maybe even drop in yourself at fifty bucks a seat in the balcony. After that you go on to your apartment, which is in a bad, I mean *baaad* neighborhood, and you unlock that gate. And then what?"

"I can't imagine."

"You don't have to imagine. You're in your own bed. Got a mattress that's just right for the shape you're in. Maybe you even got an electric blanket. Got pillows with real feathers inside, maybe even that down stuff from the hind end of a couple hundred ducks. Nighty night."

"So now I'm sure I'm human?"

"So then the sun comes up and what do you say? You say what that spider says. Halloo, old sun up there, had me a good sleep in my own web and now I get to eat some more fat flies. Halloo, says the toad, now I get to spend the day in this hot mud some more. Halloo, says the bear, now I get to dance some more with this rope around my neck. Halloo, says this guy, Alberto Perera, now I get to go to the library again and talk to this guy who can't figure out why he can't halloo the sun with the rest of them."

A flush had spread over the fellow's face, over the pallor and over the pits, over all that was more appallingly obvious today. From his parka he brought out the Arafat headpiece and hid his face in it, coughing up in there something tormentingly intimate.

Alexa Okula, head librarian, passing by and hearing the commotion, paused a moment to look in, and Perera held up his hand to calm her fears for his safety. Nothing escaped her, only all the years of her life in the protective custody of tons of books and tons of granite. Soon to be released, just as he was to be, all she'd have was her stringy emeritus professor of a husband and her poodles. Unlike himself, who'd have the world.

The fellow sat staring at the floor, striving to recover from the losing battle with his cough.

"You suppose I could spend the night in here?"

With *unthinkable* on the tip of his tongue, Perera said nothing. Accommodations ought to be available for queries of every sort at any time in your life.

"Looks like it ought to be safer in here."

"Unsafe in here, too," said Perera. "This fortress is in a state of abject deterioration. The last earthquake did some damage, along with the damage done by the budget cuts, along with the damage by vandals. Time's been creeping around in here, too. The whole damned thing could collapse on you while you slept."

"I can handle it," said the supplicant. "Nobody's going to throw lighter fuel on me and set me on fire in here. Nobody's going to knife me in here, at night, anyway. Lost my bedroll. I left my stuff with this woman who's my friend, she got room in her cart. I had a change of shirt in there, I had important papers, had a letter from a guy I worked for up the coast. I was good at hauling in those sea urchins they ship over to Japan, tons of them. They love those things over there, then there wasn't any more. Where the sea urchins were, something else is taking over, messing up the water. I'm telling you this because I don't drink, don't do dope, don't smoke, so I sure would not set this place on fire if I was allowed to sleep in here." He was talking fast, outrunning his cough. "The cops took her stuff, took my stuff, dumped it all into the truck. Ordered by the mayor. She lost family pictures, lost the cat she had tied to the cart that sat on top. She was crying. I was in here talking to you."

"It must be damn cold in here at night," Perera said.

"Maybe, maybe not, and if it's raining, maybe the roof don't leak."

"Dark, I imagine," said Perera. "I've never thought about it. I suspect they used to leave a few lights on, but now it's dark. Saves money. Let's say that once the lights go out you can't see a thing. Your sense of direction is totally lost, you're blind as a bat, and I'm nowhere around to guide you to the lavatory, and I wouldn't know where it was myself. You might be pissing on some of the noblest minds that ever put their thoughts on paper."

"I wouldn't do that."

"They do get pissed on, one time and another, but not by you or me. So let's say you're feeling your way around, looking for a comfortable place. Okula has a rug in her office, and it's usually warm in there. She exudes a warmth that might stay the night. But how to get there?"

"I know my way around."

"You do seem to," said Perera.

"What you could do when you take off, like your day is done, see? You could just leave me in here and close the door. I wouldn't care if you locked it."

"I can lock it," said Perera, "but not with you inside."

"Is there some of that coffee left?"

Perera, pouring, was planning to wash that porcelain cup thoroughly. If it was pneumonia gripping this young man, it would get a more merciless grip on him, twice as old. Or if it was tuberculosis, it would bring on his end with rapacious haste and just as he was about to embark on his most rewarding years.

This time the guest took longer to drink it down, the hot coffee feeling its way cautiously past the throat's lacerations.

"Let's say it's like that darkness upon the face of the deep," Perera said. "That same darkness the Creationists are wanting to take us back to. Dark, dark, and you need to find yourself a comfortable place. Now let's say you're at the top of our marble stairs and you don't know it. You take a step, and down you go. Come morning, they open up and find you there."

"You think so?"

"You'll be on the front pages in New York, Paris, Tokyo. A homeless man, seeking shelter in San Francisco's main library, fell down in there and died. A library, imagine it, that monument to mankind's exalted IQ. I'll say you dropped by to chat about poetry. I'll say we spent many pleasant hours discussing Darío's *Filosofía*."

Contempt in the eyes meeting Perera's. "What're you telling me? You're telling me to lie down and die?"

"Not at all. All I'm saying is you cannot spend the night in this library."

Scornfully careful, the fellow placed the porcelain cup on the desk. "You want me to tell you what that poem is saying? Same thing you're saying. If you can't halloo the sun, if you can't go chirpity chirp to the moon, what're you doing around here anyway?"

"That is not what it is saying," said Perera.

"To hell with you is what I'm saying."

Gone, leaving his curse behind. A curse so popular, so spread around, it carried little weight.

Closing time, the staff and lingering patrons all forced out through one side entrance and into the early dark, into the rain. Perera hoisted his umbrella, one slightly larger than the ordinary, bought in London the day he met the actress, years ago. It will never turn inside out, the clerk promised, not even in Conrad's typhoon. And it hadn't yet. Lives were being turned inside out, but this snob of an umbrella stayed up there. A stance of superiority, that was his problem. A problem he always knew he had and yet that always took him by surprise. And how did he figure he was so smart, this Alberto Perera? Well, he could engage in the jesting the smart ones enjoy when they're in the presence of those they figure are not so smart. He could engage in that jovial thievery, that light-fingered, lightheaded trivializing of another person's tragic truth, a practice he abhorred wherever he came upon it.

Onward through this neon-colored rain, this headlight-glittering rain, every light no match for the dark, only a constant contesting. *There is a certainty in degradation.* You can puzzle over lines all your life and never be satisfied with the meanings you get. Until, slushing onward, you've got at last one meaning for sure, because now its time had come, bringing proof by the thousands wherever they were this night in their concrete burrows and dens. There was no certainty in anything else, no matter what you're storing up, say tons of gold, say ten billion library books, and if you think you can elude that certainty it sneaks up on you, it sneaks up the marble stairs and into your sanctum, and you're degraded right along with the rest.

For several days at noontime, Perera looked for him in the long line at St. Anthony's, men and women moving slowly in for their free meal. After work he climbed the stairs to Hospitality House and looked around at the men in the collection of discarded chairs, each day different men, and each man confounded by being among the unwanted many. Here, too, he knew he would not find him. The fellow was a loner, hiding out, probably afraid his cough was reason to arrest him.

A rolled-up wool blanket, a large thermos filled with hot coffee, a dozen packaged handkerchiefs, a thick turtleneck sweater, a package of athletic socks. Perera carried all this into his office, piecemeal, as the days came and went, and these offerings had the same aspect of futility that he saw in the primitive practice of laying out clothing and nourishment for the departed.

He braved the Albatross Used Books store not far from the library, trying not to breathe the invisible dust from the high stacks of disintegrating books, and in the dim poetry section came upon some unexpected finds. Ah ha! Michaux, *My life, you take off without me,* and Trakl, sad, suicidal soul, *Beneath the stars a man alone,* and Anna Akhmatova, *Before this grief the mountains stoop,* and Ah! Machado, *He was seen walking between rifles.* Comments in the margins, someone's own poem on a title page, bus schedules, indecipherable odds and ends of penciled thoughts intermingling with the printed ones. He wanted to keep these thin volumes for himself, and instead he did as planned. He bought a green nylon parka in a discount place on Market Street, slid the books into the deep pockets, and folded the parka on top the pile.

On the morning of the twelfth day, before the hour when the public was admitted, Perera entered by the side door, bringing a pair of black plastic shoes, oxford style, made in China, recommended for their comfort by a street friend wearing a pair. The door guard silently led him to the foot of the marble stairs, where Okula, cops and paramedics and librarians were gathered around a man lying on the lowest step.

Perera had never fainted and was not going to faint now, even though all the strength of his intelligence was leaving the abode of his head to darkness.

"Mr. Perera," Okula was saying but not to him, "was an acquaintance of this man. Wasn't he?"

Nobody was answering, though Perera gave them time.

"Occasionally," he said, "he stepped into my office. My door is usually open." Sweat was rising from his scalp. "Did he fall?"

"More like he lay down and died." The paramedic's voice was inappropriately young. "TB. Take a look at that rag."

"You say you knew him?" A cop's voice. "Do you know his name? He's got nothing in his pockets."

"No," said Perera.

"Any idea where he concealed himself in here?"

"Hundreds of places." Okula, responding. "We check carefully. However, anyone wishing to stay in can also check carefully."

"What you might be needing is a couple of dogs. German shepherds are good at it. Dobermans, too. A couple of good dogs could cover this whole place in half an hour."

Kneeling by the body, Perera took a closer look at the face, closer than when they sat in the office, discoursing on the animal kingdom. The young man was now no one, as he'd feared he already was when alive. The absolute unwanted, that's who the dead become.

"Did this man bother you?"

It would take many months, he knew, before he'd be able to speak without holding back. Humans speaking were unbearable to hear and abominable to see, himself among the rest. Worse was all that was written down instead, the never-ending outpouring, given print and given covers, given shelves up and down and everywhere in this warehouse of fathomless darkness.

"He did not bother me," he said.

The door to his office was closed but unlocked, just as he'd left it. Scattered over his desk were what appeared to be the contents of his wastebasket. But unfamiliar, not his. So many kinds of paper scraps, they were the bits and pieces his visitor had brought forth from that green parka. Throwaway ads, envelopes, a discount drugstore's paper bag, business cards tossed away. On each, the cramped handwriting. By copying down all these stirringly strange ideas, had the fellow hoped to impress upon himself his likeness to these other humans? A break-in of a different sort. A young man breaking into a home of his own.

Perera sat down at his desk, slipped his glasses on, and spread the scraps out before him as heedfully as his shaking hands allowed.

Two Tragedies, With Preface

Every dusk there gather in the trees
birds whose bodies lean heavy as
magnolias on the bent and swaying branches.

Every dusk, in trees, birds gather,
looking heavy as magnolias or
the shadows of magnolias, since in color

birds are darker; and since they scatter, turning
to reassemble on their branches, burning
slowly in their song, they are, this evening,

the ashes of magnolias, and in every
way an utter fiction like the very
one I tell you now:

*

                    Imagine a married
couple on a weekend at the sea—
long-married people, not unfriendly

with each other. Let us picture them
smiling, even when rain hems
the details of their bodies from

our sight, and lays on everything a grayness,
false as coals concealing light. Now suppose
our husband, as his wife unpacks, sees

shadowed on the darkening sea a skiff
capsized, and figures in the waves as if
his watching put them there, and made his life

and his green eyes the truest water
into which they sank. He doesn't wonder
what to do, nor can he think to answer

when she asks, "What? What is it, hon?"
Before a word forms in his throat, he's gone.
And she, drawn slowly toward the window then

(the dream-like steps, her bridal stride!),
arrives in time to watch him join, side-
by-side, a line of men; their lengthening braid,

the only seam, now stretching, thinly, in
the swath of storm. The tiny boat they strain
to reach is lifted once and pitched again,

before two bodies drift to view, and swell
above the roiling tide. A smallish girl
is pulled to shore; a sodden dog, that's paddled

to the beach, shakes off his coat, sniffs at
the child; and then—it's over. The rain gives out.
The ocean soothes. The girl, beneath her blanket,

moves. And under others lie her parents—
still. Someone's called an ambulance.
The rest wait, shuffling, on the sand.

Suppose our husband turns to face the window
then. Or that his wife has met him down below.
Or that our lifeless parents rise to go,

holding their grateful child between them. Say
the words could make it so; and that our wife has always
loved her husband, loves him even more today.

Imagine hope there, burning through the gray,
turning like the light of the ambulance
that takes the girl away.

Letter from the Garden

Three days of spring winter and suddenly,
birds everywhere. The sky and garden
are not enough for them. They beat upon
the pane of glass through which I watch them, wanting
entrance. It was wrong to think that they
were happier than I, or that nothing
was denied them, when I, myself, had shut
them out. My love, paradise is lonely
for you, and your dream of redemption, but
a fleshly longing that makes my life even
lonelier still. There's a place for you here
at the teeming window, where I promise,
I will not touch you again, or punish us further
with any desire, any desire but this.

Running Lights

A faint afterglow of red behind the hills,
and the tops of the pine trees
are all mist and woodsmoke now.
Up the darkening headwaters of a little trib,
the swifts give way to bats.
Nobody's going to find you, no one
is even looking. Time measured
in the tick of insects against the screened-in porch
where you are falling asleep in a chair.
The lake is very still, slate-gray all the way to a sky
nailed down with a few evening stars.
The night is all water, water is all night.
So this then is loneliness, awakening
at some indefinite hour after midnight,
a small boat with its running lights on
moving over the water, fishermen going home
or heading out for the day.

Circe's Grief

In the end, I made myself
known to your wife as
a god would, in her own house, in
Ithaca, a voice
without a body: she
paused in her weaving, her head turning
first to the right, then left
though it was hopeless of course
to trace that sound to any
objective source: I doubt
she will return to her loom
with what she knows now. When
you see her again, tell her
this is how a god says goodbye:
if I am in her head forever,
I am in your life forever.

Penelope's Stubbornness

A bird comes to the window. It's a mistake
to think of them
as birds, they are so often
messengers. That is why, once they
plummet to the sill, they sit
so perfectly still, to mock
patience, lifting their heads to sing
poor lady, poor lady, their three-note
warning, later flying like
a dark cloud from the sill to the olive grove.
But who would send such a weightless being
to judge my life? My thoughts are deep
and my memory long; why would I envy such freedom
when I have humanity? Those
with the smallest hearts have
the greatest freedom.

The Errancy

The cicadas again like kindling that won't take.
The struck match of some utopia we no longer remember
                                    the terms of—
the rules. What was it was going to be abolished, what
restored? Behind them the foghorn in the harbor,
the hoarse announcements of unhurried arrivals,
the spidery virgin-shrieks of gulls, a sideways sound, a slippery
                                    utterly ash-free
delinquency
and then the subaqueous pasturings   inexhaustible
phosphorous handwritings the frothings of their own
                                    excitements now
erase, depth wrestling with the current-corriders of depth...
But here, up on the hill, in town,
the clusterings of dwellings in balconied crystal-formation,
the cadaverous swallowings of the dream of reason gone,
hot fingerprints where thoughts laid out these streets, these
                                    bracelettings
of park and government—a hospital—a dirt-bike run—
here, we stand in our hysteria with our hands in our pockets,
quiet at the end of day, looking out, theories stationary
while the freight, the crazy wick, once more slides down—
marionette-like its being lowered in—
marionette-strung our outwaiting its bloody translation...
Utopia: remember the sensation of *direction* we loved,
how it daggered forwardly for us,
and us so feudal in its wake—
speckling of diamond-dust as I think of it now,
that being carried forward by the notion of human
perfectibility—like a pasture imposed

on the rising vibrancy of endless diamond-dust ...
And how we would comply, someday. How we were *built* to fit and
comply—
as handwriting fits to the form of its passion,
no, to the form of its passionate bearer's fingerprintable i.d.,
or, no, to the handkerchief she brings now to her haunted face,
to the race she represents, lifting the sunglasses to wipe away
the theory—or is it the tears?—the freight now all
in her right hand, in the subaqueous place we'd pull up
through her wrist—we'd siphon right up—
marionette with her leavening of mother-of-pearl—
how she wants to be legible, how the light streaks her shades now
growing *vermilion,*
which she would *capture* of course, because that, she has heard,
from the rumorous diamond-dust, is what is required,
as also her spirit—now that it has been swallowed
like a lustrous hailstone by her unquenchable body—suggests—
the zero
at the heart of the christened bonfire—oh little grimace, kiss, solo
at the heart—growing refined, tiny missionary, in your
brightskirted host,
scorched comprehensions—because that is what's required,
her *putting down* now the sunset onto that page,
as an expression of her deepest undertowing sentiment,
which spidery gestures, tongued over the molecular fibrous
whiteness,
squared-out and stretched and made to resemble emptiness,
will take down the smoldering in the terms of her passion
—sunglasses on the table, telephone ringing—
and be carried across the tongue-tied ocean,
through dusk, right through it, over prisons, over tiny clapboard
houses,
to which the bartender returns, exhausted, after work,
over flare-ups of civil strife, skeletons rotting in the arms of
skeletons, the foliage all round them gleaming,
the green belly-up god we thought we'd seen the last of,

shuddering his sleep off, first-fruit hanging ripe—oh bright red
                                                    zero—
right there within reach, that he too may be nourished,
you know this of course, what has awakened which we thought we'd
                                        extinguished,
us still standing here sword in hand, hand extended,
frail, over the limpid surface of the lake-like page,
the sleep-like page, now folded and gently driven into
its envelope, for the tiny journey, over offices, over sacrifices,
to its particular address, at the heart of the metropolis,
where someone else is waiting, hailstone at the core,
and the heat is too great, friend, the passion in its envelope,
doors slamming, traffic backing up, the populace not really
abandoned, not really, just very tired on its long red errancy
down the freeways in the dusklight
towards the little town on the hill—the *crystal-formation?*—
how long ago was it we said that? do you remember?—
and now that you've remembered—and the distance we've
traveled—and where we were, then—and
how little we've found—aren't we tired? aren't we
going to close the elaborate folder
which holds the papers in their cocoon of possibility,
the folder so pretty with its massive rose-blooms,
oh perpetual bloom, dread fatigue, and drowsiness like leavening I
feel—

Schoolyard with Boat

*"The child plays at being not only a shopkeeper or
teacher but also a windmill and a train."*
—Walter Benjamin, "On the Mimetic Faculty"

At dusk the ring of the horizon turned brown,
folded open, then dropped lower, like grain.

But there was no grain. And it was dawn again.
The wind blew odd furrows through the field.

Snow covered the field and made children cheer
in its white and again play, the strong snow

chalked fierce and clouded in the bully wind.
There was no time between the lines of breath.

Dawn and not, reflected, moved down presently.
Culled of dawn, the snow darkened and was now.

Barren in the field, which rested on dull
color, barren in the morning row, wind brushed

down and gathered. What when not repeated
the wind. When the bright snow sheared and dulled

(the field of acts brushed by the wind fell).
Children pulled blind against the field of play

when the wind blew. Sight clouded the wind, still
cusped: it repeated my sight without cause:

waves darted out of the snow, turned to wind.
The snow waved as if under a flawed window.

I did not learn it. I knew the gate started and rang.
I knew the gate already but not now. The gate

blown rang black between kindness and the row.
I erred but did not wander. No note guards the gate.

*

Not words alone pleased me, says the ringing flag.
Its white cord rings on the pole. Choices of sight,

the lines on the flag, hands that do not meet,
ring. I have held back even the crop that returns.

The cold is only in sight. So children learn words.
The flag holds ground in the wind, again, back,

and the snow lifts, the snow is a thorn of it.
Thought is not the steel share between thoughts

when children work. But learning is work only
in this separate palette, the flag. The flag sees

but work, but the words blowing ripe, but work.
Thought is not the steel share. I did not work.

But I learned of slavery. The cold is only sight
and the flag hangs back, knowing its one mind

billeting in the wind, the resistance, in wind
that knows resistance but does not measure in it

the color of the stoppage of work. A gull shrieks.
Its call is quick-held-back, again, slower

lines of it, the long shadow of its bright ring.
The gull cups the wind. But only children speak.

What *learns*? Not what is to be learned. What
learns? When snow folded on the threshing snow:

when the lesson is valuable only after real pain
though always beautiful. I believe you

no matter if you were to say it again, no matter.
The wings in sharp eaves fold. The lesson gains

rows foxglove-burnt. I believe you no matter.
The gull sweeps from markings on its breast.

The gull sweeps and its shadow shakes furled
into bright snow—like snow and its own

breathing motion, upheld by itself, of itself,
that would cause us to leave still, the snow

like a bird shaking the snow from its crest.
Harbinger of space, white winter, white wake,

crest and decision of the field, work with me
while I live. When I do not, do not work.

Common Will

Pleasure is the widow, circulating.
She walks and her dress unfolds like a stream
folds in clear seams. The bright willow streams down
the bank. Where she walks the stream flashes bright
windows, a creed of windows. She weeps through
the river and the changing flower of foam.
Pleasure is the widow. So some pleasure
is misspent. So the burnished riverbed
pulls its bright petals in a bed of wind.
She burnishes the metal flower of foam,
the metal of the answer. Cold opens
down (in the city where sparrows cry down
brick, and brick, and light the cracks of a bank).

The widow walks for pleasure, though it moves
pleasure close to her, in rivers closing,
though she is not what moves her. She is not
what pleases. She asks not what we may give.
And her walk pours out night into the sea,
pours a wildness in the serial night
through shrieks of its wheel. Through the pouring night
a whale shrieks in the pouring night because
a light could unfold from the sea. Because
she is not what she has gained in the question.

The Hole in the Ocean

Hovering in the air were two luminous shapes.
They turned, balanced in a pose of surrender. Water
poured out into the lower world, through channels
unsolved by busy rats, tides, and fish.
Then a phrase of music is misheard, and the green
Orpheus descends, striking the prison bars
of the sky like a lyre as he falls,
a counterweight to time rising beatifically.

The sea lies flat and waits to be upheld.
Time rises and the seabed shakes. The shadows
cast, buoyant, on the light and steady shore.
The Marines stay. The shore proves the current
while an old tune plays. Then Marines barge
in and stay. Time rises and the seabed shakes.
The end of the choice proves two stars
are covenant and listen to the growing music apart.

Color Comes to Night

In the line of trees part of the mirror grows
a harder forest through them. A pallor
is the storm. Blossoms through the trees, the mirror
of rain, flow hard as a fever. We hear the marble water
dressing, dressing. The middle of rain sours
the skin. The mist is combed through, pulled apart,
having woken. We wanted to remember
these lines of trees, where the garden planned. The rain
lifts its hair on a stone. The lines of trees grow
facing the ready. Their dark grid, fresh against
the dark, separates. This is one paradise.
We hear, as if we had paused, a separate breath.
We wake, wake, listen to rain, the falling meter
as if it meant us, where there was real meter.
The map of rain accumulates. The remainder,
that parts the mist, that parts, leaves this forward rain.
I do not know what is next. That is, I know.

Outside it is very clear through the white blinds.
I can tell, outside of print, what is a dream.
The determined white, the white print, rolls in wind.
No law. No law. Then law is more than their speech.
Women are then poor. When color comes to night
there are trees of dreams, red trees hanging the night
north and south, burning with natural and now
artificial light. I do not know what is next.
I think it is late, but not late for candor.
I could walk in the night close to fire. But there
is the hanging. I did not speak but I dreamed.
I did not dream, then. The winged smoke moves from rain
to fire, rain to fire. There is an instance. Work
must be hard as a mirror, not a mirror,
hard in color to keep out time, to keep it.

LINDA GREGERSON

Fish Dying on the Third Floor at Barney's

The clothes are black and unstructured this fall,
                    enlivened
          here and there by what appears to be monastic

chic: a crucifix of vaguely Eastern pro-
                    venance,
          a cowl. My friend, fresh out of drama school,

explains to me how starkly medieval woolens
                    were cut:
          few seams, to spare unraveling, the neck-

notch centered in a single length of cloth.
                    High season,
          maiden season at the uptown store, austerity's

a kind of riff in suede and silk. Sumptuous
                    charcoals,
          lampblack, slate. And lest the understatement

lose its edge, glazers have installed
                    these fine
          aquaria, within whose bounds, superbly

not for sale, not just at present, swim
                    the glories
          of a warmer world. The sun

was always a spendthrift, wasn't it?
                    —cadmium
          yellow, electric blue, and lines that parse

as eat-your-heart-out. Nature's own
                    extra-
          vagance, and functional, in fins and tails.

But something's wrong. The angelfish
                    near gloves
          and belts is on its side and stalled, gro-

tesquely heaving at the gills. Says the
                    shopper
          to her boyfriend, "What's it *doing*?"

and she's horrified. Frank
                    dying
          makes a fearful sign of life in here,

it puts the people off their food.
                    Your mother,
          said my father when I teased

her once, and nastily, Your mother always
                    liked
          to save. And who should know

but he and I, who'd lived on her prevenient
                    thrift?
          He didn't say, Uncluttered

is the privilege of the rich these days.
                    Or: In
          a world of built-in obsolescence, saved

means saddled with. He said much later,
                    This
          —I held his hand—This is a bad

business. Nailbeds blue, blue
                    ankles,
          dusky ears. His mucus-

laden lungs and their ungodly labor.
                    Father,
          while there's air to breathe, I mean

to mend my manners.

June, June

What are the sounds that crowd the path
And linger above the unmown field?
Do you hear? —The winds of heaven are talking
In the language of the heart. "June, June,"
They say. "June. The lilacs are gone."

Wonderful things are weary of me:
The groaning meteors on the August road;
The pressed grasses where the great dog
Lay, that is fallen from the moon;
The heart that speaks in tongues, "June" and "June."

The snows are asleep in their treasuries,
With crossed feet. They are not yet thought.
At evening we see the ferry depart
Northeastward, at the appointed time,
Into the night and oncoming storm.

The ferry crosses from shore to shore
And disappears into the dark.
The grasses speak louder, "June, June."
The man and woman at the rail
Say to one another, "Who *could* have thought

What is spoken in the language of the heart!"
In the dark the ferry arrives
At the other shore. —And the snow?
The snows have come a long way, afoot,
And still have a long way to go.

ROBERT COHEN

The Old Mistakes

Having begun the day with a headache, Bonnie Saks was not particularly surprised to find herself finishing it the same way. Pain, in her experience, never disappeared; it merely retreated for a while and then came back when least convenient in another form. Like men, she thought.

All afternoon there had been a chilly, puttering rain; now, though the sky had cleared with the onset of dusk, she could feel the dampness lingering in her sinuses, her extremities. Perhaps she was coming down with the flu. She hoped so. Stuck in rush-hour traffic, the tinny roar of the heater her only comfort, she conceived a vision of herself dozing in bed, sipping fatty soups, watching TV, and acting generally like the pampered creature she was destined but for circumstance to be. Oh God, she hoped to hell it was the flu. But she did not really think it was.

Meanwhile there was this pain in her head, which was considerable, and which she now undertook by small means to relieve. She massaged her temples. She listened to some jazz. She performed a deep breathing exercise. When none of these worked, she fished in her shoulder bag for the aspirin she had resolved some time ago to start carrying there but as yet, apparently, did not. Just as well. Her stomach wouldn't have been able to handle them, anyway.

Her stomach, of course, was the *real* problem; it had been queasy for days. Now it was running through its full repertoire of post–red meat convulsions, trying to cope with the enormous trapezoidal hamburger Alex, her eight-year-old, had (as he did every second Tuesday of the month) overcooked for her, and which Bonnie, standing at the sink with her coat on, staring dolorously into the charred, soapy skillet, had bolted down in record time. Alex's hamburger, truth be told, had actually tasted pretty good. She regretted it now, of course, on her way to the school meeting. But that, it appeared, was her character, if not her fate: to do and to regret.

"When's Cress coming?" Alex had asked, watching her eat.

Bonnie checked her watch. "Ten minutes ago. As usual."

"It's not fair. Why can't we stay alone?"

"Because you can't."

"Why not?"

Bonnie allowed her eyes to close, just for a moment, as if savoring the delicious witticism that was her life. "Because," she sighed, "you can't."

"It's not fair," Alex repeated. "I can put Petey to bed, you know. I've done it lots of times."

"I thought you liked Cress. I thought you had fun with her."

"I *do*. I'm just saying, we don't *need* her. All she does is watch TV, anyway."

"She's a babysitter. They're paid to do that. Someday if you play your cards right people will pay you to watch TV all night, too."

As he hunched over his plate, his eyebrows knit together in skepticism, Bonnie, for one painful moment, recognized in the boy the coiled, recalcitrant DNA of his father. "Yeah, right," he said.

"Baby, please. It's been a rotten day. Give me a break, okay?"

He made a grudging frown.

"Is there anything left in the fridge for Cress?"

"Not much. Couple of apples. Mustard."

"All right, so I'll leave my credit card. If she's hungry she can order a pizza."

"Large or small?"

Bonnie waved her hand in exasperation. "Whichever she wants."

"I thought we were so *broke*," Alex sneered.

Half an hour later, sitting on the padded floor of the preschool's gym, Bonnie tasted the hamburger again, and while she was at it, everything else she had eaten that day. Things were backing up on her. Her gaze swept over the wrestling mats laid out around her like some pale, meandering dream. Life is containment, she thought: a bird feathering a cage. The problem was very deep. It was not, for example, just the meetings. It was not the five-figure debts. It was not the lousy apartment, the lousy sinuses, the succession of lousy jobs. Nor was it her daily existence with the kids—the weekends lost to laundry and videos, the evening grind of dinner-bath-story, and then the hour or so of studying, that small rhetorical gesture meant to impress upon herself that she did indeed have a will of her own, a *life* of her own, before she surrendered to exhaustion and fell heavily into her unshared, and often unmade, bed. No, what afflicted her was larger than any one thing. Possibly it was even larger than the dissertation which lay, half-formed and loveless, across the solid pine door she used for a desk. The door had once opened to a burgeoning closet; now, scarred by coffee rings, it led only to the narrow little sub-basement that was her despair.

"Hey, Bon."

Larry Albeit, Anya's father, sat down beside her on the wrestling mat and officiously zipped open his jacket. "Better get comfortable," he said. "We're in for a long one."

"Oh no. Not tonight."

"Oh yes." He loosened his tie. "Next year's budget. Remember last year? It'll go on for hours."

"But it can't. I told the sitter I'd be home by nine."

Larry Albeit shrugged, and offered her a wide-angle view of his high white teeth. What did he care? A lawyer in a litigious culture, meetings were the connective tissue of his life. Besides, at home he had his cheery wife, Kip, reading *Madeline* to the girls, free of charge.

"Listen," he said, "I'm getting coffee. Want some?"

"Yeah, okay."

"Caf or decaf?"

She hesitated. One would have thought from the amount of time it required that the choice was a profound one. "I'll have decaf," she said, more to herself, as it turned out, than to Larry, who had already sprung up and bounced gallantly away to fetch it.

"Okay, guys," said Geoff Dahlberg, brandishing his clipboard. "I move that we get started. Lots of business tonight."

First the secretary, Bill Lake, went over the minutes from the previous month, which had to be accepted by voice vote into the record. Then Bethany Freitag gave the membership report, Eileen Smith reviewed the curriculum proposals, and Howard Peeler gave an update on the physical plant renovations. After which the treasurer, Alice Orkin, was called upon to give her report, which she most forcefully did. It so happened the school was actually in the black for a change, though barely, and that wasn't taking into account the rent increase and the all but certain rise in staff salaries that would come in the spring. To cover these expenditures, tuition would have to go up, but then tuition went up every year. The only question was how much.

Alice, smiling, brandished one of her CPI charts. A photographer's assistant, she spent her days behind the scenes, fetching props, soothing models, fiddling with lights and shadows; only on the second Tuesday of each month could she emerge with her laser-printed graphs and charts and command everyone's attention. Not that Bonnie begrudged her. She, too, often dreamed of stepping out from the shadows and into the light. But armed with what?

"Thank you," Geoff said, bobbing over his clipboard. "Those are fine reports. We all appreciate the work you guys put in."

Alice, Howard, Bethany, Eileen, and Bill nodded in acknowledgement.

"Okay, if there's no other old business, I move we proceed to the memo you received in your boxes last week, concerning the benefits package. Now, those of you who survived last year's meetings may recall these budget issues get kind of delicate, and tend to generate some pretty strong emo—"

"Geoff?" A hand was in the air, bunched into a fist. It belonged to Ginny Stern, whose kid, Jason, was the precocious darling of Petey's class. Why shouldn't he be? He had a bright, principled, outspoken mother who took him to museums on the weekend and to France in the summer so he'd grow up bilingual, and the presence of whose hand in the air just now did not bode well, Bonnie thought, for the pace of the evening.

"I'm confused," Ginny said. It was her standard opening, and as usual not even remotely true. "Why are we using Styrofoam again?" She pointed accusingly to the nearest coffee cup, which happened to be Bonnie's, and was in fact comprised of materials that would outlive them all. "I thought we settled this issue months ago," she said.

Geoff, his brow furrowed, looked around for help.

"She's right," said Bill Lake, checking his notes. "September 17: unanimous vote."

"I'd like to know what happened to the mugs my committee went out and bought for replacements," Ginny said. "I gave them to Sara myself."

All eyes turned to Sara Montague, the waifish assistant director, who was sitting in the back of the room with her knees up, stitching flowers on a macramé tablecloth. It was Sara's job to stock the kitchen. Several times in the past, this had brought her into direct engagement with Ginny Stern, often on the losing side. But now her expression was serene. "Mugs?" Sara asked faintly, as if recalling some benign distant obsession.

"There were three dozen. They had dancing cows on one side."

"Oh, those were no good. I had them inspected."

"Inspected?" Ginny looked dubious.

"By a ceramicist. She said they were improperly fired, and anyway there's too much lead in the glaze."

"But they're from *Conran's*."

"Well, they're a health hazard."

"So's Styrofoam," Ginny shot back.

"Yes, but that's environmental. It's completely different."

All this time Bonnie was staring at the soggy toes of her shoes, wondering: her mugs at home—weren't a couple of them from Conran's, too? Was she poisoning the kids? Wait, but the kids didn't drink coffee. Thank God, she thought: she was only poisoning herself.

"Listen, folks," Geoff said, "I don't mean to cut off this discussion, but we've got a long agenda. I move that in the interests of time we go ahead and use the Styrofoam tonight, and meanwhile let's ask the food committee to purchase new mugs, safe ones, for next time. Anyone want to second?"

Several people rushed to second it. Bonnie, sipping surreptitiously from her contraband cup, would have, too, but did not dare open her mouth. Already she had acquired a reputation as something of a loose cannon: fickle in her loyalties, wanting in seriousness, slow to volunteer. Doubtless it was all true. She simply did not feel like a good citizen these days. She lacked the time, the energy, the patience; ultimately, she lacked the will. It was a shameful thing to admit at this point in global culture, but she'd about had it with participatory democracy—she'd have been happier just writing out a check every month and letting paid professionals make all the decisions; or, better, to give herself over to a benevolent fascist dictator for a while, to have at least a few of the trains in her life running on time.

Kevin, she thought. At times the name rose inside her reflexively, like bile.

It was Kevin who had talked her into this cooperative preschool in the first place. Parent involvement, he'd said, was the coming thing: responsible, statistically persuasive, and cheaper to boot. Which was approximately the same line of reasoning he'd applied a few months later to getting divorced.

But that wasn't altogether fair. Strictly speaking, Kevin had been no more to blame in the matter than Bonnie herself, who had after all done no one any good by sleeping with an old boyfriend, Stanley Gottlieb, at the M.L.A. in San Francisco, for reasons that remained shrouded in fog even now. She'd been five months pregnant with Petey at the time; she remembered thinking, rather magically in retrospect, that the extra layers of flesh would somehow insulate her from consequence. But they hadn't, of course. And now here she was. Stanley still made an occasional appearance, flying in to read a paper at a conference and, almost incidentally, to screw up her life; but Kevin, that dear, sweet, narcissistic mess, was gone—decamped to Ecuador, where he was finishing his post-doc and working with a psychoanalyst to overcome his innumerable blocks. He must have been making some progress down there, too, because of late his child support checks had begun to arrive roughly the same month they were due.

No, it was no longer quite so easy as it once was, blaming Kevin.

"...and now," Geoff was saying, "if you'll turn to page three, you'll see the charts drawn up by the personnel committee, detailing the various benefit packages available to the staff..."

Bonnie dutifully studied the charts. The fact that they were incomprehensible to her, though discouraging, was predictable enough—she had never done well in statistics—and after the first few seconds her eyes began skating giddily over the numbers, making figure eights and pirouettes in the margins, fanciful little doodles that seemed to illustrate perfectly the chaotic, trivial nature of her thoughts. The mind, she'd once read, is just a piece of paper blown around by the wind. But the nice thing about meetings was that she could just sit there and let these competent, initiative-seizing people—the *grown-ups,* she caught herself thinking—bear her along. She could coast. Coasting, under the circumstances, was a rare pleasure, the kind of minor indulgence, like getting high in the bathtub or devouring a quart of ice cream, in which embittered people seek consolation for their grievances, and Bonnie would have been perfectly capable of enjoying it if not for her headache, and the way Alex's hamburger had settled in her stomach, and the test she would have to give herself the next morning, of which the hamburger, in its small dyspeptic way, was a reminder.

"Can I say something?" asked Lucia Todd-Frazen, interrupting a discussion of the dental plan.

Geoff, sitting in a yoga position at the front of the room, nodded beneficently.

"I just want you all to know that Harvey and I—and I think I speak for both of us even though he's not here tonight? Because we really love you guys on staff, the work you do, you're like part of our family, your patience, your involvement, your . . . and we believe in labor, we do. We support it. Even though we're not technically working class ourselves, of course, and sometimes, like with the Teamsters, or the restaurant workers downtown, a couple years ago, those indictments? . . . But what I want to say is that this measure, we support it, both of us do . . . completely."

The tremulousness of Lucia's voice and the circuity of her phrasing were of a nature so profound that a kind of collective sigh went up at the end of her speech, that any additional pain might be spared her. Such is the tyranny of the shy. But her message had touched a nerve. A weight of self-consciousness descended, tilting the proceedings rather heavily in the direction of posturing. Parents of both genders began to let fly with the most ringing pro-labor sentiments heard in these parts since the McGovern days. What kind of lousy package were we *offering* our staff, anyway? Dental was one small part of an intricate puzzle. What about, for instance, workmen's comp?

"Work*persons*," grumbled Thea Doyle.

What about mental health? Job security? Paternity leave for the men (both gay, as it happened) on staff? A flurry of amendments were proposed; each had to be discussed for a while before being tabled and referred to the appropriate committee chairperson, that it might be studied and further discussed at the next meeting. Several voice votes were taken, anyway. Bonnie tried to participate, but her mouth, for some reason, had lost the talent to issue sounds. One by one, her powers were deserting her. Pretty soon it was nine-thirty, and she had to go to the bathroom again, and even Larry Albeit in his five-hundred-dollar suit was beginning to look a little rumpled.

Then Lucia cleared her throat again, and everyone froze.

"I just want to say this issue, the one we're discussing? I've had it for a long time. Because my life, it used to be a different... a different... like that proposition for the farmworkers, back in '81? I worked on that. Harvey didn't want me to at first, he thought it took too much time away, I guess, I don't really remember what he thought. But I said, Harvey? I believe in labor. I believe people who work hard, and who have families like us, should make as much as we make, and should have benefits that are just as good, and, and, this is very important for me. I have a real issue with—"

Jesus Christ, thought Bonnie. Gimme a break.

And then an odd thing happened. Lucia halted; her face went white; and one hand flew to her mouth to stifle a sob. It was as if through some dreadful ventriloquism Bonnie's thoughts had been heard by everyone. Which was impossible. And yet there Lucia stood, damp-eyed and immobile on the wrestling mat. From the clench of her hands, she might have been grappling with an angel.

Under normal circumstances, the sight of Lucia Todd-Frazen getting emotional at a meeting was no more surprising or upsetting a phenomenon than the buzzing of the sodium lights in the parking lot outside. But tonight it seemed to Bonnie that the evening's very skin had been punctured. Horrified, she tried to remember: *Had* she said the words aloud? She'd done everything else wrong that day, why not this, too? Oh God, her nature, her *true* nature, had finally revealed itself: She'd said something bitchy and awful, severed the cord that bound civilized, cooperative people together, and now they'd all hate her. And meanwhile it would be Petey, who was already tormented nightly by dreams, who could not even count past three, whose skinny nose, a small parody of her own, could not be persuaded to stop running—it would be Petey who'd suffer the consequences.

Abruptly, she stood, muttering something about the bathroom—it was true, she really *did* need to go—all the while hoping no one would notice the tremble in her voice, or the inflamed condition of her cheeks and nose, or the tears that were now in her eyes, too. There was no accounting for them; they'd simply arrived, dumbly, brutishly, like strange orphan children towards whom she felt no family feeling but for whom she understood herself somehow responsible. Room would have to be made, but where? There was no room left.

Only when she was alone in the bright tiled shelter of the bathroom did the anxiety subside a bit. Standing at the sink, she splashed cold water on her face, sensing that some personal crisis—she could not have said what—had just been narrowly avoided. Nonetheless she was left feeling somewhat depleted. Lucia's speech, in the momentary stillness, continued to galumph indignantly through her head. *I have a real issue with this.* When had issues become possessions, Bonnie wondered, and why didn't she own more of them herself? But then she did, didn't she? She owned plenty. What would it matter, if she added to the pile one more?

There were no paper towels, so she wiped her hands on her jeans, which she intended to throw out soon, anyway, because they were threadbare and shapeless, like so much of what passed for her wardrobe, from when she was pregnant with Petey.

Back out in the hallway, she lost a moment or two to indecision, trying to establish whether it was better to return to the gym or maybe just leave. Either way she would be late getting home.

So she stopped at the phone in the hallway to call Cress.

The line was busy, of course. Cress was a popular girl. Though rather plain to look at, to say nothing of her feckless and unimaginative babysitting skills, Cress emanated something, a kind of low, gravitational hum, a calm, that strongly endeared her to other people, particularly children and men. Or were these two different categories? Standing at the phone, the busy signal pounding away angrily at the protective insulation of her heart—what now? what now?—Bonnie turned to look over the construction-paper cutouts of lions and monkeys that the two-year-olds had done that week (Petey's, she was relieved to discover, was no more crude or haphazard than any of the others'), and two of the tears she had worked so hard to suppress back in the gym finally worked their way free.

"Hey, Bon?" Larry Albeit was approaching her with a concerned look. "You okay?"

Bonnie touched a finger to her cheek, where it was warm and wet. "Okay?" she said.

"You're crying."

"So?"

"So nothing. I just thought maybe there was, you know, something wrong. Sometimes it helps, you know, to talk about things."

Bonnie shook her head. Talk? Things? Things were the problem. Talk was the problem. Men were the problem. Nothing that Larry Albeit was offering could possibly be of any constructive benefit. "We should probably get back," she said. "The meeting."

"Ah . . ." Larry waved his wrist cavalierly and—unless she was out of her mind—actually blushed. "Fuck the meeting."

"Really?" Despite herself, Bonnie giggled. The sound it made in the hallway was so loud, so awful and garish, that it might have issued from the wall of paper jungle animals behind her.

"Listen, come on out to the car. I've got a joint in the glove compartment that has your name on it."

Bonnie hesitated. Lately all the junctions in her life's road seemed to be marked by this same sign: Where Do You Want to Be Least? But it so happened that she had never seen such a thing as a joint with her name on it before, and it was partly in hopes of making up for a lifetime of such deprivations, or so she told herself, that she followed Larry Albeit out to the parking lot. There his Volvo lay gleaming under the streetlight's yellow halo, enormous and sleek, a vehicle for all the soul's burdensome dreams. Larry got in behind the wheel, and Bonnie, quickly, so as not to change her mind, climbed in on the passenger's side. The position gave her an odd sensation of backwardness, of the self inverted by mirrors—she was accustomed to being the driver, not the driven—but in the end she decided that it was no stranger, in fact, than anything else.

"Now..." Larry, bent over, was fumbling in the glove compartment with his right hand, creating in the process no small amount of incidental contact with Bonnie's right knee. "Where'd I put that little sucker?"

"Never mind," she said. "It doesn't matter."

"It doesn't?"

"Not to me. I'm happy just to be out of there."

Larry, face pressed sideways to the wheel, mumbled vaguely.

"I'm living the wrong life," she said.

"Mmm..."

"I mean, let's face it, these college towns...these people with their issues, their meetings that go on forever, their perfect kids who just happen to go to private schools, their potluck dinners with tabouli and lasagna—how do you stand it?"

"Actually," Larry admitted, "I kind of like lasagna."

"Oh," she said bitterly, "so do I. At least I think I used to. That's what's so awful. All these things I used to really like, and now I can't stand them anymore. Do you think something's terribly wrong with me?"

"Oh no, I wouldn't say *wrong*..."

"Well, I don't care if there is. I mean, good lord, she was crying over dental benefits in there."

"Lucia," Larry allowed mildly, "has strong convictions."

"Well, so do I. And one of them is she's wacko."

"Oh, she's not really so bad. Everyone, you know, they just want to do things the right way for the kids. Avoid the old mistakes. Sometimes it makes people clumsy. But all in all they're doing their best."

"Yeah, yeah. I know."

Bonnie leaned against the door, too cold (she'd left her coat in the gym) and too tired, all of a sudden, to be properly ashamed of her own small-mindedness. The door itself was so much more substantial a piece of metal than the door of her shitty little Subaru that she found it hard to believe both could be accurately described by the same word. "Can you turn on the heater?" she asked. "I've been cold all day."

"Sure."

Larry turned his key in the ignition, and the car purred to life. The heater made virtually no noise at all.

"What is it with you lawyers?" Bonnie asked, watching him resume his search for the wayward joint. "How come you're the only people who smoke dope anymore?"

"Our work is very taxing," he said.

"Psh. Whose isn't?"

"It's a question of degree. There's a great deal of money, you know, that rides on our ability to make fine discriminations, draw little lines between their side and our side. Some of these lines, they're so tiny, so arbitrary, that they're almost invisible. This causes a lot of strain. You come home, you want to release some tension, blur a few of those lines. Let things get a little sloppy, you know?"

Oh, thought Bonnie grimly, I know.

"Plus we can generally afford the good shit."

"Oh yeah? So where is it?"

"Funny. I stuck one in here the other day. I wonder if Kippy might have—"

"Kip smokes?"

"Sure, like a chimney. Ever since the chemo."

"Whoa, wait . . ."

"Oh, that was, you know, two or three years ago. We had a scare, but it's in remission now, and they assure us the prognosis is very . . . ah, wait, here we go." He extracted a fat joint and reached into his pocket for some matches. When it was lit, he blew out a jet of smoke and handed it over to Bonnie, who had fallen silent.

"It's terrible what I'm doing," he said after a while. "Isn't it?"

"I don't know about terrible. Irresponsible, maybe."

"No, I mean talking about Kippy. Married people aren't supposed to talk about their spouses in a revealing way, especially to members of the opposite sex. It's a violation of any number of unwritten conjugal codes."

"What should married people do? Walk around feeling bottled up and lonely instead?"

Larry considered the question. "I suppose so," he said, and laughed a nervous laugh.

It really was good shit. It must have been that, or the late hour, or the unlikely surroundings, or else merely the promiscuous way that such things as germs and laughter travel between people—in any event, Bonnie began to laugh a little herself. At least she assumed it was laughter. It had been a while. Was laughter supposed to make her stomach so bitter, her cheeks so streaky and hot?

"Bon?" Larry was leaning forward again, his eyes small reddish stones on the placid pond of his forehead. "You okay?"

"I think I'm pregnant."

It was in the nature of an experiment, saying it aloud, and once the words were out, part of her continued to listen carefully for some kind of explosion, but nothing happened. Absolutely nothing.

Larry nodded soberly. "I thought so."

"You thought so? What kind of crazy thing is that to say?"

"Just a feeling," he said. "I saw you back there when I first sat down. You looked kind of haughty and impatient, like you were cut off from everything and didn't care. Usually this connotes something medical." He stubbed out the last of the joint, then closed the ashtray with a snap. "I figured either someone died or else you were pregnant."

"Actually, Larry, you were right on both counts. I'm pregnant, and someone *is* going to die."

He considered this for a moment. "Forgive me for prying," he said gently, "but I take it the father's not in the picture?"

"The father? The father is a hot young turk post-structuralist. The father won't even concede that an author is responsible for his own book. What's he going to make out of this?

"Also," she added wearily, "he lives in Toronto. With a woman.

Maybe two women. It's not entirely clear."

"Well, that's a tough situation," Larry said, and rubbed his jaw.

"Yep."

"Is there anything I can do?"

"Do?" She tried to look out the window, but the glass was fogged with her own breath, and she lacked the energy to wipe it clean.

"Sure. You know…"

She wheeled around to face him. "What are you talking about? I hardly know you. Our kids happen to go the same preschool. What the hell could you possibly do—adopt us?"

"Okay, okay. Take it easy. I'm only trying to help."

"What *is* it with you people, anyway? Where do you get your confidence? Tell me the truth: Was it Mom? Did she love you so much you think you can just go around *do*ing things? Like what do you have in mind, Larry? Form a support group? Have a bake sale? Just what are you proposing?" Her stomach flopped over like a salmon. "Oh, shit," she wailed, "oh, filthy mother of—"

"Sometimes just talking," Larry said gently, soothingly, as he inched closer across the leather seat. "Just letting it out…"

Though she did not herself subscribe to this theory, in truth something did happen to Bonnie as the tears fell: Her head became very heavy and at the same time remarkably light. She could feel it taking off on a bobsled run of its own, circling giddily for a while and then slowing, easing itself towards the smooth, solid topography of Larry's shoulder—the surface to which all earthly gravity would consign her. All right, okay: she let it go. And, yes, the sensation *was* luxurious, damn it, rather like dropping into a wide, silken net. And she deserved it, too. She deserved it for all her hard work, for every paper she had written or graded, every diaper, every omelette, every load of laundry, every aimless night she had passed staring at the crack in the wall above the toaster, wondering how not to fall in. Yes, she had worked hard, very goddamned hard, and now she was due…well, *some*thing, she was certainly due *some*thing…

Her head touched Larry's shoulder. Then, immediately, in its stubborn, cork-like fashion, it bobbed right up again. "I have to get back," she said, reaching for the door handle.

"Are you sure? All those people, they'll be——"

"No, no," she said, "I mean *home.*"

But once she had extricated herself from the car, the wind caught her, whipping around like a shroud, as if to expose—or perhaps, she wondered briefly, enfold?—her. Overhead, through the skeletal branches, she could see the cold clear eye of the moon. It was getting late. Parents were beginning to push through the double doors and head for their cars. She could not make out their faces in the darkness, but she recognized them by their good bulky winter coats: Geoff Dahlberg, Lucia Todd-Frazen, Howard Peeler. Alice Orkin and Thea Doyle were hugging goodbye; Bethany Freitag was leaning into Ginny Stern's car, hammering out some detail of car pooling; Arthur Browning was talking into his cellular phone, informing his wife to stick his dinner in the oven, he was on his way. The meeting was over.

Bonnie was almost to her car when she remembered her coat back in the gym. For a moment she was tempted to leave it there. But she had always liked that coat, and it had another year or two left in it, and she could not afford another right now. So she turned and headed back to the double doors.

The hallway was deserted. Of the forty-odd people who'd attended the meeting, only Sara Montague, locking up the kitchen for the night, remained. Sara looked tired but content; apparently the Styrofoam debate had been resolved to her satisfaction. She put her keys back in her shoulder bag and wound her scarf loosely around her neck. "Forget something?" she asked brightly.

Bonnie made a theatrical flailing gesture with the palms of her hands. "My coat."

"I think Geoff locked the gym when he left. He usually does."

"Oh. Oh, well——"

"I can open it for you, though."

But when they got the gym door unlocked and flicked on the lights, Bonnie looked around with a dry mouth and a sinking heart. No coat was in evidence.

"Let's try the lost and found box," Sara suggested.

The coat was not there either, though she did find one of Petey's T-shirts, mislaid since early October. She clutched it with both hands as she followed Sara out. *This,* she decided, was what had been due her. Not reward, but punishment; not escape, but a deepening of her hole. After all, she had been digging it for years; it would take more than a little hanky-panky with Larry Albeit at this point to vault herself free.

"Hey," Sara said. "Is that it?"

Bonnie blinked. There, just outside the door of Petey's room, was her coat. It had been folded and draped, with some delicacy, across one of the tiny plastic chairs. There was a rise to the shoulders she hadn't noticed before; in her present condition, she was reminded of wings.

When she unfolded the coat, a slip of paper fluttered off and fell to the floor. Bonnie paused; she was aware of being a little bit stoned at the moment, and also of Sara Montague, keys in hand, holding the door that led to the foyer, watching. Hurriedly, she bent over to retrieve the slip of paper, dirtying the knees of her jeans in the process.

The note, written in a mother's careful hand, read: "Does this belong to Bonnie Saks, Petey's mom? If so, please make sure she gets it."

Suddenly a gate rose in Bonnie's heart, and all its channels flooded at once. She was here, she was known, she was being looked after. Things would be delivered to her.

Driving home, through an infinity of green lights, Bonnie gave some thought to the many people in her life who had been irritating her so. She thought of the kids, of Cress, of Lucia and Ginny and Larry, and Kip, poor Kip. She thought of Kevin, and even Stanley, that wretched bastard, who were after all to be pitied, she decided, not hated, for their estrangement from what they had wrought. And she thought of the writer of that unsigned note, who could have been any one of the parents at the meeting, tired, harried, earnest, squeezing good works without recompense from their busy schedules. Larry was right: Everyone was trying so hard to avoid the old mistakes—of course it made them clumsy, it makes all of us clumsy, she thought, all of us but not all the time.

When she got home, she found Cress at the kitchen table, thoughtfully smoking a cigarette. "How were they?" Bonnie asked.

"Monsters."

"Sorry. I tried to call."

"That's okay." Cress waved her wrist, dispelling the smoke. "I guess the meeting ran long, huh?"

"Yeah." She glanced half-heartedly at the dishes piled in the sink. Was any pizza left? She was famished.

"Well..."

Cress stubbed out her cigarette and reached for her bag.

"Let me just sit for a minute, okay? Then I'll call you a cab."

"Okay, cool."

So they sat there a while. Cress put down her bag and lit another cigarette, pausing every so often to tap the ashes into a teacup, and whatever obsessions were running through her head, she chose to retain there. Bonnie, too tired to shrug out of her coat, allowed her eyes to fall closed. She was not thinking about the long evening she had just passed, or the dishes still to be done, the lunches still to be made. She was thinking only of this moment right now, this space that did not demand to be filled because it was not in fact vacant, but merely hanging, suspended in time's web, between past and future, in a state of pure potentiality. And it occurred to Bonnie that in the final analysis she was a very capable person, capable of more, oh, much more than she could possibly envision, perhaps even capable of being happy...

Then Cress yawned. "Can I go now?"

And Bonnie, her eyes still closed, purse clutched to her stomach, thought clearly and without bitterness, *This is going to cost me, too.*

Pursuit of Happiness

Ned loved Betsy, a blond waitress who lived in the suburbs.
Only Betsy was in love with Peter, the race-car mechanic,
who had muscles and a black Corvette, and wore a cross
inside his T-shirt. But Peter was half-crazy over Anne, his
    beautiful X-
lover, who said, "You're nothing but a loser," and
left him to marry Chet, the insurance salesman, who was boring
    in bed
but who was climbing hand over hand up the corporate ladder.
At the dress rehearsal, Chet's sister Jane met Betsy,
and her heart had leapt with the force of a gazelle.
It was hopeless of course. Betsy couldn't stop talking about Peter:
his opalescent eyes, his enormous biceps. After months of despair,
Jane tried to hang herself, awoke in the Community Hospital
in the same room with Margaret, a nun from Minnesota
admitted for irritable bowels, and who reminded Jane
of her sixth grade teacher, also a nun, who'd kissed
her ear one day after school. Jane had a religious conversion
right there in the hospital, left her job as secretary at Finch,
Legatt, and White Legal Services, and joined the order—
Sisters of St. John of the Cross. Margaret, the nun, passed
away from complications. Betsy met a cross-dresser and
ran off with him to Venezuela. Peter enrolled at the local college
    to study
sanitation engineering. Anne had four children and gained thirty
    pounds.
Ned remained at home caring for his aging father,
a retired dentist, who ate spoonfuls of blender food till he died.

Three Poems

Narcissist #1

I'm so amazing I could lick myself.

Narcissist #2

Did you see how well I licked myself?

Narcissist #3

I was so upset. They barely noticed the way I licked myself.

Her Body

1. The Fingers

They are small enough to find and care for a tiny stone.
    To lift it with wobbly concentration from the ground,
        from the family of stones, up past the pursed mouth—

for this we are thankful—to a place level with her eyes
    to take a close look, a look into the nature of stone.
        Like everything, it is for the first time: first stone,

chilly cube of ice, soft rise of warm flesh, hard
    surface of table leg, first and lasting scent of grass
        rubbed between the tiny pincer fingers. And there is

the smallest finger poking the air, pointing toward the first heat
    of the single sun, pointing toward the friendly angels
        who sent her, letting them know contact's made.

2. The Eyes

We believe their color makes some kind of difference,
the cast of it played off the color of hair and face.

But it makes no difference, blue or brown,
hazel, green, or gray, pale sky or sand.

When sleep-burdened they'll turn up into her,
close back down upon her sizeable will.

But when she's ready for the yet-to-come—
oh, they widen, grow a deep cool sheen

to catch the available light and shine
with the intensity of the newly arrived.

If they find you they'll hold on relentlessly
without guile, the gaze no less than interrogatory,

fixed, immediate, bringing to bear what there's been
to date. Call her name and perhaps they'll turn to you,

or they might be engaged, looking deeply into the nature
of other things—the affect of wall, the texture of rug,

into something very small that's fallen to the floor
and needs to be isolated and controlled. Maybe

an afternoon reflection, an insect moving *slowly,*
maybe just looking with loyalty into the eyes of another.

3. *The Toes*

Who went to market?
Who stayed home?
This one goes,
this one doesn't.
This one eats

the flesh
of grass-eating mammals,
this one does not.
In the seventeenth century
Basho—delicate master

of the vagaries of who
went where—
wrote to one he loved
not of market
and not of meat,

but something brief,
abbreviated,
like five unburdened toes
fluttering like cilia
in the joy of a drafty room:

> *You go,*
> *I stay.*
> *Two autumns.*

4. *The Soul*

Who knows how they get here,
beyond the obvious.
Who packaged the code

that provided the slate for her eyes,
and what about the workmanship
that went into the fingers

allowing such intricate movement
just months from the other side?—
Who placed with such exactness

the minute nails on each
of the ten unpainted toes?
And what remains

beyond eye and ear, the thing
most deeply rooted in her body—
the thing that endlessly blossoms

but doesn't age, in time
shows greater vitality? The thing
unlike the body that so quickly

reaches its highest moment only
to begin, with little hesitation,
the long roll back, slowing all the way

until movement is administered
by devices other than those devised
by divine design? The ageless thing

we call *soul,* like air, both resident
and owner of the body's estate.
But *her* soul, only partially

unpackaged, sings
through the slate that guards it,
contacts those of us waiting here

with a splay of its soft,
scrutinizing fingers.
Her soul is a sapling thing,

something green, dew-damp
but resolute, entering this world
with an angel's thumb pressed

to her unformed body at the very last,
a template affixed to her body
when they decided it was time

to let her go, for her to come to us
and their good work was done.
An angel's thumbprint, a signature, her soul.

Ethics of Twilight

"As it leaves dawn behind and advances into day, light prostitutes itself and is redeemed—ethics of twilight— at the moment it vanishes."
—E. M. Cioran

Ethics of secrets and vanishings,
    of sunny downfalls and cloudy coverups.

The reign of commonsense has ended
    and strangeness floats through the air.

Deceptive moonlight, dusky erasures—
    night welcomes us with open blue arms

to its plots and betrayals, desires
    wafting like music through our bodies.

We go forth to our furtive daydreams—
    our unaccountable, inadmissible motives—

and come home to lie down again
    alone or together, drifting obliviously

into the vacant coffins of sleep.
    Ethics of nightmares and dawn advancing...

Days of 1968

She came to me with a mind like fire
and a name written in smoky letters on the wind.

She came to me with the grief of a fallen angel,
with white arms that should have been wings

and skinny legs sadly rooted to the ground.
She came to me barefoot in a sleeveless dress,

playing air guitar and talking about the gods
who said she never should have been saddled

with a body in the first place, with a human
past and a disembodied voice flickering

like a small candle in the endless dark.
"I believe in being reincarnated," she declared—

my pure psyche, my haunted half-girl turning
back into the spirit she wanted to become.

In the Backyard

This morning a hawk plunges
straight for the squirrel at my feeder
and leaves only
its signature: blood on the snow.

All morning it circled the yard,
then dove, stunning itself
on the glass sky of my window,

and in minutes returned, braving
the thin, perilous channel
between hedgerow and house. I was watching
its path as it fell, its persistence,

and the squirrel, how it dashed
for the downspout, finding itself
motionless under the heat
of the hawk's body,

the claws in its rib cage, the sudden
tearing of wind as it rose
over the fence, the feeder,

the tops of maples and houses.
All morning it stays with me, not
the squirrel's terror, the hawk's
accuracy, but only

how it must feel to be lifted
out of your life, astonished

at the yard growing smaller, the earth
with its snow-covered fields tilting,
and what must be your shadow
flying across it, farther
and farther below.

Dust Storm

A secret like a lodestar, a ball of pure lead, I thought
about tasting him long enough for a life to wither,
a new planet to come into view. I imagined the smell
of his genitals, so common, so indescribable.
Wyoming and summer. Thunderheads galloping
in a stark yellow light. Or puffball clouds white
as eggs streaming over eye-piercing cobalt skies.
Grasses and hyssop. Jewelweed and coneflower.
Through the long evenings we would lean against
fences telling our lives more precisely than they had
ever been told. Desire rang bell-deep in my pelvic bone.
Two foxes looping along a ridge, or two coyotes.
Moon licked clean the sleek backs of his geldings.
Wherever I slept, my body spiraled then glided.
Distant ancestors appeared in dreams and spread
embroidered robes and silken scarves before me,
opened lacquered boxes filled with blue dust.
The prairie winds caught that dust. Even the crickets'
scrapings grew muted. One can over-think a thing.
The road skirled dust into tiny funnels, the funnels
to waves, the waves to a sea. I never slept with him,
but grew remote as a watch. Windswept plains,
sagebrush, tumbleweeds, and later, contrails
that crosshatched a shock-pink sky. His cattle
began to look painfully dumb. All were castrated.
My blood had grown too thin in Wyoming's thin air.
A woman out of her element, adrift on a high plateau.

First Marriage

Drought summer I broke my foot and hobbled on crutches.
Stood staring, crutches against the counter, refrigerator door
open, blank light spilling. Your mother, all hours, weeping
upstairs, her widow's heart splitting her chest apart.
Home after nine, or later, vacant as a ghost, you would swallow
me with a hot mouth, grime visible on your neck, your hands.
A tire dropped like a scream from the beech, then the children's
sandbox with its litter of plastic toys, the rusted jungle gym.
A clothesline that spun and squeaked in storms. Two neighbor
farms against the sky to the north, but everything else blank.
Crickets, and louder, cicadas, and still louder, frogs.
Sometimes cows lowing or the long low wail of the freight
trains passing through Carmargo. Was it the foolishness
or the emptiness that mattered? Remember the barn swallows
chirping before dawn and how happiness entered us then
as rapidly as spring took the prairie? Milk soured so quickly
and I would scrub that kitchen till it glistened and a silence
opened in the long afternoons. Some days I longed to bite
into the light and vanish. Light brushing windows, stepping
across the paneled walls. The old torn couch on the porch,
you over me and forcing me and with cars passing a half-mile
off; your mother upstairs; the thrumming of sixteen-wheelers.
You sold feed. You traveled. The sky passing new clouds
east that would thin out and dissolve, or gather illuminated
in the evenings, or in the afternoons, heavy and dark with rain.
After all the cats died and your mother went back to Florida,
a dizziness once watching the dust a truck blew up and wind
carried off, the baby asleep in his playpen, dogs not barking.
Chicory blue behind the barn, Queen Anne's lace, goldenrod.
This happened. I lived there with you. We were young, stumbling
and half-asleep in our existence on this earth. There were children.

Fifth Amendment

The fear of perjuring herself turned into a tacit
Admission of her guilt. Yet she had the skill
And the luck to elude her implacable pursuers.
God was everywhere like a faceless guard in a gallery.
Death was last seen in the auction room, looking worried.
She hadn't seen him leave. She narrowly avoided him
Walking past the hard hats eating lunch. Which one was he?
She felt like one of those women you sometimes see
Crying in a hotel lobby. But he couldn't figure her out.
She wrote him a letter saying, "Please don't phone me,"
Meaning, "Please phone me." And there were times when she
Refused to speak at all. Would this be one of them?
On went the makeup and the accessories. Her time was now,
And he could no more share her future than she
Could go to college with him twenty years ago.
She would have had a tremendous crush on him
Back then, with his scarf flying in the wind like
The National League pennant flying over Ebbets Field
In Brooklyn, borough of churches, with the pigeons on the sill
And the soprano's trill echoing in the alley.

Ninth Inning

He woke up in New York City on Valentine's Day,
Speeding. The body in the booth next to his was still warm,
Was gone. He had bought her a sweater, a box of chocolate
Said her life wasn't working he looked stricken she said
You're all bent out of shape, accusingly, and when he
She went from being an Ivy League professor of French
To an illustrator for a slick midtown magazine
They agreed it was his fault. But for now they needed
To sharpen to a point like a pencil the way
The Empire State Building does. What I really want to say
To you, my love, is a whisper on the rooftop lost in the wind
And you turn to me with your rally cap on backwards rooting
For a big inning, the bases loaded, our best slugger up
And no one out, but it doesn't work that way. Like the time
Kirk Gibson hit the homer off Dennis Eckersley to win the game:
It doesn't happen like that in fiction. In fiction, we are
On a train, listening to a storyteller about to reach the climax
Of his tale as the train pulls into Minsk, his stop. That's
My stop, he says, stepping off the train, confounding us who
Can't get off it. "You can't leave without telling us the end,"
We say, but he is already on the platform, grinning.
"End?" he says. "It was only the beginning."

Tenth Commandment

The woman said yes she would go to Australia with him
Unless he heard wrong and she said Argentina
Where they could learn the tango and pursue the widows
Of Nazi war criminals unrepentant to the end.
But no, she said Australia. She'd been born in New Zealand.
The difference between the two places was the difference
Between a hamburger and a chocolate malted, she said.
In the candy store across from the elementary school,
They planned their tryst. She said Australia, which meant
She was willing to go to bed with him, and this
Was before her husband's coronary
At a time when a woman didn't take off her underpants
If she didn't like you. She said Australia,
And he saw last summer's seashell collection
In a plastic bag on a shelf in the mud room
With last summer's sand. The cycle of sexual captivity
Beginning in romance and ending in adultery
Was now in the late middle phases, the way America
Had gone from barbarism to amnesia without
A period of high decadence, which meant something,
But what? A raft on the rapids? The violinist
At the gate? Oh, absolute is the law of biology.
For the pornography seminar, what should she wear?

Eleventh Hour

The bloom was off the economic recovery.
"I just want to know one thing," she said.
What was that one thing? He'll never know,
Because at just that moment he heard the sound
Of broken glass in the bathroom, and when he got there,
It was dark. His hand went to the wall
But the switch wasn't where it was supposed to be
Which felt like déjà vu. And then she was gone.
And now he knew how it felt to stand
On the local platform as the express whizzes by
With people chatting in a dialect
Of English he couldn't understand, because his English
Was current as of 1968 and no one speaks that way except
In certain books. So the hours spent in vain
Were minutes blown up into comic-book balloons full
Of Keats's odes. "Goodbye, kid." Tears streamed down
The boy's face. It was a great feeling,
Like the feeling you get when you throw things away
After a funeral: clean and empty in the morning dark.
There was no time for locker-room oratory.
They knew they were facing a do-or-die situation,
With their backs to the wall, and no tomorrow.

Twelfth Night

His first infidelity was a mistake, but not as big
As her false pregnancy. Later, the boy found out
He was born three months earlier than the date
On his birth certificate, which had turned into
A marriage license in his hands. Had he been trapped
In a net, like a moth mistaken for a butterfly?
And why did she—what was in it for her?
It took him all this time to figure it out.
The barroom boast, "I never had to pay for it,"
Is bogus if marriage is a religious institution
On the operating model of a nineteenth-century factory.
On the other hand, women's lot was no worse then
Than it is now. The division of labor made sense
In theories developed by college boys in jeans
Who grasped the logic their fathers had used
To seduce women and deceive themselves.
The pattern repeats itself, the same events
In a different order obeying the conventions of
A popular genre. Winter on a desolate beach. Spring
While there's snow still on the balcony and,
In the window, a plane flies over the warehouse.
The panic is gone. But the pain remains. And the apple,
The knife, and the honey are months away.

After Rosa Parks

Ellie found her son in the school nurse's office, laid out on a leatherette fainting couch like some child gothic, his shoes off, his arms crossed over his chest, his face turned to the wall. "What's the deal, Kid Cody?"

When he heard her voice, he turned only his head toward her, slowly, as if he were beyond surprise. "I have a stomachache," he said.

"Yeah?" Ellie sat down beside him and stroked his bare arm. "That's the message I got."

"It's a nervous stomachache, Mom. It's right in the middle." He pointed to his belt buckle, a nicked metal casting of a race car. "It's right where Mrs. Schumacher said my nerves are."

Cody was in kindergarten, and he did not like school. He told anyone who would listen that he did not like school. Yesterday, from just inside their back door, Ellie overheard him telling their next-door neighbor Mrs. Schumacher that school gave him a bad feeling behind his stomach, "the kind of feeling," he said, "that you get before something happens." Ellie stood still in the doorway and watched as Mrs. Schumacher looked up from grooming one of her half-dozen cats. Mrs. Schumacher was a stringy, wild-haired widow—dirt poor, bone thin, and half-crazy with loneliness and neglect. Sometimes when Cody and Ellie would haul trash back to the cans in the alley, she'd wave and call out her kitchen window to Ellie, "You pull those shoulders back, girl. Divorce is no sin." Yesterday she picked cat hair out of a long metal comb and told Cody, "There are two kinds of stomachaches, you know. Now a sick one just swirls through your gut like a bad wind, but a nervous one sits real still." She pressed one gnarled hand to Cody's belly. "Almost like you've swallowed a baseball," she said. "And it glows."

"That's the one I get at school," Cody told her. "That's the one."

After he said it, Ellie pressed her head against the cool storm door and felt sorry for herself, sorry she lived in the only run-down pocket of this suburb on probably the only street for miles where a woman could put her hands on her child and tell him such things.

The school nurse, a young, red-haired woman strangely over-dressed in a carnation-pink suit, came from behind her desk to the couch. Ellie leaned back as the nurse ran her hand over Cody's forehead. "He doesn't have a fever, as far as I can tell. But he won't take the thermometer in his mouth. He says he wants it under the arm."

"Axillary," Ellie said. "That's how we do it at home."

Cody lay still under the nurse's hand. "I told her that," he said.

"Well, at school we do it by mouth," the nurse said. "You need to try doing it that way at home so it won't be new at school."

Cody and Ellie both looked at the nurse, then Cody looked back at the ceiling. "It's a nervous stomachache, Mom," he said softly. "I can tell."

"Let's sit up, Cody," Ellie said. "You look sicker than you are like that, and lying down is not what you need. A break is what you need. Put your shoes on now." Ellie stood up and took the nurse's elbow, led her to a window that looked out over an empty play yard. "He gets nervous," she said quietly. "It seems to happen most often when too many people treat him like a child." The nurse looked at her. "I mean when too many people try to tell him what to do," Ellie said. "See, he's an only child, and he lives half his time with his dad in their house and half his time with me in ours. So he's accustomed to partnership, you know, to being a partner in his own management. I mean, you live alone with a child, and there's none of that usual 'us versus him' kind of thing. You live alone with a child, and he's part of the us."

"Oh," the nurse said. She took a step back. People often did that when they learned how Cody lived. A social worker, new to their city from California, had concocted the scheme during the divorce. To Ellie and her ex-husband, it had sounded humane, but Ellie and her ex-husband did not live in California. They lived in an old and mostly refined Midwestern suburb, a place where tall trees and wide driveways led back behind big houses to double and triple garages. "I'm wondering," the nurse said, "if I have the correct home phone number for you. A man took the message when I called." She looked Ellie in the eye, insinuating now. "I think I woke him up."

"That's my brother. He's been staying with us to help out." Disappointed in herself for revealing more of their life than was necessary to this woman, Ellie added, "I'm sure you did wake him up. He's ill today."

Cody looked up from struggling with his shoelaces. "Uncle Frank is a night person," he said. "When I'm asleep, he's awake. He does life the opposite."

Ellie smiled at him and looked back at the nurse. "Frank works nights, is what he means." The nurse's face said that even this fact made her suspicious. "Look, I think Cody just needs extra time is all," Ellie said. "This is his first year of school. He didn't go the play group and preschool route. His father and I kept him home so he could get wise to both of us still being there for him, even though it was in different houses. He's fine about that, but he's no wise guy when it comes to school. Are you, Cody?"

Cody stood up and smiled. "I get stomachaches," he said. Both his shoes tied, he was ready to go now. Ellie saw that he believed the hard part of this day was behind him. Next to her, the nurse narrowed her eyes at his sudden good humor, and Ellie felt her hesitate, weighing for a moment whether Cody was a liar or only a new and distinct form of damaged child. Then she looked at Ellie, and Ellie saw that what the nurse had decided was that Cody was an odd child, that he was an ill-equipped child—a child with a strange and probably damaged life—and probably, Ellie understood the nurse was thinking, probably it was Ellie's fault. They stared at each other a moment. Then Ellie went to Cody and took his hand.

"I'll just take him now. We'll just be on our way. We'll try school again tomorrow, right, Cody?"

"Okay," he said.

"You have to sign him out." The nurse pointed to a binder on her desk. "For our records."

"Right," Ellie said. "No problem."

. . .

They drove away slowly from the school. Cody rolled the window down and rested his head on the doorframe so that the wind lifted his hair off his forehead. Ellie didn't know if he was pensive or only relieved. Maybe he had sensed what the nurse thought of her. Or of him. She turned the radio on low.

"Do you want to drive by the lake?" she said. "It's warm today. We could climb down the rocks to the beach." The beach was where Cody told Ellie things, where he confided in her. The wide expanse of sand and water loosened something in him. It was there, digging a hole one day last spring with a new miniature folding spade, that he had looked up and said, "Do you want to hear something secret?"

"Sure," Ellie told him, and then he recited, nearly word for word, an ugly desperate argument she and her ex-husband had had just before they gave it all up. He recited it so precisely that the night came back to Ellie. She'd made a formal dinner in the middle of the week—cornish hens stuffed with herbs and rice. A friendly Greek man at the liquor store had helped her choose a nice wine which she served in their wedding crystal. She'd left the bottle on the table, tucked in a hammered silver ice bucket, while she and her ex-husband said horrible, hurtful things they'd never said before or since. On the beach that day, Cody recited it all. He paused in his digging and looked up at her. "I was under the table," he said. "You just didn't see me there."

For a moment, Ellie believed him. Then she remembered another moment, carrying their salad plates to the kitchen, when she'd been so ashamed she'd gone back to Cody's room to check on him. He lay sideways in his youthbed, one foot wedged between the bars. From the doorway she listened to his breathing before she went to his bed and straightened him, sliding his foot from the bars, folding his quilt up over his shoulders. On the beach, she felt the same relief she'd felt at his door. He'd been asleep. He'd slept through it. She watched him dig the hole, throwing sand over his shoulder, hunkering down to his work, and suddenly she was shaken again.

"Daddy didn't tell you those things, did he? Did Daddy tell you those things?"

"No." He looked up from his digging, a little wary of her.

"Oh."

"Daddy says I probably dreamed it."

They were both quiet then. He finished his hole and sat back on his heels to admire it. It was deep, the deepest he'd dug, and he fingered his new shovel lightly. Then he crawled into the hole, tucking his legs up to his chest and folding his arms around them. "Cover me up, Mom," he said, smiling then.

She slid the warm sand over him as he watched her. When the sand covered the tops of his knees, she smoothed it around his chest. He looked up at her. "I did see it," he said.

She took her hands away from him and sat back. "I know," she said. "I know you did."

Now, in the car, she looked at him. "How about it?" she asked.

"No thanks. I don't feel like the beach."

"We could try the library."

"No," he said. "Thanks."

"Well, I need a milkshake. I'm going to pull into that hot dog stand under the train tracks and have a chocolate shake."

He didn't answer, but Ellie pulled in anyway, and settled him outside under a striped umbrella, where she brought his milkshake out to him. He drank it quickly, tipping his head back, while Ellie looked up at the train platform, where a few late commuters stood next to their briefcases. She was glad now she and Cody were not going anywhere, glad she had taken the rest of the day off when she got the call at the office, glad they could sit here half the morning and then stop at the park if they felt like it. The gift of her child was that, in his presence, life lengthened and uncoiled. Though it was nearly eleven o'clock, this day spread out before them as sweetly as at dawn.

"I like ice cream in the morning," Cody said. "This is the first time I've had ice cream this early."

"It's a quiet pleasure," Ellie said. "That and the weather. This is the warmest January we've ever had, I think."

"I remembered this was your day," Cody said. "So I told her to call you and not Dad."

Ellie touched his wrist. "You were right. Exactly right. You're getting very good at this. You're becoming a big boy."

Cody looked out over the parking lot. The umbrellas rippled in the breeze like sails, and above them late commuters swayed lightly like distant buoys. "I would kick a bad guy in the stomach if he came near our table."

"That would do it," Ellie said.

"I'd karate-kick him in the stomach and then in the knee."

"He'd go limping off to the other side of the world," Ellie said. This was something new for them that had started with school—this imagined violence, her child's sense of himself as a warrior and her quiet affirmation. School had forced Ellie to see how divorce had changed her—that she had become a cautious person, a person who lived as if she were allowed only one mistake in life and had already made it—and school had forced her to see that she was sending her son off into the world with the rigid moral sense of a saint. He'd see a child steal another child's hat in the play yard, and he'd suffer it all day. When he came home, he'd tell her the story of the theft and then lie on the rug, exhausted, looking up at her to say, "That was a terrible thing, don't you think, Mom? Don't you think that was an awful thing to do?"—as if he'd witnessed a murder. So now she let Cody talk this way, imagining his own power, and lately she had begun to surprise him with figures from a set of fierce dinosaurs and cavemen as a way of making up for all the early years she'd encouraged a pristine sensibility.

"Cody, did anything happen today? I mean, before you went to the nurse with a stomachache?"

"No."

"Nothing?"

"Well, the playground lady made me take a time-out."

"Why was that?"

"I was swinging on my belly."

"Uh-huh."

"And that's all." He rolled the edge of his cup around one finger. "There's a rule against swinging on your belly."

"I didn't know that."

"I didn't know that, either, but the lady said that now I would know and now I would remember."

"Oh. Well, I guess she's the boss."

"She is."

Ellie ran her hand along the rough close-cropped hair at the nape of his neck. He looked away from her when she did it. "So then what happened?"

"I had to sit on the ground by her feet for a while and then I had to say I was sorry."

"Did you?"

"Yes."

"And then what?"

"Then she called me Cory and told me I could go."

"She called you by the wrong name."

"Uh-huh. Yes."

"Did you tell her?"

"No." He leaned against her then and tilted his head back to look into her face. "I didn't want her to know me by my right name, Mom."

She put one arm lightly around his shoulders and rested her chin on the top of his head. "What should we do now?" she said softly.

"Go home."

At home, Frank was on the couch, an afghan pulled over his legs, watching the noon news.

"You're awake early," Cody said.

Frank looked up. "You're home early."

Cody quieted when he said it. He dropped his knapsack under the hat rack, pulled out his box of dinosaurs and cavemen, and began to arrange them delicately, as though he were being watched. Frank raised his eyebrows at Ellie. She shook her head. "I guess I'll make soup or something," she said.

A few minutes later, Frank joined her in the kitchen. He moved stiffly to the sink, leaned there a moment, then drew a glass of water from the tap and sat down at the table.

"It's vegetable soup." Ellie turned from the pot on the stove. "Can you tolerate it?"

"Not today." He raised his glass. "Today I'm drinking water." Frank suffered from colitis—at least that's what he said it was. He'd been a medic in the Army and learned just enough about medicine to believe he could treat himself. Last week, though, he'd been so sick that Ellie had convinced him to let her drive him to the VA hospital for some tests. Nudged into a pocket of darkness between two high-rise office buildings, the hospital was a spooky place—cavernous and forbidding and full of old and middle-aged men shuffling the hallways in paper slippers. "This is awful," Ellie whispered to Frank as they stood in some line. "Why don't you get real health insurance?"

"Forget it," Frank said. "I spent three years of my life defending the Golden Gate Bridge to earn this." She noticed as he walked away from her that day, and again this morning as he came into the kitchen, that he had begun to look like those men at the VA. He'd begun to look like a damaged man. Though he was tall and thick with muscle, he carried himself lightly, his arms held away from his body, as though he were hollow. Today his rumpled hair stood up from his head. Under each eye was a white translucent spot of pain. "You look pale, Frank."

"I feel pale."

"Did you call on your test results?"

"They said they'd call me."

"You should check."

"They said they would call, Ellie."

She turned back to the stove and then shouted, "Soup in twenty minutes, Cody."

"And biscuits, please," he shouted back.

"Okay, and biscuits." She peered into the refrigerator, looking for the plastic container of dough.

"That is not a sick child," Frank said.

"He was nervous. Something happened on the playground."

Ellie went about her work quietly, spreading flour on the countertop, rolling out the dough, but she felt like Cody had looked in the other room a moment ago. She felt like she was being watched. Frank sat at the table, the glass of water between his broad hands. Her brother was an odd man. There was such power to him, in his hands and legs and the set of his jaw, but around other people—even Ellie and Cody—he was always quiet and watchful, slightly ill at ease. Ellie believed that life—real life, life in society, whatever it was she was living—was a confusion to

Frank. She wasn't sure why. Sometimes she blamed the Army. Frank had been one of the last men drafted into Vietnam. Though the war ended not long after he finished basic, the Army had changed him—perhaps in ways worse than a year fighting in the jungle might have changed him. She didn't know. She wasn't even sure exactly what he had done during those years or what had been done to him. Occasionally, he'd written to Ellie of demotions, restrictions, extra duty, a few short stays in the brig. She had tried to imagine what circumstances could have landed her brother in a military jail, in a cage. As a boy he had been cocksure and strong-willed, and sometimes he'd had a smart mouth, but all boys had seemed like that to Ellie back then.

When the war ended, Frank wrote again to say that he was glad, but for an odd reason. If he'd gone to war, he'd written, his resistance might have become inflated even in his own mind into some kind of grand refusal. He might have gone the rest of his life thinking that what he had learned was that he could not kill anyone or that a big country should keep its nose out of a little country's affairs. Then he would have missed what he said was the only real lesson of the Army, which was that people who tell you what to do—no matter what reasons they claim—are performing an act of aggression. You're in their way, is what Frank had written to her; they'd just as soon you die.

When he was discharged, he roamed the world—Ellie imagined he roamed it with that credo—crewing sailboats to New Zealand, working illegal shrimp boats out of Key West, leading tourists across the Yucatán Peninsula. For fifteen years he lived like that, never settling long enough for anyone or anything to impose itself upon him. That he came when she needed him had surprised her—though both their parents had died and there was no one else to help her. Frank spotted her first at the airport, and when she recognized him, it was by the easy certain smile she remembered. When she came close, though, he stepped lightly away from her. He shook her hand first and then he shook Cody's.

The nature of his support was also a surprise. He said very little, never entered into the acrimony of her divorce, never said more to her son than a benevolent stranger might say. He simply sat nearby while she found a job, a place to live, a car, while she went about the business of solving her life, and each Saturday morning, on the hall stand outside her bedroom door, he left two one-hundred dollar bills folded under an old candy dish of their mother's.

Only once, just after he arrived, while they sat next to each other on a commuter train bringing them back from the court-room where she had been ordered to sell her home, had he spo-ken up. "You're getting screwed," he told her.

"I know."

"You're just standing there letting it happen."

"It's worse if you make a fuss. I tried that once and even my own attorney yelled at me. You're just supposed to stand there and take it. It's all a glorified trip to the principal's office." She looked out the window when she said it.

"You're nuts. You're only seeing what's in front of you." When she didn't turn around, he leaned closer to her and lowered his voice. "For what you'll end up paying that lawyer, we could buy a little guest camp I once stayed at in Bali. It's real popular with the Australians, but far enough away that you'd never be found. Cody could grow up knowing how to catch his own dinner."

Still looking out the window, she considered it. She could take a few books, a bag of mementos, and her son, and disappear into a tropical life of light, loose clothing, modest shelter, balmy breezes. She turned to Frank. Perhaps this was how he had solved his life—not so much by running away from danger as by following closely the slender path of peace. "It's against the law," she said.

He shook his head. "If you're not careful, that's the law you're going to leave your kid. You have a choice, you know."

Ellie looked out the window again. Maybe she had never known she had a choice. She was a woman, a divorced mother of a young child. For a long time, her life had been one of necessity and ultimatum, not choice. But Frank was different, and she real-ized that his time in the Army most likely marked the beginning of a deal he'd struck with himself, because since those years ended, she could not name one thing he had done that he had not chosen to do. She turned to face him again. "I can't do it, Frank."

He looked at her then with the same expression she had seen flash over him in the courtroom earlier that day. His face became blank and quizzical as an aborigine's. As he settled back into his seat and looked past her at the city dimming into twilight, she saw something else, too. She saw his resignation. Never would they live together in a tropical guest camp. She had slipped, somehow, away from him. She felt that loss carve out a hole next to the loss of her marriage, her home, the life she had believed would be hers and her son's, and she felt the nature of Frank's love for her, and of her for him, change from hope to regret.

Moved suddenly at this memory, she sat down with him at the kitchen table. She felt tears behind her eyes and pressed the palms of her hands against them. "What?" Frank said.

"Nothing. I don't know. Maybe I should talk with his dad. We could put him in a different school, I guess."

"All schools are the same." Frank placed his thick hands flat on the table and looked at them. "They're the same man in a different hat."

"Maybe he'll get used to it. Maybe it just takes time."

Frank took a small sip of water and then looked to the pot of soup which was boiling too fast on the stove. "Look," he said. "Why don't you go back to work? I'll watch him. You can work late and make up the hours. He and I'll walk up to the chicken place for dinner and then I'll get him to bed."

She looked at him, suddenly tired, but acquiescent, too.

"Go on," he said.

She worked until past nine that night, leaving for home when lightning from a sudden thunderstorm flickered the lamp at her desk. On the drive home, the rain turned to a fraudulent snow— huge wet flakes out of a sentimental movie. She could still hear thunder out over the lake, though, rumbling distantly like doom, and she leaned over the steering wheel, anxious to be home. More and more lately, the thought came to her that in all the world, she had only two blood relatives. In the company of that fact, she felt skittish and threatened, as if two blood relatives were too slender a tie to bind her to the world.

The front of the house was dark except for the flicker of the TV in the living room. Frank was asleep on the couch, his breathing ragged and shallow. She stopped to turn off the TV and then saw the slant of light from Cody's doorway down the hall.

"Hey," she said. He was sitting up in bed with a big book open in his lap.

"Uncle Frank felt sick so I'm reading my own night story."

She came to sit beside him. "That was good of you. But it's late. Lights out."

"We went to Chicken in a Basket and I got a Coke. A large. That's why I'm so awake."

"Still." She closed his book and slid him down so that his head settled on his pillow.

"I saw the snow. Is that why you're late?"

"I worked extra so I could take you to story hour at the library tomorrow."

"Oh," he said, already drifting off. Then he opened his eyes. "After dinner, we watched the freak feature on TV. It was about giant ants that hide in the sewer. Have you seen that one?"

"I think so. It's a scary one. Don't tell about it now. You'll have bad dreams. Tell about it in the morning."

He closed his eyes again and rolled on his side to sleep. She stroked his hair off his forehead, and he took her hand and tucked it under his chin. Without opening his eyes, he said, "I'm going to tell Daddy, too, when I see him, and I'm going to find out if they have that giant ant movie at the movie store so he can watch it, too."

"You're full of plans," she said, leaning down to kiss him. Before she had sat up again, he was asleep, and he had let go of her hand.

In the kitchen she gathered their paper cups and the boxes of chicken bones. At the trash can she stopped, holding the lid open with one hand, and stared at four empty beer cans. Drinking was something Frank had chosen not to do in her home. He never used the word *alcoholism*, but he had asked her when he moved in not to keep liquor in the house. "It distracts me," he told her. For the first month or so of his time with them, he drank a lot of everything else—water, soft drinks, iced tea—and he slept a lot. Occasionally, too, he took long hushed phone calls from men Ellie believed must belong to AA or some support group— extremely polite, low-voiced men, men she thought of as veterans of another kind. She closed the lid of the trash can and moved to stand by the sink, still holding the chicken boxes and paper cups.

Frank came in then from the living room. "What's up?" he said when he saw her face. "Is Cody okay?"

She set the trash back on the kitchen table. "You drank."

"I know."

"Well, why? I mean, what am I supposed to do now, Frank? Am I supposed to kick you out?"

"You're not supposed to kick me out. Jesus, Ellie. You're supposed to drive me downtown to detox or something."

She sat down at the table, the vision of those men in paper slippers at the VA clanging around in her head. Frank filled a tall glass with water from the tap and sat down across from her. When she looked at him, he straightened his spine and set his shoulders, but his eyes drifted unsteadily. He lowered his head. "What's going on?" she asked.

"The VA called."

"What is it? Is it colitis?"

"A long time ago it was probably colitis." He looked at her. "Now it's cancer, Ellie."

She put her hand on his. He leaned back in his chair, and she felt his privacy, his strict isolation. His hand was still on the table beneath hers. It did not seem fair that he be forced to suffer more isolation. "I'm sorry," she said and took her hand away.

He shook his head. "It gets worse," he said, smiling lightly. "They went ahead and scheduled me for more tests and then this clerk called back and told me I don't qualify for treatment. 'This is not a service-related ailment,' he told me. 'The VA treats only the indigent and service-related ailments.'"

"You didn't know that?" she said softly.

He rubbed his temples with both hands and pushed his hair roughly away from his face. "No."

"So what this means..." she began slowly.

"What this means is I have cancer and no health insurance."

She sat back in her chair, stunned by the precision of this cruelty. Her brother had stepped off a plane just over a year ago tanned and strong, his only weakness that he would not keep track of rules. He had balked even when she suggested he get a driver's license. She closed her eyes at the memory. She was the reason he'd come back to this place where his weakness could turn on him so cruelly. "We'll figure it out, Frank. We'll figure something out."

"No. No. I've already done that. I just hate to leave you in a bind. I've got a little money I was saving to go back to Negril this spring. I'll leave you some of it and still make out pretty well there myself."

"What are you saying?"

"I'm saying I'm going to Negril." He looked sad for her when he said it, as if he believed she were the one with the greater loss. "I'll leave in a couple days."

"Frank, my God. You have to take care of this. You can't just walk away from it."

"I'm not walking away, Ellie. There are doctors in Negril. I'm not saying I won't take care of it. I'm just saying I can't take care of it here."

He was lying, she thought. He had decided somehow that to die whole on ground he understood would be better than struggling here. She sat rigidly across from him, her mind wildly in search of hope, of a kindly Jamaican doctor down there who would take Frank in and cure him for no more reward than the satisfaction of having preserved such a man. But she had never met a doctor like that. She wasn't sure the world was a large and varied enough place to hold even one doctor like that. "How can I stop you," she said, "from doing this?"

"You can't." He pushed back his chair and stood up. "I'm tired, Ellie. I'm going to go to bed now."

He didn't go to bed. For hours she heard his silence as he moved through the house. She wondered if perhaps he was saying goodbye to the house, to its small comforts, but then she understood that he no longer saw her home as a safe place. She was frightened for herself, knowing that. He stood in the kitchen a long time, the house so quiet around him she felt she could hear his resolve building. Then he went into Cody's room. She sat up in bed and put one foot on the floor, listening until he came out again.

When she opened her eyes next, Cody stood at her bedside. "Is it morning?" he asked.

She looked to the window. Outside the snow was gone and the sun shone brightly. "Yes."

"I had a bad dream. I had a dream someone got into our house."

"Uncle Frank was up late last night. You probably heard Uncle Frank."

"I dreamed it was someone else."

"It wasn't," she said. "It was Uncle Frank."

They washed and dressed hurriedly, though it was still early. Ellie let Cody watch cartoons as he ate, grateful for the noise and distraction. As they were leaving, she lingered in the quiet front room, looking down the hallway to Frank's closed door. Cody stood in his coat and hat, watching her. "Let's go now." She took his hand. "Time to go."

They were early to Cody's school, and his teacher looked up surprised from a table in the back of the room, but she came to greet them in the hallway. "A new day and a new start," she said merrily. Cody reached up to hold on to a corner of Ellie's jacket. "Today the Green Star group is going to spend the morning at the sand table," his teacher said to him. "Why don't you hang up your coat and get started?" She looked to Ellie. "Cody is in the Green Star group."

Ellie nodded.

"I have to tell my mom something," Cody said.

"Well, hurry along. We don't want to make Mom late for work or whatever."

"Okay," Cody said, and then stood mute next to Ellie, still clutching her jacket. His teacher watched him for a moment and then went back into the classroom. "Hurry along," she called. "I'll take the top off the sand table."

Cody stiffened and began to cry as Ellie slipped his coat off his shoulders. She took his hands, warm with the moist heat of emotion and fear. "What is it you want to tell me, Cody?"

He shook his head, his eyes a little desperate and lost.

"You don't know what it is?"

He shook his head again.

She nodded and pulled him close. "I love you, child," she said into his ear. Then she drew him away from her. "I think you can do this. I think it's important that you do this." He wouldn't look at her when she said it.

Pulling up to the school that afternoon, she saw his face at the door, a bobbing pale moon in the glass that drew an ache up from her own stomach, but he ran down the slope to her car like the other children, trailing his knapsack behind him. "Did it go okay?"

"Yeah." He closed his door, locked it, and drew the seat belt around him. "At the bad parts, I just pretended I was somewhere else. I pretended it wasn't really happening."

They were early to story hour, and Cody hovered near the librarian at her desk, telling her the story of the giant ant movie he had seen. She was a kind older woman, wise in the ways of children, and she listened raptly to Cody's story, then led him off to a far corner of the children's room. Ellie sat with their coats in a small low chair and watched the other mothers and children arrive. A few minutes later, Cody came running back carrying some books the librarian had found for him. They were junior novelizations of old monster movies: *The Mummy, Frankenstein,* and *King Kong.* "Oh, these are too scary for you, Cody. These things even give me the willies."

"Mom," he said. "She gave them to me. I was going to show them to Uncle Frank."

"Oh. Well, let me see." She flipped the pages while he leaned against her shoulder. Mainly they were just a collection of black and white stills from the old movies.

"Maybe they give you the willies because the monsters are always after a lady." Cody pointed to a picture of the Mummy carrying a woman into a dark wood.

"Maybe," she said, closing the book. "I don't know."

"Could I show them to Uncle Frank? They won't scare him, I bet."

"Sure," she said. "I guess."

He crawled into her lap then, and Ellie watched the preparations for story hour while Cody paged through his books. "I read the sign," Ellie said. "Today is a special puppet show for Martin Luther King's birthday."

"Our teacher told us about him in school."

"I'm glad. He was a good brave man."

"Once nothing was fair for brown-skinned people."

"Martin Luther King changed some of that, though."

Cody turned around and looked at her. "He got killed," he said.

"I know. I was a girl. It was very sad."

Cody leaned back against her then and fingered his monster books. His body grew slack against hers, and she thought he must be tired, but then she felt heat move out of him, the same heat she had felt in his hands that morning. She turned him around in her lap. "What's wrong, Cody?" He shook his head, and she remembered this morning, how he had wanted to tell her something he didn't know. "What is it?"

"Don't tell Daddy," he said.

He had never spoken those words to her before. Perhaps because of the way he lived or perhaps because of his own good nature, Cody had always been unstintingly fair in his attachments to each of his parents. "I don't know," Ellie said. "Why not Daddy?"

"It's not a man's secret."

"It's a woman's secret?"

"Uh-huh. I think so."

"What is it?"

"I'm afraid about dying. Do you just fall down one day and then it hurts forever?"

After he said it, she pulled him close. Children did this, she had read somewhere, picked up the unspoken cues and terror in their homes. "It doesn't hurt," she told him. "It stops all the hurt." She drew her hand across his forehead. "It feels like this," she said.

She knew when she said it that something was terribly wrong with her. To portray death to her own child as more dignified and easeful than life was some sort of abomination larger than she could fathom. But she did not take it back. She rocked Cody gently as the librarian rang a small bell and called for the children to gather around the puppet theater. She sat blankly, Cody curled against her, as the show began with a cardboard cutout of a strictly segregated bus—a cluster of white circles at the front, a cluster of black circles at the back. *Before Rosa Parks,* the caption under the bus read. Then the librarian explained to the children that Rosa Parks was tired and believed she had as much right to sit down and rest as anyone else.

It's a woman's secret, Ellie thought. This was what her son believed. How he must have wondered to find a woman's secret in his own mind, to understand that to the teeming power and circumstance of the world he would lose many things—one day even his life. Cody's head lolled against her shoulder. She realized he was asleep in her arms. The monster books slid out of his hands, and she held them a moment, looking into the shy, quizzical pain on King Kong's face. She shook Cody lightly. "We have to go," she said. "We have to hurry."

At home, Frank was on the couch in front of the news. He smiled briefly when they came in, then looked back at the television. Cody ran to him with the monster books. He wanted Frank to read them to him.

"In one minute," Frank said. "When the news is over, I'll read all three."

While Ellie hung up their coats, Cody eased himself onto the couch next to Frank and sat stiffly next to him, thumping his feet against the cushion. Frank lay one hand on his knee to quiet him. An old newsreel of Martin Luther King's last speech was playing on the TV. "I saw him at the library," Cody said. "A picture of him. It's his birthday."

"Monday," Frank said.

"My friend Bennie's dad is off work Monday, and Bennie doesn't have school, but I do."

"How come you have school? I thought everyone was off," Frank said. "It's a holiday."

Cody was quiet then, and Ellie saw that he was a little teary, blinking and looking away from Frank to the TV. "I don't know," he said. "I just do."

Frank shook Cody's knee gently. "Well, that stinks," he said, smiling. "That's not fair." He shook his knee more roughly until Cody began to smile, too, and then he leaned close to him. "Just don't go," Frank said. "Stay home."

Cody looked at him. Ellie could see that Cody had not consid-

ered that an option before, that he had never completely understood he had an option before, and next she knew he was going to
look to her. She turned away quickly to the front window, afraid
to watch the idea of freedom dawn in her son's face, but outside
in the evening sky growing up at the end of her block, she saw it
anyway—the sudden knowledge loose in his mind, spreading like
the shadows that spilled from under stoops, crawled across lawns,
and bloomed up from the dark center of even her own scraggly
hedgerow. Her son was free. Behind her, music signaled the end
of the news. It was late. She knew she should turn around, start
on dinner, but she stood a moment longer, staring out at the
dark, and felt rising in her own mind the strangest and most fearsome comfort.

The Dead

A good man is seized by the police
and spirited away. Months later
someone brags that he shot him once
through the back of the head
with a Walther 7.65, and his life
ended just there. Those who loved
him go on searching the cafés
in the Barrio Chino or the bars
near the harbor. A comrade swears
he saw him at a distance buying
two kilos of oranges in the market
of San José and called out, "Andrés,
Andrés," but instead of turning
to a man he'd known since childhood and opening his great arms
wide, he scurried off, the oranges
tumbling out of the damp sack, one
after another, a short bright trail
left on the sidewalk to say,
Farewell! Farewell to what? I ask.
I asked then and I ask now. I first
heard the story fifty years ago;
it became part of the mythology I
hauled with me from one graveyard
to another, this belief in the power
of my yearning. The dead are everywhere, crowding the narrow streets
that jut out from the wide boulevard
on which we take our morning walk.
They stand in the cold shadows
of men and women come to sell
themselves to anyone, they stride

along beside me and stop when I
stop to admire the bright garlands
or the little pyramids of fruit,
they reach a hand out to give
money or to take change, they say
"Good morning" or "Thank you," they
turn with me and retrace my steps
back to the bare little room I've
come to call home. Patiently,
they stand beside me staring out
over the soiled roofs of the world
until the light fades and we are
all one or no one. They ask for
so little, a prayer now and then,
a toast to their health which is
our health, a few lies no one reads
incised on a dull plaque between
a pharmacy and a sports store,
the least little daily miracle.

Forty Years

Work boots in the basement thrown against
a wall. The garden dies in the mind—

nasturtiums entwined on a chain-link fence.
The gods he carried nothing but dried

crusts. That vintage bottle on the table
crushed more each time he hammers it.

The Sign

Bird shit streaking down
the backs of Adirondack
chairs, a naked woman
sketching. Is the point
of art to know what hands
will do? For a moment
she looks up, then resumes.

Wind/Breath, Breath/Wind

But later, to teach myself humility I worked
exclusively with breath, with the insubstantial, with what
does not last, not leave a record behind

those streamers, those ribbons we trail from our bodies

banners, flags of the living

excrement of the mouth and lungs, though we
do not like to think that

the spirit is the waste of the body. Oh, yes, I started
with something grand as wind and when I said
w-i-n-d slowly tasting the wine in the word

I could hear the high-pitched plaintive cry
of a dog intoxicated with grief

the whip and whinny working itself up to new heights. Up there

the wind sucks itself inside out like a glove

the wind is graspable, a shaft, a pole, a tree nothing can
topple, nothing uproot the wind
by its own hair except the wind.

Once upon a time, the winds had names. But you know that.
Aeolus. Boreas. Zephyrus. Now they are anonymous
as crowds in a subway.

I am part of the great leftover, the way dragonflies
are part of what moves, the male pushing

into the female, the wind
pushing him pushing into her, how it blows
through them with an excitement different from their own

the rush through the nostrils audible
as the start of an alphabet, that place where the singer gasps
her breath forcing the music wider, now it

has to include the body, its limps and stutters.

I wanted something we all had in common, a material
ordinary as air, inexpensive, easily available

there must be as many breaths as brushstrokes, some thick
and impastoed, others phlegmy or drooling spit

How useless the saw and drill, how useless to think of patina
the shine water takes, the gleam of ice. Air takes
no shine, is passed through the mouth

where animals are chewed up and blood, where semen and saliva
where kisses and the tongue sucked in and out, throbbing

Sometimes I think there are two people breathing
inside me, one running in terror
at last gasp, the other in hot pursuit, a killer, a maniac

I am the hysteric caught in between, I hold them
here in my chest where they begin
to warm and take on the shape of my ribs, they leave

their mark in me, the way a boat leaves an impression
in the wet sand and even after the boat
breaks up and falls to pieces
its stain, its shadow like an x-ray I feel inside me, it passes

now from my mouth to your ear, my tongue ungluing
each whorl, each labyrinthine, though
we are not lovers and isn't it strange when we take the air

into our mouths, it is renamed breath and the fact
that we can change air into breath and breath
back into air is what proves

we are alive, the muscles of the breath
which are the movers, all covered with a thick network
of sinews, and some breaths are like strong

swimmers swimming one inside the other, passing
through narrow portals and the way

the glassmaker's breath bubbles into the glass
an effervescence, intoxication
of the diver, the molten pulled by lips and forceps—

or do I mean the breath?—how the body keeps giving it away,
profligate, the ease of it, the uncaring.

Terza Rima for a Sudden Change in Seasons

Probably God laughs at us, down here, entranced
As, to quiet us, He tosses down another season,
And we ooh and ah—like infants silenced

By the jangling of keys above a playpen—
At the all-effacing green or white or gold,
Or even something small: a stem, a robin,

A brittle smattering of stars across a field,
As if we hadn't seen it all a year ago
And every year before that, since an arm first held

Us to a startling, milky window, saying, "Snow."
Maybe it started as a temporary subterfuge,
To distract us while He carved each gaudy "No"

In the tablets he was making for His protégé;
He never dreamed that we'd have been so thick.
Hadn't he made us in His own image?

Could this possibly be what He was like?
Utterly bamboozled, year after year,
By the same, not all that complicated, trick?

Once you tilt the earth's revolving sphere
The rest of the stuff is pretty automatic...
But who could have imagined all our fanfare,

The way each unhinged leaf makes us poetic,
Or a single, all-inclusive blast of snow?
Especially here, in my converted attic,

The skylights blank with white, the wall-sized window
Which usually lets in every local circumstance
Just framing what the trees no longer know.

(They've forgotten where their branches are, for instance,
The houses, fences, toolsheds, swing sets, power lines,
The stiff cabal of mountains in the distance.)

What can God be doing with these afternoons,
With us so busy ogling the newest change
That we don't bother Him with choirs, organs, carillons,

Petitions for forgiveness, cash, revenge.
Maybe He's trying to write another book
In which Ishmael and Esau finally avenge

Themselves, Hagar and Leah get another look
And God reveals that on those forty nights
When Moses was supposedly on Sinai, he really took

Several whirlwind tours of Canaan's highlights—
Hebron, Jericho, Moriah, Zion—
The usual tourist binge of the holy sites

That he was meant to glimpse from atop a mountain;
God didn't have the heart to keep him out.
Unless, perhaps, it took greater compassion

To spare Moses from having to find out
That the Promised Land was just another place.
From a mountaintop, you can remain in doubt

Of a region's basic ordinariness—
What city doesn't look best from a distance?
No stench, no cars, no cockroaches, no mice,

Just towers, bridges, seeming effervescence,
The unobstructed line of each façade...
As if Moses were on Bellosguardo, seeing Florence

Or staring at Manhattan from the Promenade;
I know that He's supposed to be autonomous,
But maybe this was the only way that God

Could seem to make good on His crazy promise.
That's when He got smart and thought of winter,
Spring, summer, autumn, each one luminous

In its peculiar way, that it might counter
Our inevitable disappointment in the land itself
As memories of Egypt each grew fainter...

Or maybe it was a way of distancing Himself.
To keep us in awe or for self-protection?
Perhaps He never recovered from the Golden Calf,

Or maybe, like everyone else, He fears rejection,
Perfectly justifiable, when you consider the trend
That began with Lyell and natural selection—

A labor-saving device that got out of hand.
It was only meant to apply to moths and tortoises;
The various human races were supposed to blend,

God assumed that all our obvious likenesses
Would outweigh any differences that might arise,
Our few disputes smoothed over with the courtesies

To which the carved stone tablets would give rise—
Let's say God got in over his head,
Which really shouldn't be much of a surprise

Since he couldn't even be sure a thing was good,
Until he'd gone ahead with its creation.
You'll remember He called us very good,

Which suggests His judgment is a bit in question,
Or, perhaps, that he had no alternatives;
He didn't have much stomach for destruction.

Unless that's just another front; maybe he thrives
On floods, earthquakes, genocides, jihads—
Maybe He put us here to make explosives,

Made science just an ornate set of leads
In an ongoing pursuit of perfect ruin.
After all, He promised, no more floods...

Maybe he wanted to see if atomic fission
Was any good. Why else create uranium?
Unless it's just a ploy for more attention

(It's been ages since anyone wrote a psalm)
Or another stopgap, like the seasons,
While He works out some unexpected problem:

Who knows? Perhaps he's running out of hexagons—
Has no idea what He will do for snow;
Maybe all these flakes out here have twins,

And He's afraid that, sooner or later, we'll know
That there isn't really any infinite thing.
Clean hands? A pure heart? I don't think so

But maybe if one of us got up to sing
Or even hummed a tune, say Vivaldi,
Or plucked it out on some obliging string—

You know the one, the winter melody,
The tour de force for solo violin—
He'd make this next millennium a bit less bloody,

Find some calmer version of adrenaline.
But maybe we can't blame Him; He's lost his way,
Gotten bogged down in crocus, lily, dandelion,

Unable to keep the spring's demands at bay
While another hemisphere clamors for fall;
The trees, without his help, refuse to sway,

The birch leaves won't go gold, won't thin, won't fall...
He's far too overworked to listen to us.
But He must hear something sometimes. A mating call?

Traffic? Rain? A graceful turn of phrase?
I bet He takes a break when there's a nightingale.
Perhaps He'll linger for a song of praise.

Character as Fate

In Mexico we danced on the edge
where the saguaro cacti stood up
like billboards of cactus in the Persian blue twilight
    of Tucson—
ah, the desert in bloom
lizards with space-gear helmets on our sill
and we in our deck chairs taking the winter sun!
Nothing to do but listen to wind in the cottonwoods
    and think
how this is certainly worth two hundred a day
yet that means we will have to leave
after, let's see, about three more days,
get up, throw our gear into the saddlebags
and fill up the old Cherokee.

Sea spray recalled the surf of snow
welling up as our sleigh sped onward,
washboard of packed powder giving the bells a shake
over the Dakota-like steppes toward the East
on whose scrub and buttes the tired sun
was shedding its light without conviction.
But we stood on the end of the pier
half a mile out into the murderous
glitter of the sea and looked back
with a touch of longing I admit at the waves
like pectorals flexing, crashing on the beach far away
and waited for the genuine helicopter, ours, to land
scooping us up into its gear,
the ritzy vibration and glamorous liftoff.

I nestled in my beaver and sheepskin
and went to the wall for my beliefs.

The state ran the camp for art
at first it was like basic training
to reverse the habit of compassion;
yet we resisted, life itself was
resistance, a kind of survival, a brotherhood.
The potato soup was cold as dock oil
but we were together every day
encouraging each other
under the photo of Scriabin
doing the polka in a sun-dappled pavilion
with a ravishing girl whose head
turned away from the camera
and watched the white caps blink on the bay.

Few of us were left, though we supported
each other and went to each other's
afternoons. The nights
were silent as birches; moonlight tugged at our hair.
I was given a room with a chair
and the very bed that Solzhenitsyn had.
No one but us in the *dacha,* and a typewriter
on the deal table covered with lace
and the old fishwife crying *you havf your londge*
now glimb back to vork.

We often considered
the delights of travel, languorous terraces
of Marrakech, picking up
important Straits porcelain for a song,
gardens sprayed with riotous colors,
the gold and diamond kerosang
that Hogan gave Shaidali.
We knew all these things, survived
all the regimes.
Exile no longer matters because
it is a state vestigial
as the appendix is to the body temporal.
Yet no one will believe

I am alive and glad here in Kuala Lumpur
where the State feels an obligation
to fund radio performances of work
by all living composers, while the books
burn quietly out back of the sports
arena, where cries go up like fireworks
and the teams smiling like bankers come
from America to compete.

Don't Wake the Cards

Since my chronic bad luck
Vanished in my love's deck of cards,
I step around them softly,
I won't open the window on windy days.

I unpin her long black hair
And strip down her dress myself,
Lest their flutter stirs the dead air
And make the cards fly.

I tell her, Don't even think
About picking up a broom
Or dancing with your boobs flapping.
Lay back in my arms

And watch the light fall
Golden over us
In a wordless silence.
Don't wake the damn cards.

My chicken soup thickened with pounded young almonds.
My blend of winter greens.
Dearest tagliatelle with mushrooms, fennel, anchovies,
Tomatoes and vermouth sauce.
Beloved monkfish braised with onions, capers
And green olives.
Give me your tongue tasting of white beans and garlic,
Sexy little assortment of formaggi and frutta.
I want to drown with you in red wine like a pear,
Then sleep in a macédoine of wild berries with cream.

On the Road to Somewhere Else

The leaves made us think
Of a letter trembling in someone's hand.
In fact, many letters in many hands,
And then they no longer did.

There was a bedraggled old woman
Walking
With two gray boards on her back
Joined into a cross
To cook her dinner with,

And then,
We were somewhere else.

The Number of Fools

Is infinite, said my wife,
Quoting Solomon,
Which made me see stars,
The vastness of the universe.
The one who is not a fool,
Like a sugar cube that fell in the sea.
The one who is not a fool
Like a tarantula
On a slice of wedding cake—
So I covered my ears.

Lone Tree

A tree spooked
By its own evening whispers.
Afraid to rustle,
Just now
Bewitched by the distant sunset

Making a noise full of deep
Misgivings,
Like bloody razor blades
Being shuffled,

And then again the quiet.
The birds too terror-stricken
To make their own comment.
Every leaf to every other leaf
An apparition,
A separate woe.

Bare twig:
A finger of suspicion.

Bowling in the Future

Glenn Thrip failed to notice the bullet hole in the rear window of his pickup until several days later, after they had removed his wisdom teeth. Snowed on codeine, he was clearing the Nissan's floor of pennies, trying to extract the keys from beneath the mat, when he looked up and saw the fresh Amnesty International emblem in the window's lower left corner. A silver filigree of cracks ran from the edges and into the safety glass. He peeled back the sticker and found an identical black and gold emblem holding the window together from the outside. The hole was nearly the diameter of his ring finger, and he tested the edge. It was too much. Glenn Thrip was only fifty-six hours past his confrontation with the oral surgeon, and at that moment, facing anything more than the rote act of driving seemed well beyond reason. He began an inching U-turn across Valentine Place. Out on East State, descending toward his now cooling order of take-out lasagna, he remembered to use the headlights.

Marni Coe. He could recall Marni Coe, yesterday on the phone, before she returned the truck, asking if he had any preferences in bumper stickers. Offhand, Thrip didn't, which surprised him, as there were definite preferences for nearly everything else. People used to think of Glenn's surname as a kind of verb. "I thrip. You thrip. We're in the grip of thrip," they'd say and laugh.

In front of his landlord's house on North Geneva, Thrip reached for the stereo, forgetting that it would be the Ramones. The Ramones or nothing, that's how the world had been for a while, as the tape was stuck in the deck. After completing a vague series of left-hand turns, and convinced that he'd undershot the lasagna, Thrip began trying to picture his navigational mistake, when the take-out place materialized at the corner. He slowed as a black Celica with smoked windows pulled quickly around him. Violet-white light spilled from the undercarriage and reflected off the wet pavement. The Celica made a left-on-red into the four-lane traffic of Route 13, sliding out on a spectral pillow of purple.

Inside Roma's the tanned kid behind the counter in a lacrosse jersey had just hung up the phone. "People always say I ordered an hour ago. Always an hour ago." His flour-dusted fingers snapped in the air. "What am I supposed to do? Feel guilty?" Thrip nodded. The remote on the counter was wrapped in plastic.

They bagged his order while Thrip examined the dining room beyond the TV as if it were a wall-sized painting. And why not? Why shouldn't it simply be another psychic law of the universe? That the person you most wish to avoid is always randomly and immediately accessible? In among the booths, Marni Coe sat across from a burly man with the beard of a physicist. She waved Glenn over.

"Greetings, Thrip." Marni apologized, but his name did still sound like a salutation. Thrip smoothed the back of his head as if to compensate for his extra height. It was a gesture he often made when faced with a surprise. Marni Coe was a horticulture grad student and tiny. A turf grass specialist with deep-set, unpredictable eyes. In truth, she was actually a friend of Eleanor's, and had borrowed Thrip's truck to move Walter's stuff into storage before he left for a post-doc in Seattle. Walter stopped dismantling the white garlic pizza and squinted. His beard appeared to have sprung from his face with no sense of direction and simply curled. Was he applied or theoretical? Glenn couldn't remember.

"You've looked better," Marni said, regarding the greenish-yellow bruises on Thrip's jaw. The sockets, the spaces where his wisdom teeth had been, still throbbed. This was better than yesterday, though, when Thrip could barely open his mouth and had to stay on the couch sucking tea bags to control the bleeding. "Walter thanks you for the truck," Marni Coe said.

And how does one bring a bullet hole up in polite conversation? It was a small one, but still. "When did you bring it back?" Thrip asked.

"This morning, but early. I thought you'd be asleep so I didn't knock. Any news from Eleanor?"

"Nope." When she wasn't doing field work in Louisiana, Eleanor lived with Thrip. It was a romantic arrangement that

Thrip, at times, thought could clearly go either way. "Soft food," he said, lifting the white bag and backing toward the door. In the truck, he saw that Marni Coe had left him a full tank of gas.

Nobody expected Thrip at work, particularly on a Friday, but the next afternoon he woke from a dream where he'd been assigned to stuff pillows into blue jars, as container ships headed for open ocean beyond his window. Thrip arched his back. He had been sitting around the house far too long beneath this shroud of left-over anesthesia. How many forgotten bowls of mashed potatoes could you stumble across before it confirmed the onset of some larger lethargy? He would go in and open envelopes, maybe use a few paper clips.

Work waited across two gorges in a cluster of half-timbered chalets at the university's fringe. Thrip did permissions—he was the Czar of Permissions—for a small academic press. He evaluated requests, reexamined contracts, hunted lost volumes, and released letters with bills attached back to the world. "In reply to your recent request we are pleased to grant you one-time rights to quote from page 237 of the Zeiss volume in your upcoming: *Bee-wolves: A Saga of Solitary Ground Nesting Wasps.*" Thrip's second-floor office had once been a kitchen.

Compensationally challenged or merely income-impaired? These were questions his older brother, the water rights attorney, asked late at night from San Antonio. "Be a big picture guy," he'd say. "Detail is a drug," he'd explain. "Have a direction," he'd suggest, as if it were a drink. This was a stopgap job, a platform to reconnoiter from after one and a half nonessential master's degrees. Thrip saw that. Yet he had been up there for more than a year, immobile and baffled, wending his way into the long term, and now he could imagine a fair portion of his life streaming by below, filling in like bitter petrified wood.

Fat number-ten envelopes were splayed across Thrip's desk like fish. Seventy-two fish, to be exact. He culled the foreign ones, saved their stamps for his niece, and paired up the duplicate requests. September was a bad time for permissions, as all the college copy shops wanted immediate action on their course packets. Even so, when the dentist saw Thrip's impacted wisdom teeth, he called this "a good window," an occasion to confront the decay. Later, during the preliminary examination, the oral surgeon gave Thrip his choice of anesthesia. Yet after she said, "These two in the bone might come out in bits," and then, "You'll be happier if you're not aware of what I'm doing," and finally, "Oh my, this one's inflamed," Thrip agreed to skip the local and take the general. One week later, his mouth dry from the pre-op tranquilizer, the needle went in, and Thrip disappeared from time. He woke as a rubbery male voice said, "Walk to the chair. Breathe!" and Thrip's feet went on ahead. After a friend from work got him home and up the steps, one of the neighbors came over, convinced that Thrip had been in an accident.

Now, an hour into the hazy control of classifying, the phone rang. "You're not recuperating," Marni Coe said.

"I am, too."

"That's likely. Know what I forgot to tell you? This woman yesterday blocked me in your driveway. Short hair? Shoulder pads? Big gray detective's car?"

"Never saw her," Thrip said. He watched the unopened pack of Juicy Fruit by the phone, the one he'd found on the street and didn't dare eat.

"She tried some keys out on your front door and then came after me to see if I lived there. What's this supposed to mean?" Marni Coe asked.

When Thrip and Marni Coe met two years ago at an improvised Thanksgiving, they argued about anthropology. Marni Coe insisted that romantic love was innate while Thrip claimed it was a twelfth-century construction. From the start, he had imagined her as someone capable of nibbling plums in the grocery store without guilt, or opening a few test bags of cookies before deciding to purchase.

"You sure you're okay?" she asked.

"I have no idea," said Thrip, to both questions.

Outside it was still dim, but Thrip felt like squinting. This town remained besieged by clouds so much of the time that you developed the need for sunglasses when it was simply bright and gray. From September to April, people traveled without shadows, which after a while began to seem nearly normal. Bands wrote songs about it.

In the truck, Thrip's foot slipped on a cluster of dimes before finding the clutch. There had to be at least twenty dollars of change at large in the cab, and Thrip left it that way deliberately, deciding it prudent to allow chaos a corner of its own. Backing out of the press lot, Thrip heard the refracted echo of field drums and a horn line, so he coasted down the wall of the valley, beneath the abandoned Ithaca Guns smokestack, and past the falls. At the high school, Thrip adjusted his sunglasses and climbed the stands until he became slightly dizzy. This appeared to be the final rehearsal before an away football game. Buses idled by the tennis courts, as the band pulled into a tight fist on the far sideline and spun through the first sixty-four bars of the show again and again. At the fifth time through, Thrip decided that there would be a message from Eleanor waiting for him at home.

Eleanor, the dreamy and inconsistent entomologist, had been piling up dissertation data for three months at a field station south of Shreveport. She would drive for five or six days at a time, hunting leaf hoppers; insects with brains the size of commas, yet smart enough to catch thermals and ride the jet stream straight to Minnesota. She was gracefully tall, freckled, and habitually look-ing for something—a place to eat, better funding, a watch with enough functions—yet always in such an indecipherable way that Thrip never understood how the parts could fit into an overrid-ing whole. Her phone messages had become increasingly vague, and now he did not know when she might be back. Two weeks ago her taped and wispy voice reported only that she'd found a Ziploc bag with a dog's heart and a condom in it at the edge of a state forest. What, Thrip wondered, am I to do with this?

The house on Valentine Place was minute, but reasonable, and Thrip had moved in a year ago last spring. Eleanor and Thrip began as roommates and evolved. Thrip initiated it, as that had been his pattern. At first he saw her as intriguing and oddly prin-cipled. She was fascinated by folk dancing, pleased that her name belonged to another generation, and refused to wear anything with words on it. In May they'd had a falling out, "a period of dis-engagement," Eleanor said, before she went south. Thrip couldn't place what had shifted or how it had moved so quickly. It was akin to working in mist. Long ago he concluded that he was simply not bright at this type of thing—B-minus at best. Instead, Thrip held the fort, a task he found much less exasperating alone. Before, he would discover Orange Milanos in the medicine chest, a garlic press behind the plates, unopened beers among the empties when he got to the deposit counter at Tops; all of which he kept quiet about, deciding that in the future these kinds of problems would simply be a given.

The zinc-toned sky had turned orange at the seams. Thrip felt a faint warmth and rested his head against the edge of the next row up. He'd played trombone in high school, and band was as close as he ever got to being on a team. From the field, though, you could never imagine what a show actually looked like. It was always too large. This band kept getting stuck at a long arc with a spiral on the north end, a spot where one side couldn't keep up and the music slipped out of phase. The director's voice sprang from the bullhorn with corrections, and everyone sprinted back to try again.

When Thrip woke up, the band and buses were gone. On the soft red track, four people ran hurdles in the rising twilight, weaving from lane to lane.

Late Saturday morning, Thrip sat cross-legged on the floor, examining a Matchline ad in the free weekly paper. "Vampire, attractive, 34, works nights, wants man for fun. Must be named Pete or Doug." Sure. Last week there was one from: "Operative, seeking aloof, athletic counterpart, indifferent to Communists." Why was he reading these at all? Thrip wondered. There were no messages from Louisiana.

Thrip's tongue toured the sockets. The oozing had stopped, but his mouth tasted like chewed yarn. It would take a year for the soft tissue to fill in. He pushed the Weather Channel's tornado video back into the VCR, and on the screen, the TV crew once again raced a black funnel along a Kansas interstate. At the overpass they sprinted from the van and took shelter up under the girders as the tornado caught up. Every time he saw this, Thrip wondered about the slow car, the one that tumbled from the frame just before the column of wind hit the bridge. Everyone under the girders survived.

Marni Coe appeared in his kitchen without knocking. Or maybe she did knock, Thrip thought, and it didn't register. Her dark hair was pulled back. She wore an ALUMINUM MAN triathlon T-shirt and deposited a container of sherbet in the freezer before Thrip could say hello.

"You're progressing," Marni said, settling into the couch. "Down, I'd say, from pumpkin head to a squirrel face." Marni Coe on the raspberry-colored couch. "Am I interrupting anything?" She looked tired and blamed it on the mockingbird. "It's a northern mockingbird and it sings every night from eleven to three-thirty, directly below *my* window." She waved at the screen. "What is this?"

Thrip explained, as a wall of black sucked up clothes, tricycles, and roofs, ground these together at ten thousand feet, and rained down the parts. He couldn't get used to it. A quick and specific swath, a cleaving of past and present. He had even been learning his clouds; the anvil shape of the nimbus, the difference in altitude and attitude between altocumulus and cirrostratus. Lately he had begun to imagine a future in meteorology.

At the fifth staccato tap on the kitchen window, Thrip made it to the back door. As soon as he opened it, a flushed, middle-aged woman with blunt hair and confident shoes stepped right up on the threshold.

"Excuse me," she said, "but I am showing this house." She crossed the kitchen as a puzzled older couple wearing tan windbreakers followed in the perfumed slipstream. Thrip looked at his bare feet and noticed that he wasn't really dressed, just sweats and a bathrobe.

"This house should be empty," the woman said, giving the seven-foot ceilings a glance of appraisal. She blocked the television screen and dusted smooth the arm of her coral jacket as Marni Coe headed for the bathroom.

Thrip tightened the belt on his robe. "Who are you supposed to be?" he asked.

"A real estate agent," the woman said, "in the midst of a tour." This was her second try, she explained, and the owner kept assuring her that the delinquent tenants had already been evicted. She gave Thrip a piercing smile and aimed the frowning couple upstairs.

A wall of wind slid across Wichita before the tape shifted to an explanation of the mechanics of tornado formation. Red and yellow spheres rose and spun like chemistry class molecules as Marni Coe emerged from the bathroom. "That was her," she whispered. "The woman who chased me."

"Why'd you hide?" Thrip asked.

"I'm not a confrontation person."

That couldn't apply to him, either, Thrip decided, at least not anymore. Some days he was barely a let's-get-out-of-the-driveway sort of person. Footsteps wound through the second floor bedrooms and congregated at the top of the stairs. Thrip heard the words "tiny" and "charm" used in several contexts. As the trio descended, the older man nodded, as if to say, That's enough.

Once they were safely out on the sidewalk, Thrip shouted, "Thanks for stopping by." Lately he'd been unable to predict how the sentences coming out of his mouth would land. "Look at me." He plucked his sweats taut. They were maroon, a pair from tenth grade. "I'm a mess."

"That woman didn't even see you," Marni Coe said. "You weren't even in the room."

She turned over the Priority Mail pouch on the coffee table. It was addressed for Louisiana and full of postcards, overseas letters, and direct-mail pleas that Thrip couldn't get around to forwarding. Marni flipped it back while Thrip tried to explain his landlord situation, in that Mrs. Tibbits actually owned the property, but Gary, her son, managed it. "He's a hammerhead," Thrip said, looking for the phone directory on the alphabetized bookshelf. He found last year's under the VCR, and Mrs. Tibbits answered on the first ring. She would be in the hospital bed that filled her parlor, watching fragments of TV with the remote in her lap. Thrip didn't know what was wrong with Mrs. Tibbits, except that it was chronic. "We've been visited by a real estate agent," he told her.

"Oh, you two." Mrs. Tibbits coughed. "Squatters. Squatters so many months in arrears that my son sent the sheriff to have you evicted." She hung up. Thrip called back, but Mrs. Tibbits wouldn't answer. Gary's number remained busy.

"I write the checks," Thrip said. "I know I do." Marni Coe ran the tornado around at double speed. "Why'd you come over?" he asked, genuinely perplexed.

"To see how you were." She gave him a quizzical look. "Besides, I needed a walk. We could also drive somewhere. I like driving things the size of your truck."

Thrip discovered his checkbook and showed off a recent rent stub. Marni hummed. Eleanor, before she left, had signed six months' worth of rent checks.

"You really should get dressed," Marni said. "We're going bowling."

"That's silly."

"Be a sport."

"I don't think I can bowl," Thrip said.

She paused the tape. "Anesthesia is fat-soluble. It's like a curse, which is why you've got to burn it away. There's only one way out. You know, that little window at the top of the room? We might as well get on with it."

Marni Coe drove, and Thrip noticed that she didn't have to readjust the seat. He filed this away as they entered the bowling alley and prepared to rent footwear.

"One good thing about bowling is that you get people's shoe sizes without asking," Marni said. "You can tell a lot about a person's personality from their shoe size."

Thrip felt his pockets for quarters. "Yeah, like usually I'm a nine and a half, but today I'm a ten?"

"Well, generally," Marni said. She paid for both pairs. "You, for instance, tend to exaggerate misfortune." Thrip thought he should have been annoyed, but she turned away so quickly that he couldn't be sure.

The bar in the bowling alley was called the Noon Gun Lounge, and initially Thrip saw this as the proper place for their discussion. He had never owned anything with a bullet hole in it. Or even an object that had been shot at. But as they walked toward the lanes, all the distant pin explosions seemed amplified, yet somehow occurring in a different time zone. It was disorienting, so Thrip went to the bathroom and did another dose of codeine. He liked the distance it gave him. However, when he emerged, the bar and the alleys had been overrun by gangs of seven-year-olds embarking on pizza parties.

Thrip tried to concentrate on his feet as he laced his shoes up next to Marni Coe. But he kept imagining how nice it would feel to launch a friendly, hand-sized rock into his truck's rear window, taking out the remaining safety glass and the bullet hole in one clean swipe. To block this away, he began to tell Marni about the condom machine in the men's room with "Don't buy this gum. It tastes awful" scrawled across the front.

"That is getting pretty standard," Marni said. She smiled watchfully and investigated the futuristic overhead projector at the scoring island. A second later, she rolled the ten-pound ball with the peanut-butter swirl along the edge of the gutter and didn't even check the two pins' worth of damage it caused. "Okay," she said, "bowl your weight."

Thrip had done that once. He'd rolled a 175 back when he was still holding the ball wrong. He only saw how to use the finger holes correctly two weeks ago from a woman in a car ad holding a bright green ball as a prop. The elemental thrill of bowling, Thrip decided, came entirely from the kinetic joy of knocking things over and then getting to do it again. Everyone is enamored by the possibility of repeated perfect events.

In the eighth frame, Thrip began to recognize certain pin groupings as distant sets of incisors waiting for rearrangement, so he asked Marni Coe about her work. He only had a thin notion of what she did, but Marni confided that it was not going at all well, which was another reason to be bowling. "Lots of bowling coming up," she explained. "A windfall of bowling." When she was working, Marni Coe created ways to make turf grass grow more slowly, mainly by developing new varieties or applying retardants. "We're lawn-addicted already," she told him, "but you save a lot of everything, energy, money, whatnot, if you make it so people can't mow *all* the time."

"And you're happy with this?" Thrip asked.

"Saving the world through turf grass management?" She gave

him a pleased and weighty look. "How many blades to an acre?"

"Depends," Thrip said, feeling sage.

"564,537,600," she said. "Average. I win lots of bar bets. Lots. That and most people spend thirty hours a year mowing. Almost a week of vacation. See, I'm lowering stress rates for the future." She balled up the empty bag of cheese doodles and began a new frame. "Thing is, you've got to try visualization."

"I do that and they all go down in the wrong lane," Thrip said.

As they climbed Route 13, away from the lake and past the lone dead car that was always on the shoulder near the crest of the hill, Marni Coe refused to explain where they were headed. "We're having a caper," she said amid the open-window rush, as Thrip began to plead. "Did your drugs run out?" she asked.

"No," Thrip said. "Why'd you cover up the bullet hole?" Marni acted as though she couldn't hear. "The safety glass." Thrip gestured, but the stickers were gone. The rear window was whole. He reached back to pat the spot.

"It really doesn't concern you," Marni Coe said. "It's fixed." She pulled into the driveway of a blue-stained split-level house and backed up to the garage.

"I'm still concerned," Thrip said.

Marni frowned in a way that said, Sorry, pal, too late. "Maybe you just need a new world view. You know, out at Walter's, there was cat throw-up on this hood and I wiped it off. Just in time. Did you a favor. The acid in it stains your paint."

Thrip felt at once outflanked and apprehended. "Whose house is this?"

"Some friend of Walter's," she said. "This guy who designs speakers that biologists use. Sub-woofers. Extremely low frequencies so they can talk to elephants in the field. It is neat, but we're here to steal a bed. Actually, it's a frame that I found and Walter turned into an issue. He hexed it."

Marni Coe pulled a key ring with a small globe on it from her pocket, yet none of the keys opened the garage. She peered in with her palm against the glass. In the cab, Thrip was preoccupied. He was remembering a time last fall when Gary broke a screwdriver off in their kitchen door while trying to change the locks. Mrs. Tibbits must have given the real estate agent her old keys, ones that never could have worked. Mrs. Tibbits, Thrip realized, had put the house on the market behind Gary's back.

Glenn Thrip reserved Sunday afternoon to deal with Mrs. Tibbits, but on the phone, Marni Coe claimed to have found another set of Walter's keys. She wanted a new try at the bed. Thrip was just waking up. The skin on his jaw felt stretched too far. "We'll do both," Marni said. "You'll come get me." And he agreed.

Marni's apartment was the second floor of a bright-aqua, World War I–era house on the flats, near the end of Lake Street. Her ancient and stooped downstairs landlord no longer had a lawn, as he had converted the entire yard to tulip beds. In the truck, Marni asked Thrip if he had a plan, an actual negotiating strategy for Mrs. Tibbits. "It is prudent to rehearse this," she explained.

"I did," Thrip said, looking cornered, "but there were lots of versions. I kinda got lost."

Mrs. Tibbits's shingled and once-grand Victorian now sported a satellite dish beside the cupola. The windows on the upper two floors were shuttered, as once Mrs. Tibbits became bedridden the activity of the house collapsed into the front parlor. The license plate of the black Celica in the driveway said BLCELICA. Gary lived just beyond, in the carriage house apartment.

Thrip announced himself through the front porch intercom. After a pause, which he timed at one minute and forty-three seconds, the lock on the leaded glass door buzzed. The hall smelled of burned toast. The runner to Mrs. Tibbits's parlor was criss-crossed with blue whorls.

"What gall," Mrs. Tibbits said. "The squatters are here, in my house." Her voice was high, almost girlish. The hospital bed had been cranked up, and she leaned lightly against it, wearing a pale sweater and matching peach slacks. Both hands held a translucent switch which was connected to a wire that ran along the oak baseboards to the front door. "Where are my funds?" she asked.

"Mrs. Tibbits—"

The buzzer interrupted. Thrip went to check the door until he understood that this was her method of controlling the conversation. "My son reports that you two have refused to pay rent for eight months," Mrs. Tibbits said. "Eight. I am through with you. I am selling the property and have not even told the child."

He was suddenly weary, weak-in-the-knees tired. He wanted to sit, but Marni already had the fan chair in the corner. He opened the envelope his bank statement came in and handed Mrs. Tibbits the canceled rent checks. She turned the first three over to examine her son's endorsement. "Could these be fakes?" she asked.

Thrip shook his head. Mrs. Tibbits set the checks on the bed as Thrip replaced them with a stack of copies. "I believe our lease is still in effect," he said, not realizing until later how ludicrous and lawyer-like it sounded.

Mrs. Tibbits waved vaguely. "Be gone," she said, crumpling a tissue. "I will discuss this."

Freeing the bed turned out to be disarmingly easy, given the right set of keys. As they drove up East Hill, Marni explained that Walter's friend, Peyton, who owned the blue-gray house and lived alone, was in the Azores taping and decoding bird calls. The bed itself turned out to be a maple, nineteenth-century beast of a thing. It came with sleigh ends, scalloped rails, and a freezer bag of hardware. When Thrip tried to help load the parts, Marni shooed him upstairs. "There's cool stuff on the walls," she said. "Wavy pastel landscapes."

In the living room, Thrip ignored the tinted and manipulated photographs and investigated Peyton's vast collection of small plastic figures. The bookshelves had been converted to dioramas. Dinosaurs battled Teutonic knights. A Redcoat waited to ambush an ambulance driving wizard. Napoleon went hand to hand with Richard Petty.

The garage door closed, and Thrip heard his truck start. The bed was roped in and veiled with a blue plastic drop cloth. It seemed to take no time at all.

Under pressure, Thrip could recognize a pattern, so as Marni Coe drove downtown, he acted as though destinations no longer mattered. He enjoyed watching her drive. He liked gliding into the corners. He didn't want to interrupt. Soon Thrip found himself behind the front window of a bar, in a chair with a loose leg and using both hands to clasp a bottle of Rolling Rock. The sky had darkened with astonishing speed, and the orange streetlights in front of Woolworth's sparked to life. Incoming cumulonimbus, Thrip decided.

Marni Coe landed a basket of golden popcorn at his elbow. "This is death to my sockets," Thrip said. "Parts'll get stuck. My face'll blow up."

"Can't have that." She moved the basket to the table behind her.

"How involved are you and Walter?" Thrip asked. The words jutted out.

"Past or present?" Marni didn't even look surprised. "Pretty much, until recently. I mean, we were kinda everywhere." She retrieved the popcorn, and Thrip took some, anyway. He attempted to guide the sharp parts toward the roof of his mouth. "See, Walter sort of thinks he's a warlock," Marni explained. "Really. I mean, he spends a lot of time lately worrying about what he's eating or how he's getting out of bed. Putting spells on viruses. He was forever a project but—I don't know. There's some reason I can't have this bed, only I'm not sure what it is. We're in mid-drift."

"Who started it?"

"I did." Marni Coe crossed her legs. Two one-way streets met at the corner beyond the glass. "I love this seat," she said. "It's bad-idea central. Traffic-violation city. Once an hour, minimum."

Thrip watched with drowsy surprise as the black Celica, the one with the purple undercarriage sheen, made an illegal left-hand turn and headed the wrong way up Cayuga Street. "Jesus," Thrip said. "That's Gary." The license plate matched. "Man oh man, is he going to have a difficult time."

"Think he knows?" Marni said. "I mean, that his cash cow's on the market?"

Thrip shook his head. "Gary's one of those people who decides you can put purple lights under your car and just become somebody else. Like you can get away with anything. You've got force-field protection."

"Nothing wrong with the concept," Marni Coe said. "It could be that simple." This she said almost to herself. "Couldn't Gary have raised your rent, not told his mom, and skimmed off the top?"

"Maybe." Thrip nearly laughed, but it stopped halfway up. "The boy's just missing that overarching view." Yet as he said the words, Thrip noticed a shift, a peculiar change in pressure. How he had arrived here, late in the afternoon in this precarious chair, right before the rain? He was not at all comfortable with the question.

"You don't often get to see a car with an aura," Marni Coe said. She draped her hand at the back of Thrip's chair and smiled into the middle distance. "It's pretty. And you're holding up how?"

The entire neighborhood was in a fog when Thrip left Marni Coe's apartment early the next morning. The streetlights had chilly halos, and Fred Lively, her landlord, was out searching for unraked leaves. "How'd you like that blue jay last night?" he asked. The rake was painted to match the house.

"Fine," Thrip said, though he didn't understand what Fred Lively was talking about. Thrip zipped up the too-large motorcycle jacket he'd found on a chair in Marni's kitchen. His thoughts were spongy. The world sounded like a tape with extra vibrato. Driving appeared impossible, so Thrip left the truck in front of Marni's house. She already had a key. She must have, he thought, or she wouldn't have been able to get the rear window fixed.

Walking up Gunshop Hill made Thrip's sockets pulse. The blood vessels felt too close to the surface, and he worried about his clots. He didn't want them to break. Yet as the fog brightened, Thrip understood that down below, on the porch, Fred Lively had meant the mockingbird. "Isn't that a stupid blue jay?" someone had shouted last night on the street, just after a bar on the corner had closed. "No, it can *do* a blue jay, but it's *not* a blue jay," the other voice explained. As Thrip drifted off, the bird began mimicking a distant car alarm. "Trwiip. Dwiip. Trwiip. Dwiip. Trwiip." Thrip had to work to ignore it.

At the higher plain of Stewart Avenue, Thrip discovered an expanse of light blue sky. The fog was in fact only a large cloud

crowded into the valley. You could walk across the top. He granted himself permission to disregard work and head toward home.

It had turned into a day far too warm for fall. Thrip woke late
that afternoon, but in his dream the oral surgeon had exclaimed,
"We have to go back! There's more to take!" Even if that turned
out to be true, Thrip reasoned, at least now he'd know what to
expect. He took a bracing dose of codeine and counted the
remaining pills while listening to a phone message from Mrs. Tibbits's daughter. It explained that all future rent checks should be
made out to Mrs. Joyce Chaning, Gary's sister, and sent to an
address in Corning.

Marni Coe appeared with the truck around dinnertime. She
wore her green-checked flannel shirt like a jacket and under that a
black top that said MAD MAX in letters that looked homemade.
"Salvation Army," she explained. "You knew I made a truck key?"

"Guessed," Thrip said. Invasive procedure or invasive personality? The phrase came from his dream.

"What if I lost yours?" Marni said. "I didn't think you'd mind,
but I wasn't sure. You're more difficult that way than what I'm
used to." Marni pointed to the bowl of mashed potatoes in
Thrip's palm. "Those you can bring in the truck," she said. "You'll
want Walter's jacket, too. It might be cool later."

Going past the airport, in a direction that seemed to spell Cort-
land, Thrip said, "If this is contra dancing I'm getting out now."
Over the years he had developed a deep fear of contra dancing.
Usually this event happened at some VFW with quilts on the
walls, and as soon as Thrip caught on, they changed the moves,
leaving him terminally on the wrong foot and propelled from
hand to musty hand. "Like being on a midway ride gone wild," he
explained. "Your face gets sucked back by unbearable G-forces."

Marni Coe had a deep and musical laugh. She turned on the
tape deck. It came up at the key change in "I Wanna Be Sedated."
From her shirt pocket, she handed Thrip a crisply rolled joint.

"Another oldie." He punched in the cigarette lighter and wondered aloud how much longer those would still be in cars. "Want
some?"

"Gotta drive," she said.

"That's admirable." A lavender motorcycle helmet rolled around in the truck bed behind him. They passed a drive-in which had succumbed to life as a mobile home dealership. Blue spruce climbed to conceal the screen. Thrip rubbed his eyes and lost track of where they were. Marni Coe, he saw, wore a friendship bracelet on her right wrist woven from brilliant tropical-colored threads.

"You still want to know what it was?" she asked.

"Sure," he said, not certain what the question referred to.

"A pellet gun," Marni said. "I did it. Walter left it loaded. I had it in the front seat sticking out of a waste basket and *phfft*, it happened. Out your rear window."

The various greens and golds making up the fields appeared to expand. Thrip could barely imagine the things he might have said, even as recently as last week. The words swelled like an impressive wave that would never make it to the beach. How could it not matter? he thought. A bullet hole? But the reflected sun kept coming at him from the rearview mirror. He tried instead to look ahead, past the vibrating pastures at the sides of his vision, to a spot where the landscape was still in miniature.

Several oiled roads later, on top of a hill overlooking Route 81 and across from the Blodgett Mills Gun Club, the Skyway Raceway sat fenced and surrounded by a freshly carved gravel parking lot. It was a low-banked dirt track: five eighths of a mile, two turns, and an infield of puddles. The blue and white numbers by the pit area were painted to match the stands. A stake-bed pickup, driven by a blond boy and hauling a water tank, circled as the heavy woman in back wielded a wand, dampening down the dust.

Marni eased in to park among the Blazers and station wagons. She paid the five-dollar cover and tossed the motorcycle helmet into the cab. "I'll put us in the family section, so no one'll mess with you," she said. Only six-packs were allowed in the family section, according to the sign.

A race had just started. The cars looked normal enough from a distance, aside from the roll bars, the wire mesh on the windows where the safety glass had been, and the hand-painted ads for siding companies and bakeries on their doors. The noise rose up to Thrip as the unmuffled roar of throaty mammoths. When they reached the family section, Marni Coe checked her watch. "Will you be okay for a while?" she asked. Marni went to wander, as Thrip grew accustomed to the question.

Alone, things became clear in a way that they were usually not. He had been left, in several senses. Decisions had actually been made months ago. Thrip now knew that. He could think of this dismantling as his idea, but it was in fact a favor from Eleanor. He was only now catching up, and embarrassed by the bits of wrongly imagined future, he had carried along.

At a quarter to eight the lights came on. The white-haired woman beside Thrip in the Agway jacket yawned, and a small bug flew into her mouth. "That about sums up my day," she said. The announcer ordered all Spectator Race contestants to bring their release forms and helmets to the start-finish line. Thrip wondered where Marni Coe was, exactly.

When the three cars and the lone white truck lined up two across for the first heat of the Spectator Race, Thrip understood. These were the cars people had arrived in. They were the vehicles they drove to work. His pickup had the inside slot on the second row. Marni Coe, wearing the lavender helmet, was behind a gold Cadillac and flanked by a Civic.

"They're here to have their hearts stopped," said the loudspeaker. "And you, in your heart of hearts, know you could be out there, too."

Three laps. The crowd thought this was hilarious. Racing with repair consequences. It was a monthly event. "Next week it's trailer races," the woman beside him explained. "They tow pop-up campers and things. Snowmobile trailers."

"That's my truck," Thrip told her. "The white one."

The woman turned to appraise him from a different angle and patted his knee. "Good for you," she said, as if he had finally begun to branch out. "Good for you."

Thrip's truck spewed clumps of mud through the long corners. It might have been a loud mural, set in motion against the deep forest. Marni Coe passed the Civic, and her back wheels made an elegant sideways hop into the following turn. This was a test, Thrip thought. He had been chosen. He saw that this might not be a compliment, but that turned into a choice the moment you could recognize it. He was supposed to be unnerved. That was the underlying game here.

The Cadillac held the lead until it blew a tire at the finish and slid across the line behind the Civic. A kind of happy pandemonium rolled through the stands. Marni came in third. She grinned and pounded the steering wheel. The woman beside Thrip hooted and said that next he'd have to worry about finding a pit crew.

As the crowd stood, Thrip gave in to examining the clouds. Altocumulus in solid regular rolls. A middle-level line of tubes over a magenta sky. Moisture masses heaped and headed in one direction, only to be cut by vertical currents of unstable air. It felt like acting, all of this, here in the family section of the Skyway Raceway. He began to wonder if on a certain level the mechanism, the way another sort of person became you, might be that simple. With a release of pressure, events would always swirl in to fill a space.

When Glenn Thrip could see the track again, the woman and the boy with the tank truck were spraying it down for the next heat. Thrip followed the white roof of his pickup into the clotted parking lot and watched as Marni, still laughing, backed into an empty space. There was nothing to stop this from continuing.

GREG SIMON

The Interpreters of Dreams

"...the Muse guides mariners
in the shape of bees."
—Philostrates

Her wild cunning hypothesis:
the Sirens in the *Odyssey*
were bees. And I imagine
two virgins, joined at the thorax—
grounded, centered, perfumed—
who could hum the Greeks' ancient
choruses, who knew all
the lullabies, the waltzes,
the songs a wife would sing
while she worked her loom.
Those honey-throated twins
who tempted first with knowledge,
then lived your life in their dreams.

Long-suffering, brilliant
Odysseus, who lusted
after motion, temptation,
change, asked his girl Circe
to recommend the best way
to meet her friends. Stuff the ears
of your oarsmen with beeswax,
she said. Let them lash you
to the stoutest mainmast—
lash every pagan part of you
except your eyes and ears
while the Sirens plow a
broad new furrow in your brain.

And now, her research complete,
she contemplates the bodies
decomposing on the green
shoreline. She wonders how they died,
or why Homer did not spare
a noble hexameter
to clarify, to explain?
The poet, who was a drone,
and a blind one at that, surely
understood the frenetic
lure of the hive, the text
those two unbridled voices
trill to all who come too near.
He was reticent, our poet,
not shy. The Sirens' hymn
persists. Others died of bliss.

Bread Lines

"Flour is a fine thing."
—Nadezhda Mandel'shtam

Bread we've all pissed away
Stale crumbs the baby dances
On sandwich she won't eat now
Vallejo's nightmares semi
Full colon hungers crackling
Like electricity be dash
Tween them a hungrier man
If we survive moments self dash
Abnegation like that
We will elect ourselves to
The pantheon of the poor
Marching to Umschlagplatz
Gateway to the Underworlds
Auschwitz   Dachau   Treblinka
Bearing a child starving
                              Start
Father will we meet Mother
& be together again
Of course my child of course
She's waiting for us there
& when will we be given
Bread Father Soon Soon Soon
It is already very near
Stop
        I think too much salt
Made that bread so bitter
Salt that was squeezed & lashed
From those who worked the korpse
Factories gunpowder kaves
For Hitler & Joe Stalin
& when 1 skrimped for loaf
Of bread kame sliding back

167

Akross the kold dead window dash
Sill at Lubyanka
A Woman knew A Husband
A Father   A Son   A Daughter
A Sister   A Brother
Joined the ranks of shadows
On the outskirts of labor
Kamps in the Taiga Osip
Mandel'shtam's widow Nadezhda
Mandel'shtam learned the price of
A little human treachery
Semi kolon full sacks of flour
Unleavened by pity or
Kare she was a Jewess
Who deklined Chekist *aktion*
Non dash akkomplice who lived due
East of the Smotheredlode
Charred in the Nazi ovens

Chaos Theory

1. Sensitive Dependence on Initial Conditions

For want of a nail the shoe was lost,
for want of a shoe the horse was lost,
and so on to the ultimate loss—a battle,
a world. In other words, the breeze
from this butterfly's golden wings
could fan a tsunami in Indonesia
or send a small chill across the neck
of an old love about to collapse in Kansas
in an alcoholic stupor—her last.
Everything is connected. Blame it on
the butterfly, if you will. Or the gesture
thirty years ago, the glance across
the ninth-grade auditorium floor,
to the girl who would one day be your
lover, then ex-lover, then the wind
that lifts the memory's tsunami,
the mare of the imagination, bolting,
the shoe that claps the nail down on
your always already unending dream.

2. Love's Discrete Nonlinearity

No heart's desire is repeatable, or,
therefore, predictable. If a few hungry foxes
gorge on a large population of rabbits,
the population of foxes increases
while that of the rabbits declines,
until some point of equilibrium is passed

and the foxes begin to vanish with
the depleted supply of rabbits, and then
the rabbits multiply, like rabbits. And so on.
The ebb and flow of desire and fulfillment
is a story as old as the world. So,
if I loved you, finally, too much, until
you began to disappear, and I followed,
would you theoretically return to love
repeatedly again? There are forces so small
in our story of foxes and rabbits
no Malthus could ever account for them.
Whole species daily disappear, intractable
as weather. Or think of a continent's
coastlines, their unmeasurable eddies
and whorls: infinite longings inscribed
by finite space and time,
the heart's intricate branchings.

3. *Strange Attractors*

Our vision is simply not large or small enough
to encompass love's fractal geometry.
Who can know the motion of whorl within whorl
entrancing that paradoxical coastline, the changing
habitat of rabbits, the possibility that,
in the clockwork attraction of the solar
system, some heavenly body may not appear
every few million years, to throw all our
calculations asunder? Which says something
for randomness, which has its own hopeful
story. It's just that the patterns of love
and loss are so limitless that chaos
makes its own beautiful picture in which
we are neither (for all our grand needs
and egos) first cause nor unrepeatable.
We are uniquely strange attractors, love's

pendulum point or arc, time's shape or fancy,
in a system with its own logic, be it
the cool elegance of eternity, or
the subatomic matrix of creation and decay.

The Brooch

Some cruel entrepreneur glued jewels onto wings
to prevent their broad, papery flowering,
the ruby or sapphire or smoky opal hump
wedged in an oval frame, its frail gold chain
blunted with a pin, so the exotic beetle,
living brooch, could plod its strict loop.
Pinned to my mother's monogrammed blouse,
that insect circled her initial, *D,* endlessly,
one arm of a clock wild with sprung tension,
symbol of *time passing* in early Bergman.
Then Mother cushioned a fish bowl with confetti,
the exiled prince plush in his glass palace,
and though she sprinkled water and crushed matzoh,
the beetle soon rocked onto its burdened back.
For days it lay among shredded funnies
because she couldn't bear to pry the jewel
from the sleek carapace, snap the foreign skull,
couldn't touch the withered roach.
No one spoke its brittle, miniature corpse.
Then Grandmother, in her gruff, Old World manner,
crumbled what remained of that conversation piece
into soot, the blue-black powder backdrop now
for the gem that flamed in her furrowed palm:
her stuck-in-the-throat history of sifting ash
from unearthed sancta of charred flesh
till clasping one daughter's heirloom brooch.

Port Townsend

A year after your death, I leaned above
My desk, and listened to gullshrieks rising off
The shoreline I imagined—shapes of driftwood,
Glistening sacs of jellyfish, whatever

Washes in—page after page of days
Misplaced in the leaden interim...
                                One evening,
I felt it before I saw the seam, the tremor
Widen—felt the shell-white, shadowed white

Roll back across the Sound—
                            And found the stair,
The switchbacks snaking up through hemlocks, tensed
Madronas drenched with salt (mist caught in the rusted
Wrecks of brambles, smoking in and out

My breath), past sidelong, nearly silent springs
Slipped out through raw cuts in the slant rock...
Crossing the headland wading wet ferns, lichens
Crumbling underfoot, I skirted the derelict,

Moss-sunk gun emplacements to the cliffedge
Crumbling, undercut—
                        And at that moment—
In that motion, pulse—the cries of warblers
Flicked across my shoulder, little flock

Of leaf-shapes into the lick of blue. Below,
Obsidian sand flats, smooth off-camber rollers...
Farther and farther out through rafts of kelp,
An eely coot winked under, coming up

With glints of fish. I watched horizons crumpling
Range on range against Mt. Noh, the slow
Heart of the lighthouse drifting—drowned—until
The left side of my face froze numb, and I

Stepped into the dusk again—its fronds and root-knots,
Oblique mists, its echoes of waveshocks even
Here—through silvery, insubstantial fir slopes,
Traces of cloudsurf far from the sound of water.

Bay of Naples

The city is still the same handful of glances,
Glimpses of alleyways like wounds laid open,
Balconies of laundry drying, names of streets
Unfolding in the smells of fishscale, kelp,
And poverty...
              Across Fleet Landing, sheets
Of blind-white glare seethe off the spires and stairflights
Through me, through my sea-pitched, sea-numb body,
Toward the sea. I'd like to drink myself
Civilian, thread my way through troughs of dusk,
Past café tables set immaculate
Beside some nondescript, scummed-over fountain,
April's glassy strata spinning itself
Apart above Vesuvius—
              But in
This rivering air of angels, algae, waves
Of language rolling through me, I can't tell
How much I've spent, or anything I've heard...
Arriving here lightheaded in the shadow
Of Castel Nuovo, reeling a bit
On solid rock, I am a memory
The hookers and gypsies sing to,
Passing through the gates into the city.

CHARLES WRIGHT

Christmas East of the Blue Ridge

So autumn comes to an end with these few wet sad stains
Stuck to the landscape,
                         December dark
Running its hands through the lank hair of late afternoon,
Little tongues of the rain holding forth
                                          under the eaves,
Such wash, such watery words...

So autumn comes to this end,
And winter's vocabulary, down-sized and distanced,
Drop by drop
Captures the conversation with its monosyllabic gutturals
And tin music,
               gravelly consonants, scratched vowels.

Soon the camel drivers will light their fires, soon the stars
Will start on their brief dip down from the back of heaven,
Down to the desert's dispensation
And night reaches, the gall and first birth,
The second only one word from now,
                                    one word and its death from right now.

Meanwhile, in Charlottesville, the half moon
Hums like a Hottentot
                       high over Monticello,
Clouds dishevel and rag out,
The alphabet of our discontent
Keeps on with its lettering,
                             gold on the black walls of our hearts...

Umbrian Dreams

Nothing is flat-lit and tabula rasaed in Charlottesville,
Umbrian sackcloth,
                    stigmata and *Stabat mater,*
A sleep and a death away,
Night, and a sleep and a death away—
Light's frost-fired and Byzantine here,
                                        aureate, beehived,
Falling in Heraclitean streams
Through my neighbor's maple trees.
There's nothing medieval and two-dimensional in our town,
October in full drag, Mycenaean masked and golden lobed.

Like Yeats, however, I dream of a mythic body,
Feathered and white, a landscape
                        horizoned and honed as an anchorite.
(Iacopo, hear me out, St. Francis, have you a word for me?)
Umbrian lightfall, lambent and ichorous, mists through my days,
As though a wound, somewhere and luminous,
                                        flickered and went out,
Flickered and went back out—
So weightless the light, so stretched and pained,
It seems to ooze, and then not ooze, down from that one hurt.
You doubt it? Look. Put your finger there. No, there. You see?

October II

October in mission creep,
                    autumnal reprise and stand down.
The more reality takes shape, the more it loses intensity—
Synaptic uncertainty,
Electrical surge and quick lick of the minus sign,
Tightening of the force field
Wherein our forms are shaped and shapes formed,
                    wherein we pare ourselves to our attitudes...

Do not despair—one of the thieves was saved; do not presume—
                    one of the thieves was damned,
Wrote Beckett, quoting St. Augustine.
It was the shape of the sentence he liked, the double iambic
    pentameter:
It is the shape that matters, he said.
Indeed, shape precludes shapelessness, as God precludes
    Godlessness.
Form is the absence of all things. Like sin. Yes, like sin.

It's the shape beneath the shape that summons us, the juice
That spreads the rose, the multifoliate spark
                                that drops the leaf
And darkens our entranceways,
The rush that transfigures the maple tree,
                    the rush that transubstantiates our lives.
October, the season's signature and garnishee,
October, the exponential negative, the plus.

OKSANA ZABUZHKO

Prypiat—Still Life

*translated from the Ukrainian by
Lisa Sapinkopf and the author*

It could be dawn.
The light, crumpled like sheets.
The ashtray full.
A shadow multiplies on four walls.
The room is empty.
No witnesses.
But someone was here.
A moment ago twin tears shimmered
On polished wood
(Did a couple live here?)
In the armchair a suit, recently filled by a body,
Has collapsed into a bolt of fabric.
Come in, look around. No one's here,
Just the breathing air, crushed
As though by a tank.
A half-finished sweater remembers someone's fingers.
A book lies open, marked by a fingernail.
(How amazing, this silence beyond the boundary!)
On the polished wood, two stains.
On the floor by the armchair an apple,
Bitten but not brown.

*Note: Prypiat is an abandoned town in
the evacuated area around Chernobyl.*

Conductor of Candles

*translated from the Ukrainian by
Lisa Sapinkopf and the author*

O conductor of candles!
>Eyes shimmer with reflections...
Black web of shadows, break apart for an instant—
Yes, for just the single gesture with which he tears off his gloves
I'd accept even more than my earthly travails!
Conductor of candles!
>Your arms, all sinews and veins,
Are bared nearly to the shoulders in the unsteady light.
Oh, I can feel all the glib, sticky smiles
Peel away from my face,
Just as fingers rub the melted residue from candles.
The stage brightens with a parching glow,
Your silhouette is distinct, indelible, even through closed lids,
O conductor of candles!
>And no one sees them but me,
These flames with which the candelabra are charged
Like guns with bullets.
In the seat next to mine a bearded oaf is snoring.
In front of me plump dresses exhale perfume.
O conductor of candles!
>And no one hears you but me,
In this hall where people doze off at their own lives.
What's the point of this, Maestro? Who needs it?
Look around—we're alone in this hall!
"The first candle stinks!
What this orchestra of yours needs is a coupla good sparklers!"
—Voices rustle in the dark like banknotes.
Without blinking, I peer into the candles' golden pupils.
O conductor of candles!
>I know the charred wicks of your fingers
Will flare up any moment into petals of living fire!

Oh, how the people will leap from their chairs, squeaking and
    shrieking,
When the splash of sparks rends the curtain of darkness,
When you burst to the ceiling like a living torch,
Shedding angry fireworks on their sleepy faces!
And when your still-warm ashes will have burned through into
    the stagnant brains
(My God, for whom, before whom, have you burned?)
I will shape a thin candle
From the pure, prescient wax,
I'll walk down the empty aisle and climb onto the stage...
I'll tear off my gloves—
The black web of shadows will break for an instant—
And I'll step up to your music stand, as Conductor of the
    Last Candle,
Until the moment I'm replaced.

Easy Lay

Hard to believe how *popular* I was. At Mt. Ephraim High School where I was in ninth grade that spring. Counted *ten, twelve, sixteen, nineteen* new friends! Not just boys in my class but popular juniors and seniors, athletes began to notice me, smiled and called me *Doll, Doll-girl, Ingrid, In-grie.* Word spreads fast, who the good-looking ninth-grade girls are. Asked me on dates, but Momma wouldn't allow it saying I was too young. Tried to get my phone number to call. Whispering, staring. A guy named Artie in jeans, a T-shirt, biker boots running his thumb along the row of ninth-grade lockers prowling the ninth-grade corridor to check *Doll-girl* out. But it was the popular boys, a better class of boys I sought. I loved it, their attention! That feeling leaves you sick and faint with excitement knowing you're *popular*! Couldn't get enough of it drifting through school corridors between classes as in a dream smiling Hello! Hi! *Hi there!* imitating the pretty popular older girls because in truth I had no friends, a horse-faced girl named Bernice who talked about me behind my back saying I had bedbugs, a boy named Jig from Mohawk Street who talked me into kissing him open-mouthed then laughed at me I started to choke and gag and somebody told me he'd written something nasty about INGRID BOONE in all the boys' lavatories at school. But I had certain friends I listed their names in code in my notebook with a star by the special ones and there was a special-special list of boys all hearts. And there was a special list growing longer with each passing day of boys and girls who had insulted me, cut me to the heart, these were marked with a skull and crossbones the way the mystery-detective novels were marked at the public library, on their peeling spines. Marked for Death. But truly I *was* pretty, and I *was* popular. Girls in my neighborhood were jealous of me the way their mothers were jealous of my mother with her blond hair, her face and figure and clothes and bronze Cougar. The clothes *I* wore, funky little tops and poor-boy sweaters and jeans snug in the rear, now I refused to wear most of what Momma sewed for me, made me look older than I was whatever age I was. And I'd started to smoke, carried my own cigarettes and a gilt-lettered matchbook from the Yewville Park Lane Hotel where one of Momma's man friends with money to spend took her certain weekends. And I was smart. My mind rattled on fast as a machine sometimes, ran its own way without my participation. So I'd know the answer to an algebra problem but not the steps to that answer. Or what a poem like Robert Frost's "The Road Not Taken" meant but not how to explain it. Stammering and going beet-red if called upon. Even by my English teacher Miss Elsworth who liked me. And the other teachers who were hopeful of me at first then grew impatient, exasperated. My problem was nerves I guess. Too nervous and excited to do well on tests unless I memorized every possible question beforehand and written them out and even sometimes if I made this exhausting effort it did no good, my blood beat too hard, my thoughts ran wild. *You're stupid. You're a bad girl. White trash. Going to hell like every other Boone.* This voice I'd never heard in my life and it was not a voice I acknowledged but at such times taking tests and exams it rang unimpeded in my head like a radio you can't shut off. But I excelled in take-home assignments and homework in general so a teacher like my social studies teacher Mrs. Hornell would think I was cheating getting help from an older student or a parent and if interrogated about this I stammered and blushed and stared at the floor scarcely able to whisper *No.* When I did my homework my grades were A's except if I lost my homework to some guy grabbing my duffel bag, turning it upside down over the oil-splotched pavement behind the high school teasing me calling me *Doll-girl* the way they did. Or maybe I'd done the wrong questions in the textbook, hadn't been listening when the teacher gave the assignment. Or I was listening but staring so hard at this guy Foxy sitting sprawled in his desk by the window at the far side of the classroom ignoring me, stared and stared at Foxy who'd hurt me and never apologized so I didn't hear the teacher's droning voice. Or it was one of my feverish days scribbling poems in my notebook! Poems about love, and dying, and flying high above the earth, and white horses with long streaming manes wild in the mountains. Cascades of words filling up pages in my notebook like the churning channels of water of Tintern Falls you can stare at until you're hypnotized but you can never determine their pattern except to know there *is* a pattern inside the falls. Or maybe I wasn't writing poems at all, maybe I was scribbling love letters to Foxy who had kissed me and run his hands over me and said he was crazy for me then hurt me squeezing my breast, turned mean when I told him stop and pinched my left nipple so I burst into tears, and he never apologized! Not a one of them ever apologized! Or letters to Dale, or Bibi, or Dorie, or Rich, or Carrie Kimble the "captain" of the varsity cheerleaders' "squad"—the senior girl I would have traded my soul, of all the girls of Mt. Ephraim High, to *be*. Or letters to Mr. Quincy our algebra teacher I wanted so desperately to please. Homely frog-face with his mean little bored half-smile, leaning his chin on his hand every day and his eyes trailing over most of his students in pity and contempt but I loved Mr. Quincy, I was terrorized by him, a clammy sweat broke out over me and my brain shuddered to a stop when he announced with his mocking smile *Spot quiz! Take out a clean sheet of paper and put away your books!* From Ingrid Boone a paper with so many corrections and X'd out problems it was virtually unreadable and no surprise when the quiz came back marked F- in red felt-tipped pen. And once that shameful sheet of paper returned to me with the usual F- but also that time a swirling indignant question mark through my scrawled INGRID BONE—I had misspelled my own name! And Mr. Quincy staring at me hunched and thumbnail-biting in my seat like I was white trash as hopeless as Bernice Urken. Or I might be writing to Miss Elsworth my English teacher who was the only teacher who liked me though the fact that she liked me qualified her in my eyes. Or I might be writing to "Bunny" Heinz the boys' gym coach who ran my afternoon study hall like a drill sergeant on TV, wisecracking and harsh and unpredictable in his moods. Or I might be writing to our principal Mr. Cantry who led us in the Pledge of Allegiance at Friday assemblies with a high ringing sincere voice pressing his right hand against his fattish torso like an upright hog, the kind of man you can't help *wanting to please. Wanting to impress* so one day maybe he'd smile saying *Hello Ingrid!* in the hall like he did with only the most popular, the very best students.

I was not popular and I was not a good student but I had my plans, my schemes. If I'd swallowed a diet pill or two given to me by my girlfriend Bonnie (I'd trade her cigarettes, five Newports for one pill) these schemes seemed to me very plausible, it was only a matter of *making them happen* but *being patient, too.* The main thing was: I had a glen-plaid wool jacket similar to one worn by a pretty red-haired JV cheerleader named Gail Ellen Ryan. And sheepskin-lined boots similar to boots worn by Carrie Kimble. These were imitations of the real things but nobody would look closely would they. Bought on sale at the Hitching Post where after school I browsed with my friends Sandy, Denise, Bonnie giggling trying on outfits in the dressing rooms working up our courage to steal (you'd put on layers of clothes under your own) but the bitchy salesgirls had our number spying on us so we'd stroll over to Bar-B-Q Diner where we'd meet guys from school, not ninth-graders but older guys sliding into our booth in the back right corner grinning at us especially me *Hi Ingrid! Got room for me, In-grie?* Some jokes about my name and BOONE which the guys would mumble-moan BOOOOONNNNE! but I ignored them. Things said of me or scrawled on walls but how would I know what, and why care. And we'd smoke our cigarettes, drink Cokes fizzing with caffeine till my head buzzed and we'd laugh, laugh like hyenas. Bonnie's sister's diet pills, real prescription pills Bonnie stole a few at a time, plus the caffeine: WOW! Talking screwing around with these cool guys, couldn't break away, why lots of nights I didn't do my homework or if I'd already done it in study hall it was taken from me for somebody else's use. Or just taken, ripped or tossed away. Funny! Wild! And if the guys took us to movies at the mall, a show starting at 5:15 p.m. getting out at 7:30 p.m. And in the dark back rows where the seats creaked when a guy you didn't know slipped his arm around your shoulders and began to kiss you forcing your head back like he wanted to snap your neck forcing your mouth open so there was the terror of choking on his tongue alive and thrusting like an eel, and his sudden fingers between your legs, poking, pinching, and if you began to choke, or clawed at his hand, or thrashed your head from side to side panicked trying to escape he would lean back panting in his seat whispering *Shit!* then get up and walk away. Or if a guy had a car or his daddy's pickup and asked to drive you home. And you knew it was an asshole thing to do but you said *Sure!* Beer cans opened in the parking lot, warm beer in dribbles down your chin. A single can and you're dizzy, two cans and you're what the guys called *smashed*. That tone of admiration and approval like Momma's drunk-marveling voice: *smashed*. And there was the old quarry road off Mohawk, bumpy treacherous with icy slush and low overhanging tree limbs heavy with snow and you squealed with laughter the car bounced so, bounced and rattled on its high tires, and already it was dark, it was night and no stars and car's lurching headlights and you'd just gotten out of school, you'd been expected to drop by Flora Wells's to meet up with your mother for some purpose long forgotten. *Oh oh oh!*—waiting to see if he would drive the clumsy car too far, skid out onto the quarry ice and the ice would shatter beneath the weight of the car and you would all sink, drown a hideous death in freezing water. That trucker behind his windshield gazing up, a pilot behind his windshield gazing up, grinning, waiting. *Doll-girl, do me, huh? You know how? Don't play dumb.* How they would go from moaning how beautiful you are, how crazy they are for you to that sound of reproach and threat, it was always a surprise. But the kissing was so sweet, even the open-mouthed kissing so sweet sometimes, and a guy's strong hands cradling your head, stroking your hair, gazing at you close-up like a lover on TV or in the movies like you *exist*, you *are there*. But sometimes the hands were hurtful, and the guy too drunk and you're not smashed enough not to be scared, and running stumbling sobbing and puking beer across a snowy debris-littered field to the rear of a neighbor's house and so through to Mohawk Street and back home where Momma was not waiting anyway. And next morning Momma bleary-eyed and pissed examining the glen-plaid jacket, sniffing the beer-vomit you've tried to wash out. *Ingrid?—what the hell are you up to?* But by then the panic was not only gone but forgotten. The swimming eyes and bruised mouth. Kept a scrupulous record of boys I "dated" but it wasn't always clear if these episodes had happened yet or were meant to happen someday soon. But if it had happened it *had happened* and was over with. And I wouldn't need to remember, or would confuse it with another time or something on TV or in a movie. Because I *was* smart: reasoning I couldn't be pregnant, the stuff that came out of him I knew to call sperm hadn't gone *in*. Just dribbled on my thighs, in my pubic fuzz. Where I'd touched it afterward examining it on my finger, just—nothing. Clear wetness a little sticky, and no smell. Like a more transparent snot. But not nasty like snot. Reasoning too I was too skinny, tiny breasts and my pelvic bones jutting, I was thirteen years old and hadn't begun "my periods" yet one of the last girls in the ninth grade according to the girls' gym teacher who kept a weird record of such things. And how strange to me that my face was so different to the outer eye than I knew it to be from inside. My fevered skin, that itched and demanded scratching. I would stare in amazement at my reflection in any mirrored surface—*Is that me?—Ingrid?* It was a sort of joke. Unless it was a trick. But who was playing the trick? The girls' lavatory bluish-foul with smoke though smoking was forbidden so I would lean close to the mirror in wonder as if to kiss the staring blond girl with the wide-set brown eyes lightly threaded with veins but the skin actually clear-looking. *My God am I pretty?—how is it possible I am pretty?* Discovering then a tiny red pimple beside my mouth, a budding dull-red lump at my hairline. *C'n I borrow a cigarette, Ingrid?* a girl would ask and my heart would swell in pride. *Sure! Take two.* How proud I was counting *five, six, nine, eleven* girlfriends. And more boys asking me out, or following me home. But were these girls I could trust?—what were they saying behind my back? Their eyes narrowing when I passed by them in the cafeteria, smirking when Miss Elsworth read my essay "Winter Riverscape" to the class, a conspicuous red A+ beside my name. That was the cruel secret of friendships at Mt. Ephraim High I was beginning to learn. But I would never give up. Each morning vowing to make a new friend, or anyway to try. Could be a girl or a boy, in ninth grade, or tenth, or eleventh, or most prized of all a senior. Because in fact I had no friends, not a single girl not even Bernice. Not a single boy who would not betray me. But I forced myself to smile like Carrie Kimble *H'lo Dale! Hi Dorie! Hi Foxy!* moving in the noontime crush jostled along the corridor to the cafeteria my eyes stark and staring as a zombie's. And later in the day taking a certain stairs hurrying from one end of the hall to the other where Kirk Belknap who was a senior dark-haired and good-looking a basketball player with a terrific smile left his biology class to go downstairs to his sixth period class which was gym and by chance I would be headed downstairs too beside him, or as close to beside him as possible *Hi Kirk!* and if he was talking and laughing with his friends he might not hear so I would say a little louder *HI KIRK!* and he would glance back at me quizzical and possibly a little annoyed not recognizing me or not remembering my name but mumbling *Yeah, hi* reddening as one of his buddies poked him in the ribs and the guys moved on together eyeing *Doll-girl* in that way that scared and excited me like somebody bringing a lighted match up close to my hair: WOW! And one afternoon after school there was Kirk in his car cruising the curb where I was walking by myself and he leaned out his window asking in the nicest voice how'd I like a ride home? And I could not believe my eyes who it was, I must have stared amazed and there was a beat or two before I managed to say *Sure!—thanks!* and lots of people were watching, girls stricken with envy, and we rode around talking and smoking cigarettes and listening to the radio and Kirk told me all sorts of things about himself I would never have guessed such as he wanted to be a doctor ministering unto the poor someday, possibly in the Peace Corps, and he had three basketball scholarships offered him by colleges but couldn't make up his mind which one to accept, and he'd had bad luck with girls, in his opinion at least, there was always some hurt feelings and misunderstandings and he was damned if he caught on why. Driving in sleety rain north of Mt. Ephraim and along the river following the railroad tracks the way I remembered from some other time unless it was a dream I was remembering, so sweet. And we stopped at a place that sold fishermen's supplies plus beer and liquor and the owner seemed to know Kirk so sold him two six-packs of ale though he was underage, this strong dark ale like nothing I had ever tasted before Kirk said takes getting used to. And in a hidden place we parked above the river and drank and talked and laughed listening to the radio and I was snuggled in

Kirk's arms like I'd been there many times, so peaceful, and we were kissing and it was gentle like no other kissing of my life but like kissing on TV or in the movies and Kirk was saying over and over like the lyrics of a song *Ingrid you're so pretty! Ingrid you're so special!* and he groaned he was so crazy for me, wanted me so, and it was a long time later I tried to wake up pushing his hands away where he was inside my clothes and he'd opened his trousers like some of the guys want to but Kirk was gentle, saying *Ingrid?—let's go in the back seat okay?* and I saw how big his penis was, big for *me,* I was proud how big it was for *me,* and I was sleepy and sort of sickish saying *Gee I don't know, maybe I should go back home?* and Kirk said *But honey I love you, I'm crazy about you* and I said in this slow dazed voice *Gee I don't know, I guess not* but he wasn't listening, pushing against me, and running his hands over me, and we never needed to go into the back seat.

An Interview with James Merrill

Words sat up and behaved when James Merrill was around. Whether poetry or prose, Merrill's writing always sounded like it fell from a tree, perfect from the start. His memoir, *A Different Person,* was no exception. In it, Merrill explored his early life as a young poet, a dutiful son, and a gay man in Europe and America. The book's intimate, candid tone may have surprised readers familiar with his poetry. As a poet, Merrill was master of convolution and indirection. However clear his diction, the emotions and ideas which informed it remained stubbornly elusive. The memoir, on the other hand, seemed to lay everything on the line, from Merrill's troubled relationship with his divorced parents to his complicated lovelife. What marked it as unmistakably Merrillean was the delicacy of its insights into art and artists, and its attention to detail.

Publishing a memoir was only one step in a career marked by its eerie perfection. Merrill's achievement could almost stand as a road map of traditional literary success. For one thing, he was prolific: After his first book, *First Poems,* was released in 1951, he published fourteen books of poetry, two novels, two plays, and a book of interviews and essays. For another, his poetry won everything there was to be won in terms of national recognition, including two National Book Awards (for *Nights and Days* and *Mirabell*), the Bollingen Prize in Poetry (for *Braving the Elements*), and the Pulitzer Prize (for *Divine Comedies*).

Of course, his best known work of poetry was the modern epic he first published in 1982, *The Changing Light at Sandover.* In it, he and David Jackson, his partner of many years, engage in extended conversations with dead friends and historical figures by means of a homemade Ouija board. Their guides in the literary underworld include such figures as W. H. Auden, William Butler Yeats, Ephraim, a Greek Jew born at Xanthos in 8 A.D., and a bat-like spirit named Mirabell who turns into a peacock. Over the course of nearly six hundred pages, J.M. and D.J., as the poem's protagonists are referred to throughout, learn about the secrets of the universe and their origins in a figure called God Biology, who himself makes periodic appearances. The plot is less confusing than it sounds in paraphrase, but it is even wilder and more implausible. Lest there be any confusion, Merrill was not strictly kidding in any of this; he and David Jackson really had been using an Ouija board since the 1950's.

Spookiness, perfection, and revelation—these words get at something important and persistent in Merrill's work in all its forms. In the fall of 1993, we conducted this brief interview through the mail, which seemed exactly appropriate when it was done. A correspondence left room for both elegance and distance, qualities essential to Merrill as he talked about *A Different Person*, *The Changing Light at Sandover*, and the state of poetry.

Merrill died in February 1995, at the age of sixty-eight.

. . .

HEATHER WHITE: Why a memoir, and why now?

JAMES MERRILL: It's hard to write about things that aren't in perspective. Forty years have passed away; so have many of those human figures. Also, I acquired a word processor. Otherwise— untidy as I am, always mislaying drafts—I would never have dreamed of undertaking a long piece of work like this.

WHITE: The surface of your language in the memoir's prose seems even more highly polished than it does in your poetry, where a dissonant emotional tone often underlies its elegance. Is that your impression also?

MERRILL: You're right. And again, it's thanks in part to the computer. I love to revise, but in the old days of retyping, scissors, and tape, I'd often settle for four or five drafts. But with the memoir I could polish—expand or simplify—to my heart's content. The dissonance you speak of in many poems came from my chronic trouble in sustaining a uniform tome. To mask this, I often relied on interruption, change of voice, and so forth.

WHITE: How does that polish relate to your sense of revealing yourself (or not)?

MERRILL: I never believed that spontaneity was the answer to self-expression. It's too raw, too messy. Loving revision as I do, I have almost a sculptor's feeling for the insight that emerges as the extraneous, the random, is chipped away. Some readers may feel the polish I aim for is a form of concealment; I don't.

WHITE: What do you think constitutes the "unsayable" in a memoir written in the nineties?

MERRILL: There's not much left that's "unsayable," is there? But the unreadable proliferates. I wonder if they don't often amount to the same thing. Things that are said so ineptly that no one wants to read them.

WHITE: Were there points in the memoir where you felt you were approaching the unsayable, in a personal or societal sense?

MERRILL: One recurring impulse, given my nature, is to think the worst about myself as a friend or lover, or "intellect." A little self-doubt goes a long way, and most readers gladly do without it.

WHITE: What are the qualities you value in a memoir?

MERRILL: I haven't read that many memoirs. One that I love is *First Childhood* by Lord Berners (the dilettante, composer, and model for "Lord Merlin" in Nancy Mitford's novels). Very casual and entertaining. At the other end of the spectrum I would put Proust: his patience with the reader, his willingness to be long-winded, to explain, his trust in language. What I most value in *any* book, if it comes to that, is style, elegance, pacing, an observer's eye. If you have those, your life can be dull but your book will be enthralling.

WHITE: Of what value or interest do you imagine *A Different Person* to be to readers of your poetry, in their reading of your work?

MERRILL: That would vary a lot. I can imagine a reader who really doesn't want this kind of clarification (if that's what it is). I myself don't drop everything to read the lives of poets I most admire.

WHITE: If we could turn to more general poetics, can you account for the emotional affect of words ordered in a particular way on a page?

MERRILL: A very hard question. Let me just say: No, I can't. Or: I know it when I see it.

WHITE: Is there some essential distinction between poetic language and other kinds of language?

MERRILL: That is the same question I just dodged so gracefully. I'd go on to say that Context is everything in these matters. The proportions, the turn of mind. I've seen some shopping lists and lists of checks written in a poem that charmed me (by Madison Morrison). What makes the difference is the writer's sense of form and style.

WHITE: Why is rhythm so important in a reader's sense of a poem's effectiveness?

MERRILL: Its importance—and I assume by "rhythm" you also mean conventional meters—is twofold. For the poet, it is vital that formal demands be made upon him (or her); attending to them leaves the subconscious free to infiltrate the poem. For the reader, there is the increased pleasure these effects bring. And the greater chance of the poem being—literally—memorable.

WHITE: Can you say to what extent you bring another poem into your own by the act of alluding to it in your poem?

MERRILL: This can take two forms. A direct, conscious allusion is usually ornamental, or one-upmanship, or a friendly nudge to the reader. The allusion of which the poet is unaware is more subtle, more enriching in the long run. That's when you really bring "another poem into your own." Is it what we mean by Tradition?

WHITE: You've written what many readers call a modern epic; what is an epic poem, today?

MERRILL: There may still be poets positively yearning to write an epic. I always found myself shying away from what I saw as megalomania. What perhaps makes *Sandover* most readable is my resistance to the conventions of epic—the grandiloquence, the universal relevance. The models in this field remain what they always were: Homer, Virgil, Dante, Milton. In all of them there are supernatural beings, celestial machinery, and so forth. This definition seems to exclude Pound and "Paterson"—so be it. Lacking a muse to fill their sails, these great modernists have short, splendid passages, but keep running into mudflats from which there's no extricating them.

WHITE: How does having written an epic inform your sense of direction as a poet (in relation to the poems you write afterwards)?

MERRILL: A number of words, which until *Sandover* had figured innocently enough in my work, acquired a new resonance. The names of colors, the senses, Sun and Moon... Right after finishing the poem I had a problem with scale. "Oh good," I thought, "now I can write *short* poems once more." But the first one I wrote reached two hundred lines before it skidded to a stop.

WHITE: What is a great poet?

MERRILL: Well, the names I've mentioned to begin with. Whitman, I suppose. Stevens in a certain light. But there are also the great lyric poets, like Sappho or Keats of the "Odes." The dramatists—Sophocles, Shakespeare, Racine. Even a miniaturist like Basho or Issa: you can't fully envision the human mind without taking them into account. What do they have in common? You tell me.

WHITE: Would it please you to be considered a great poet?

MERRILL: Certainly not. Or not since I was fifteen. It must have been around then that my ambition ceased to be cosmic and became a matter of craft and tone. Some Great Ideas were forced upon me by the "epic" convention, though, as I said, and I fought them off as best I could. Besides, "great" is an adjective we more and more reserve for guests on talk shows. It should be applied in earnest, if at all, posthumously.

WHITE: Is there a sense in which you consider yourself a poet "of your time"?

MERRILL: I don't choose topical themes or subjects for direct confrontation. However, peripheral vision takes in a good deal. I'd like to think that we can "witness" out of the corners of our eyes. Stevens said that in terrible times the poet needs to press back against the pressure of reality. That notion never left me.

ABOUT TIM O'BRIEN

A Profile by Don Lee

The good news is that Tim O'Brien is writing fiction again. In 1994, after his sixth book, *In the Lake of the Woods,* was released, he distressed his many fans by vowing to stop writing fiction "for the foreseeable future." Then, a few months later, he published a now famous essay in *The New York Times Magazine* that described his return to Vietnam. With his girlfriend at the time, he visited My Lai, where on March 16, 1968, a company of American soldiers massacred an entire village in a matter of four hours—women, children, old men, chickens, dogs. The body count ranged from two to five hundred.

From 1969–70, O'Brien had been an infantryman in the Quang Ngai province, and his platoon had been stationed in My Lai a year after the massacre. Then and now, he could feel the evil in the place, "the wickedness that soaks into your blood and heats up and starts to sizzle." In the *Times* cover story, O'Brien elaborated on the complex associations of love and insanity that can boil over during a war, almost inevitably exploding into atrocity. But he went a step further, drawing parallels between the "guilt, depression, terror, shame" that infected both his Vietnam experience and his present life, especially now that his girlfriend had left him. Chillingly, he admitted, "Last night suicide was on my mind. Not whether, but how." This time, his fans were not the only ones concerned. Friends and strangers alike called him: shrinks to sign him up, clergymen to save his soul, people who thought he had disclosed way too much, others who thought he had disclosed too little.

Today, O'Brien has no regrets about publishing the article. He considers it one of the best things he has ever written. "I reread it maybe once every two months," he says, "just to remind myself what writing's for. I don't mean catharsis. I mean communication. It was a hard thing to do. It saved my life, but it was a fuck of a thing to print." After taking nine months off and pulling his life

PHOTO: JERRY BAUER

back together, O'Brien started another novel, intrigued enough by the first page to write a second, propelled, as always, by his fundamental faith in the power of storytelling.

Born in 1946, O'Brien was raised in small-town Minnesota, his father an insurance salesman, his mother an elementary school teacher. As a child, O'Brien was lonely, overweight, and a professed "dreamer," and he occupied himself by practicing magic tricks. For a brief time, he contemplated being a writer, inspired by some old clippings he'd found of his father's—personal accounts about fighting in Iwo Jima and Okinawa that had been published in *The New York Times* during World War II. When O'Brien entered college, however, his aspirations turned political. He was a political science major at Macalester, attended peace vigils and war protests, and planned to join the State Department to reform its policies. "I thought we needed people who were progressive and had the patience to try diplomacy instead of dropping bombs on people."

He never imagined he would be drafted upon graduation and actually sent to Vietnam. "I was walking around in a dream and repressing it all," he says, "thinking something would save my ass. Even getting on the plane for boot camp, I couldn't believe any of it was happening to me, someone who hated Boy Scouts and bugs and rifles." When he received his classification—not as a clerk, or a driver, or a cook, but as an infantryman—he seriously considered deserting to Canada. He now thinks it was an act of cowardice not to, particularly since he was against the war, but in 1969, as a twenty-two-year-old, he had feared the disapproval of his family and friends, his townspeople and country. He went to Vietnam and hated every minute of it, from beginning to end.

When he came back to the States, he had a Purple Heart (he was wounded by shrapnel from a hand grenade) and several publishing credits. Much like his father, he had written personal reports about the war that had made their way into Minnesota newspapers, and while pursuing a doctorate at the Harvard School of Government, O'Brien expanded on the vignettes to form a book, *If I Die in Combat, Box Me Up and Ship Me Home.* He sent it first to Knopf, whose editors had high praise for the book. Yet they were already publishing a book about Vietnam, *Dispatches* by Michael Herr, and suggested that O'Brien try the editor Seymour Lawrence, who was in Boston. "He called me at my dormitory at Harvard," O'Brien recalls. "He said, 'Well, we're taking your book. Why don't you come over, I'll take you to lunch.' It was a big, drunken lunch at Trader Vic's in the old Statler Hilton, during the course of which we decided to fire my agent. Sam said, 'Look, you're not going to get much money, there's no way, might as well fire the guy. Why give him ten percent?'"

If I Die in Combat was published in 1973, just as O'Brien was being hired as a national affairs reporter for *The Washington Post,* where he'd been an intern for two summers. "I didn't know the first thing about writing for a newspaper, but I learned fast," says O'Brien, who never took a writing workshop. The job helped tremendously in terms of discipline, which, O'Brien confesses, was a problem for him until then. "I learned the virtue of tenacity."

After his one-year stint at the *Post,* O'Brien simply wrote books. In 1975, he published *Northern Lights,* about two brothers—one a war hero, the other a farm agent who stayed home in Minnesota—who struggle to survive during a cross-country ski trip. *Going After Cacciato* came out in 1978. In the novel, an infantryman named Cacciato deserts, deciding to walk from Southeast Asia to

Paris for the peace talks. Paul Berlin is ordered to capture Caccia-to, and narrates an extended meditation on what might have happened if Cacciato had made it all the way to Paris. The novel won the National Book Award over John Irving's *The World According to Garp* and John Cheever's *Stories.*

The Nuclear Age, about a draft dodger turned uranium speculator who is obsessed with the threat of nuclear holocaust, was released in 1985, and then, in 1990, came *The Things They Carried,* which was a finalist for both the Pulitzer Prize and the National Book Critics Circle Award. The collection of interrelated stories revolves around the men of Alpha Company, an infantry platoon in Vietnam. The title story is a recitation of the soldiers' weapons and gear, the metaphorical mixing with the mundane: they carried M-60's and C rations and Claymores, and "the common scent of cowardice barely restrained, the instinct to run or freeze or hide, and in many respects this was the heaviest burden of all, for it could never be put down, it required perfect balance and perfect posture." A central motif in the book is the process of storytelling itself, the way imagination and language and memory can blur fact, and why "story-truth is truer sometimes than happening-truth."

In his latest novel, *In the Lake of the Woods,* which is now in paperback, O'Brien takes this question of how much we can know about an event or a person one step further. John and Kathy Wade are staying at a secluded lakeside cottage in northern Minnesota. He has just lost a senatorial election by a landslide, after the revelation that he was among the soldiers at My Lai, a fact he has tried to conceal from everyone—including his wife; even, pathologically, himself—for twenty years. A week after their arrival at the lake, Wade's wife disappears. Perhaps she drowned, perhaps she ran away, perhaps Wade murdered her. The mystery is never solved, and the lack of a traditional ending has produced surprisingly vocal reactions from readers.

"I get *calls* from people," O'Brien says. They ask questions, they offer their own opinions about what happened, they want to *know,* missing the point of the novel, that life often does not offer solutions or resolutions, that it is impossible to know completely what secrets lurk within people. As the anonymous narrator, who has conducted a four-year investigation into the case, comments in a footnote: "It's human nature. We are fascinated, all of us, by the implacable otherness of others. And we wish to penetrate by hypothesis, by daydream, by scientific investigation those leaden walls that encase the human spirit, that define it and guard it and hold it forever inaccessible. ('I love you,' someone says, and instantly we begin to wonder—'Well, how much?'—and when the answer comes—'With my whole heart'—we then wonder about the wholeness of a fickle heart.) Our lovers, our husbands, our wives, our fathers, our gods—they are all beyond us."

O'Brien feels strongly that *In the Lake of the Woods* is his best book to date, but it took its toll on him. He is a meticulous, some would say fanatical, craftsman. In general, he writes every day, all day. He does practically nothing else. He lifts weights, watches baseball, occasionally plays golf, and reads at night, but rarely ventures from his two-bedroom apartment near Harvard Square. He'll eke out the words, then discard them. It took him an entire year to finish nine pages of *The Nuclear Age,* although he tossed out thousands.

Always, it will begin with an image, "a picture of a human being doing something." With *Going After Cacciato,* it was the image of a guy walking to Paris: "I could see his back." With *The Things They Carried,* it was "remembering all this crap I had on me and inside me, the physical and spiritual burdens." With *In the Lake of the Woods,* it was a man and a woman lying on a porch in the fog along a lake: "I didn't know where the lake was at the time. I knew they were unhappy. I could feel the unhappiness in the fog. I didn't know what the unhappiness was about. It required me to write the next page. A lost election. Why was the election lost? My Lai. All of this was discovered after two years of writing."

But when O'Brien finished *In the Lake of the Woods,* he stopped writing for the first time in over twenty years. "I was burned out," he says. "The novel went to the bottom of the well for me. I felt emotionally drained. I didn't see the point of writing anymore." In retrospect, the respite was good for him. He likens the hiatus to Michael Jordan's brief leave from basketball: "He may not be a better basketball player when he comes back, but he's going to be a better person."

Of course, the road back has not been easy, particularly with the loss of his editor and good friend, Sam Lawrence, who died in 1993. "Through the ups and downs of any writer's career, he was always there, with a new contract, and optimism. Another of his virtues was that he didn't push. Sam didn't give a shit if you missed a deadline. He wanted a good book, no matter how long it took." For the moment, O'Brien has yet to sign up with another publisher for his novel in progress, which opens with two boys building an airplane in their backyard. He prefers to avoid the pressure. "Maybe it's Midwestern," he says. "When I sign a contract, I think I owe them X dollars of literature."

And in defiance of some editors and critics, who suggest he should move on from Vietnam, he will in all likelihood continue to write about the war. "All writers revisit terrain. Shakespeare did it with kings, and Conrad did it with the ocean, and Faulkner did it with the South. It's an emotional and geographical terrain that's given to us by life. Vietnam is there the way childhood is for me. There's a line from Michael Herr: 'Vietnam's what we had instead of happy childhoods.' A funny, weird line, but there's some truth in it."

Yet to categorize O'Brien as merely a Vietnam War writer would be ludicrously unfair and simplistic. Any close examination of his books reveals there is something much more universal about them. As much as they are war stories, they are also love stories. That is why his readers are as apt to be female as male. "I think in every book I've written," O'Brien says, "I've had the twins of love and evil. They intertwine and intermix. They'll separate, sometimes, yet they're hooked the way valances are hooked together. The emotions in war and in our ordinary lives are, if not identical, damn similar."

ABOUT MARK STRAND

A Profile by Jonathan Aaron

Born in Summerside, Prince Edward Island, Canada, in 1934, Mark Strand spent much of his childhood in Halifax, Montreal, New York, Philadelphia, and Cleveland. As a teenager he lived in Columbia, Peru, and Mexico. Upon graduating from Antioch College, he went to Yale to study painting with Joseph Albers. Turning from painting to poetry "wasn't a conscious thing," he says. "I woke up and found that that's what I was doing. I don't think these kinds of lifetime obsessions are arrived at rationally." After spending 1960–61 in Italy on a Fulbright scholarship, studying nineteenth-century Italian poetry, Strand attended the University of Iowa Writers' Workshop for a year, and then taught there until 1965, when he went to Brazil. A year later, he and his wife and small daughter moved to New York City. He taught at Mt. Holyoke College in 1967 and at Brooklyn College from 1970–72, then held visiting professorships at various places, among them Columbia, the University of Virginia, Yale, and Harvard. In 1981 he accepted a full-time position at the University of Utah, Salt Lake, where he remained until 1993. Strand is now the Elliott Coleman Professor of Poetry at Johns Hopkins University, where he teaches in the Writing Seminars.

Strand's many books include eight volumes of poetry. He has received fellowships from the Ingram Merrill, Rockefeller, and Guggenheim foundations and from the National Endowment for the Arts. In 1974 he was awarded the Edgar Allen Poe Award by the Academy of American Poets, and in 1979 the Fellowship of the Academy of American Poets. He received a MacArthur award in 1987. In 1990 he was chosen to succeed Howard Nemerov as Poet Laureate of the United States. In 1992 he won the Bobbitt Prize for Poetry, in 1993 Yale's Bollingen Prize for Poetry.

Mark Strand's attitude toward his own writing is frank, unfussy, and wry. When he talks about himself, it's always with a sense of humor that underscores the absence of solemnity in his

PHOTO: DENISE EAGLESON

seriousness. *Reasons for Moving* (1968) and *Darker* (1970) gained him a national reputation as a poet. The disturbing power of their dark conundrums stemmed from the vividness of their comically incongruous details. The tenor of his work shifted in *The Story of Our Lives* (1973). Reflecting "an emotionally strenuous period," its poems "were more ambitious, longer, and involved than any I had written," as he said at the time. Highly rhetorical, they sought to express sorrow in elevated, passionate terms. *The Late Hour* followed in 1978, its poems "shorter and more lively," containing "more of the world in them and less of myself."

The Monument, published that same year, showed that Strand had not lost his faith in the uses of self-mockery. A book of "notes, observations, instructions, rants, and revelations" satirizing the notion of literary immortality, it was Strand's answer to a question he'd heard asked at a translation conference: "How would you like to be translated in five hundred years?" Strand thought it a "fabulous question. It stumped everyone." The book was his answer. Harry Ford (Strand's editor then at Atheneum and now at Knopf, to whom Strand has always been devoted) turned *The Monument* down, thinking "it would ruin my career. I think he meant that it was bad, tasteless, and would offend my contemporaries." In its playfully barbed irreverence, the book seemed out of keeping with Strand's ostensibly more serious writing. It looked then to some like a wrong move. Today it seems a brilliantly prescient entertainment.

After *Selected Poems* came out in 1980, Strand hit something of a wall. "I gave up [writing poems] that year," he says, looking back. "I didn't like what I was writing, I didn't believe in my autobiographical poems." He began to concentrate on journalism and art criticism. He wrote the sweetly freakish comedies collected in *Mr. and Mrs. Baby and Other Stories* (1985), which featured the likes of Glover Bartlett, who reveals to his wife that he used to be a collie, or the nameless narrator who's certain his father has returned to life as a fly, then as a horse, and finally as his girlfriend. In settings that ranged from contemporary Southern California to the Arcadia of Greek myth, Strand explored new approaches to parody and satire and, in doing so, began to work himself free of what he felt were the imaginative and stylistic limitations of dramatic self-regard. "And then," he says, "in 1985, I read Robert Fitzgerald's translation of *The Aeneid.* I decided I'd try a poem, and I wrote 'Cento Virgilianus,' and I was off and running."

The Continuous Life, Strand's first book of poems in ten years, appeared in 1990, containing both poems and short prose narratives. More varied in dramatic scope and tone than his previous collections, its humor pointed yet ruminative, *The Continuous Life* offered dryly poignant views of disappearing worlds ("The Idea," "Cento Virgilianus," "Luminism," "Life in the Valley"), its prose pieces piercingly funny send-ups of various aspects of the literary enterprise ("From a Lost Diary," "Narrative Poetry," "Translation"). It signaled Strand's complete recovery of poetic purpose and poise. His most recent collection, *Dark Harbor* (1993), a long poem in forty-five parts, reads like a book of dreams and reports on dreams. An episodic journey full of both daily and mythical incident, it amounts to a fearful perception of the self as Dante-like in a twilit world full of beauty and menace, pervaded, finally, by a deep sense of mortality.

When asked what his next book will be like, he replies, "I just can't predict. I suppose *Dark Harbor* was a step toward what I'm doing now, which is completely cuckoo. But I don't care. I'm just amusing myself." He's a little reluctant to amplify. "I'm not sure how clear I can be on this matter, because I'm not very scrupulous in keeping track of myself. I think there's a certain evenness of tone that I used to try to establish in my poems, which I now try to disrupt. I try to fracture the poem, crowd the poem with shifts or changes which I might have found too crazy or too disturbing in the past." After a pause, he adds, his voice softer, conspiratorial, "Verbal high-jinx—without that, there's not much of a difference between poetry and prose, is there?"

Strand aims to read all of Proust during the coming winter. Asked what poetry he reads, he replies, "I tend to read my friends—Joseph Brodsky, Charles Simic, Charles Wright, Jorie Graham." He keeps returning to Wordsworth's *The Prelude.* "And the Victorians—I don't read Browning, but I do read Tennyson, not necessarily the best poems, but I love 'Marianna.' And any number of Christina Rossetti's lyrics, which are so dark and seem to come off so well."

He's written a book on Edward Hopper. The painters William Bailey and Neil Welliver are especially close friends. Moreover, his poems themselves are often pictures—he makes a point of speaking through images that capture what Charles Simic, thinking of Strand, calls "the amazement of the vivid moment." So it's something of a surprise to hear him say that looking at paintings doesn't help when he feels blocked or stuck in his own writing. "No, when I can't write, I read John Ashbery, oddly enough." John Ashbery? "There's a tremendous vitality there, and he's very unpredictable. Ashbery befuddled me in the old days, because I was always looking for the wrong kind of sense in his poems. I kept trying to paraphrase him. Not that you can't paraphrase him, but if you do, you miss the point of his poems. Anyway, now that I don't try to translate Ashbery anymore, it all makes perfect sense." He laughs. "'I'm Tense, Hortense.' That's the title of a poem I'm writing. It's very Ashberyesque, don't you think?"

Jonathan Aaron's most recent book of poems is Corridor *(Wesleyan/New England). He teaches writing and literature at Emerson College.*

THE MASTER LETTERS *Poems by Lucie Brock-Broido. Knopf, $20.00 cloth. Reviewed by Wyn Cooper.*

Rarely does a book of poems appear that takes us back to poems and poets we know we should read again. Even more unusual is a book that sends us back to these poems with an entirely new way of reading them. *The Master Letters* is such a book. Based loosely on three unsent letters—addressed "Dear Master" and "Recipient Unknown"—that Emily Dickinson left behind, Lucie Brock-Broido's second book is a series of fifty-two poems and letter-poems that serve as "Terrible Crystals" of the history of poetry in English, complete with its accompanying madness.

Though many of Brock-Broido's poems refer to Dickinson's work, an almost equal number allude to a broad range of other poets, from Shakespeare, Wyatt, and Donne, to the Romantic poets, Hopkins (whose influence is firmly felt), and Americans from this century. For example, here are the closing lines of "When the Gods Go, Half-Gods Arrive": "Once you knew the powers / Of conversion, white powder cut / With nothing on the scales, / Delicate, Pythagorean, bold as a compass / / Needle pointing—North, a commerce / Of tiny clean white envelopes, / / Your letters to me long since / Lost, I've been loving you so long." The title is from Emerson, the last line from Otis Redding, the dash from Dickinson, the closing couplet "sprung" from Hopkins, but the voice is pure Brock-Broido, lilting and staccato by turns, made all the more powerful by the echoes.

The contents of these poems tell us much about Dickinson and her peculiar role as woman writing what were arguably the most radical poems of the nineteenth century. Brock-Broido quotes snippets of letters Dickinson wrote to men, refracts her poetic techniques, and slips into and out of the personas of Dickinson, Master, and contemporary poet, all the while nodding to other voices. The book is a difficult history, but Brock-Broido shows us there are anxieties more cruel than influence.

Like Dickinson, Brock-Broido flies in the face of convention while constantly alluding to it. She uses old poetic devices as means to new ends. She pushes alliteration to the jagged edge. It would all be so much trickery if it didn't have such a full and beating heart. The words Brock-Broido uses in the preamble to describe Dickinson's Master letters could apply to her own poems: "These are gracious, sometimes nearly erotic, worshipful documents, full of Dickinson's dramas of entreaty and intimacy, her distances—the Queen Recluse, little girl, the mystic, the breathless renouncer."

The Master Letters requires the kind of attention and open mind so helpful when first encountering something so utterly new. Imagine living in the nineteenth century and suddenly coming across a sheaf of poems by Dickinson. Now you don't have to imagine it, because Brock-Broido has conjured and conjugated Dickinson for the end of the millennium. She adds her own layers of sound, allusion, and drama until a simple, if skewed, nineteenth-century drawing room becomes a Gothic mansion. It's hard to know what will turn up in the next room, but the surprise, like the book, is well worth the wait. Fortunately, there are five pages of very helpful notes that follow the poems. This is not an easy book, though it does not require a thorough knowledge of Dickinson in order to satisfy. It is an elaborate homage that is by turns hypnotic, frightening, and hilarious, and at all times brilliant.

Wyn Cooper is the author of The Country of Here Below, *a book of poems now in its third printing. He has work forthcoming in three poetry anthologies. He teaches at Marlboro College in Vermont.*

DANGEROUS MEN *Stories by Geoffrey Becker. Univ. of Pittsburgh, $22.50 cloth. Reviewed by Fred Leebron.*

For fifteen years, the Drue Heinz Literature Prize has been awarded to a first book of stories by an enormously talented writer, and this year's selection, *Dangerous Men* by Geoffrey Becker, is no exception. Marked by precise and evocative language and a vision of the world as injurious but not always fatal, Becker's fiction is populated by musically inclined characters, most of them in their late teens or early twenties, who are willing to abandon all comforts for a chance to dance with danger.

In the title story, three bored Boston music school summer students swallow a lot of acid and ambivalently quit their apartment in the hopes of finding a few homosexuals to terrorize. It is the night of Nixon's resignation, and their search is convoluted by a car accident and their own increasing paranoia. Virtually every page is filled with surprises in language and plot. "There was a kind of purity to the moment, as when a thick August afternoon finally transforms itself into rain," says the narrator. "This was where we'd been heading tonight, after all. If we couldn't beat up fags, we could at least beat up each other."

"The Handstand Man" chronicles the doomed relationship between Jimi-John, a handstanding busker making his way through Europe, and Jenny, a wanna-be theater type with indeterminate but decisive ambitions. To win her over after she ditches him back in New York, he transforms his wretched apartment into a beach scene from Spain, replete with a roomful of sand, a palm tree, and a blue ceiling, and announces that he is going back to Europe. When Jenny tells him she's staying put, he is "surprised to find that this didn't really disappoint him. It was as if the place in him that had ached for her all this time had grown so large that, like an expanding star, it had given up all its energy. Instead, he felt only a quiet, spinning coolness." In this story and in others, Becker never uses his characters' youth as an excuse for a simplicity of emotion, but instead reveals a profound depth of fear, hope, and despair.

In "Magister Ludi," seventeen-year-old Duney is trapped in the boredom of the summer before her departure for college, wishing "something would really happen sometime." While she is "sentimental about the dumbest things: certain buildings in town that she's never been inside, an ancient bike rack that used to be as tall as she was, a particular section of cracked, heaved-up sidewalk she's walked over a thousand times," she wonders what it is that she and her best friend are "hoping so much to preserve, and whether five years from now they'll be sorry they tried." Duney gets more than she bargains for in the form of a twenty-three-year-old rock guitarist named Riggy, who takes her for a swim in an isolated quarry. Even though she tries to keep her distance in the water, she can't help but allow him to catch up. Here, and throughout *Dangerous Men,* Becker's characters must embrace the danger that only they create, for it is both part of their passage to the adulthood which they so desperately seek, and a form of expression which provides a certain and absolute release.

Only three of the eleven stories feature characters without any connection to music. "Taxes" is a deeply felt and ambitious story about two black brothers, Ronnie and Pretzel, and an old Jewish accountant, Fishman, who is Pretzel's piecemeal employer. While Ronnie is the dangerous man Pretzel has worked so hard not to become, he is also the vehicle for danger that Pretzel cannot, ultimately, avoid. Their conflict is resolved with a broken bottle and a knife: "Pretzel swings high toward Ronnie's face, feels himself connect with the side of his head, feels for just a moment a wonderful satisfaction, as if he has solved an impossible math problem. Then a bright comet of pain in his side as the knife enters almost effortlessly, his head seems to come untethered from his body, and the sound suddenly goes away." The intimacy accomplished in this section speaks to the vision of an author in touch not only with the music of music, but with the music of portraying difficult characters with dignity and grace.

Throughout *Dangerous Men,* Becker's young men and women dance to a vivid and distinct language, in a world that waits to consume them while all they want to do is prevail. It is a heartbreaking and striking collection.

Fred Leebron's first novel, Out West, *will be published by Doubleday in 1996. He is the co-editor of the forthcoming* Postmodern American Fiction: A Norton Anthology.

NEW AND SELECTED POEMS *Poems by Donald Justice. Knopf, $25.00 cloth. Reviewed by Liam Rector.*

Donald Justice's *New and Selected Poems,* which includes work from six of his earlier books and features fifteen new poems, begins with this two-line poem, entitled "On a Picture by Burchfield": "Writhe no more, little flowers. Art keeps long hours. / Already your agony has outlasted ours."

It's a befitting opening to the book, since there is something very abiding about the poems of Donald Justice, both in their subjects and in the very fluid sense of form that variously provides their ground, air, and horizon—their music here on earth. There is something enduring about his work as well. I suspect readers will be pulling *New and Selected Poems* off their shelves for years to come to make sense of the major and minor occasions of their lives.

Justice seems never to have published a poem or a book of poems before its time. Few other poets—Frank Bidart among contemporaries and Elizabeth Bishop among moderns—can lay claim to less having been so much more. Each of Justice's books has been a kind of publishing event, and this one is no exception.

Books of selected poems used to be published only towards the end of a poet's life, to put a cap upon a lifetime's work. Now we inhabit a culture wherein a book of poems (or to say most books) has a shelf life roughly comparable to that of yogurt. Books of poems go out of print quickly, and volumes of selected poems are needed *en route* to acquaint and reacquaint readers with a poet's ongoing body of work. Hence, Justice's earlier *Selected Poems,* published sixteen years ago. Notwithstanding newer work still, *New and Selected Poems* now replaces that earlier *Selected* as the definitive edition of Justice's work in progress.

The book also includes an excerpt from *Bad Dreams,* a verse play, and adds back in several poems omitted from the earlier *Selected,* including the unforgettable "Sestina on Six Words by Weldon Kees." The new poems in the book—especially "Body and Soul," "Pantoum of the Great Depression," and "Dance Lessons of the Thirties"—stand among Justice's finest work. The first stanza of the latter poem exemplifies vintage Justice moves and rhymes: "Wafts of old incense mixed with Cuban coffee / Hung on the air; a fan turned; it was summer. / And (of the buried life) some last aroma / Still clung to the tumbled cushions of the sofa."

New and Selected Poems reminds us not just of Justice as a master of inherited forms, but also as a master of the tones and emotions of nostalgia, a bittersweet longing for the things, persons, and situations of the past. From his earliest work, Justice has looked upon time from the vantage point of an older man. He writes not only of the powers that be, but also of what he calls the "Powers-That-Once-Were." His are poems of strong sentiment, though never sentimental, and their emotions will endure because, to twist Pound a bit, they have been objectified by such a strong style. Pure style—what Donald Hall has called "the glass of water."

Philip Larkin once said facetiously that he cared only for content in his poems, and the mockingness of his remark might also apply to Justice's work. With a stylist as accomplished as Justice, it often seems, as a consequence of his music, that we are in the midst of sheer, pure content.

Liam Rector is the author of two books of poems, The Sorrow of Architecture *and* American Prodigal. *He directs the graduate Writing Seminars at Bennington College.*

SISTER TO SISTER: *Women Write About the Unbreakable Bond. An anthology edited by Patricia Foster. Anchor Books/Doubleday, $22.95 cloth. Reviewed by Kathryn Rhett.*

For the anthology *Sister to Sister,* Patricia Foster has gathered twenty compelling pieces on an essential subject: the relationships of sisters.

Foster writes in her introduction that she opened her eyes one night to see her sister standing in a doorway "watching me just as I was watching her." She realized that her sister lived in "a narrative that fixed me in the center of her vision, just as I'd fixed her in mine." One of the anthology's contributors, Maria Flook, expands on this notion of shared consciousness, stating: "My sister walks ahead of me through these pages. She's holding a shoe box of scraps, notes with her half of the story."

It is not surprising, then, to see so many writers in the book dwelling on a sister's absence, either because of geographical or emotional distance, or illness, or death. Flook's sister ran away at age fourteen, disappearing for two years, a void that "keeps regenerating like a flowering vine." Lucy Grealy writes about a twin sister and the bond everyone expected them to have, "about how my sister did not mean for me the things other people told me she should." Robin Behn's sister converted to Buddhism, becoming remote and silent, abandoning a shared life of music in which she and Robin played flute together, becoming, for a few minutes, "gods, mutual makers of inviolate time." Bonnie Friedman's sister is hospitalized with multiple sclerosis; Louise DeSalvo's sister committed suicide; Donna Gordon's sister is homeless. Debra Spark writes: "Cyndy is dead, of course. That is why I wear her black coat now. She died of breast cancer at age twenty-six, a fact I find unbelievable, a fact that is (virtually) statistically impossible."

However inseparable sisters are (Foster writes, "My sister has lived so long, so restlessly in my psyche, that it occurs to me only as an aberration that we are not joined"), they do, of course, have separate experiences and destinies. Thus, differences, as well as divergent choices, are explored here: a sister who is less pretty, or more trusted by her parents, or who stays near home, or exiles herself to California. Comparisons, after all, are inevitable. As Bonnie Friedman comments, "A sister's life interrogates yours, saying, Why do you live this way?"

Along with engaging stories, the anthology offers the pleasures of intellect. Lori Hope Lefkovitz's "Leah Behind the Veil" cleverly examines the male fantasy of men coming between sisters, from the Bible to Woody Allen's *Hannah and Her Sisters*. Erika Duncan's "What Is Cinderella's Burden?" uses good sister/bad sister mythology to deconstruct her experience, in which two sisters switch roles in their adult lives, and their mother parcels out final rewards.

A resistance to finality pulses throughout the book, because no word on a sister can ever feel final; one writer even added an afterword to say that she and her sister had become much closer since she'd written her essay. And yet, the good writing in *Sister to Sister* evokes whole, satisfying realities, demonstrated by bell hooks, who describes Saturdays when six sisters and their mothers straightened their hair: "While one of us sat in the chair with her back to the stove, getting her hair pressed, the rest of us gathered at the table to drench white bread in hot sauce and pick tiny bones from the bodies of fried fish, to eat homemade french fries and drink ice-cold pop. Such moments of shared female ecstasy haunt me, linger in the shadows of a grown-up world..."

Kathryn Rhett's poetry and nonfiction have appeared in The Antioch Review, Grand Street, Ploughshares, *and elsewhere. She is currently editing an anthology called* Survival Stories: Memoirs of Crisis, *which will be published in 1997.*

*Books Recommended by
Our Advisory Editors*

Andre Dubus recommends *Moving Violations,* a memoir by John Hockenberry (Hyperion): "You don't have to be in a wheelchair to love this book, which reaches a conclusion about the U.S. that I've never read before."

George Garrett recommends *Omniphobia,* fiction by R. H. W. Dillard (Louisiana State): "Four stories and three novellas by a master of American metafiction. A virtuoso demonstration of the virtues of the avant-garde."

Marilyn Hacker recommends *In the Crevice of Time,* poems by Josephine Jacobsen (Johns Hopkins): "The collected and new work of a poet who is truly one of our 'unacknowledged legislators.' Josephine Jacobsen's keen intelligence and moral acuity are perfectly matched to the precision, elegance, and wit of her words: and that fit never ceases to surprise and amaze. She's a compassionate and unsparing participant in the human predicament she observes. Her poems are extraordinary instances which reverberate in the imagination while eliciting new awareness in the conscience. And the new poems are among her best."

Maxine Kumin recommends *Late Summer Break,* fiction by Ann B. Knox (Papier-Mache): "A delightful series of interwoven short stories, mostly with female protagonists, set on the fringes of rural life, in which the author explores interaction between the generations in ways that touch all of us."

Maura Stanton recommends *Improvising Rivers,* poems by David Jauss (Cleveland State): "*Improvising Rivers* is an impressive book of technically accomplished poems. The surface details, as on a river, float gracefully over hidden but powerful currents."

Chase Twichell recommends *Vortex of Indian Fevers,* poems by Adrian C. Louis (TriQuarterly): "More passionate, funny, dead-serious poems from one of the most overlooked poets in America."

*New Books by
Our Advisory Editors*

Andre Dubus: *Dancing After Hours,* a new collection of thirteen stories, two of which were originally published in *Ploughshares,* from a short-fiction master—America's resident Chekhov. (Knopf, Feb. 1996)

Bill Knott: *The Quicken Tree,* new work from a truly original and brilliant poet, whose language, ideas, and images always bedazzle. (BOA Editions)

Alan Williamson: *Love and the Soul,* a third collection of poems that eloquently addresses psychological and spiritual questions about love. (Univ. of Chicago)

Miscellaneous Notes · Winter 1995–96

ZACHARIS AWARD *Ploughshares* and Emerson College are proud
to announce that Debra Spark has been named the 1995 recipient
of the John C. Zacharis First Book Award for her novel, *Coconuts
for the Saint.* The $1,500 award—which is funded by Emerson
College and named after the college's former president—honors
the best debut book published by a *Ploughshares* writer, alternat-
ing annually between fiction and poetry.

Debra Spark, who is thirty-three years old, was born and raised
in a suburb of Boston. She grew up in a family of professionals—
lawyers, doctors, professors—with artistic inclinations. After graduating from Yale University in 1984 with a degree in philosophy,
Spark attended the Iowa Writers' Workshop at the University of
Iowa, where she received her M.F.A. Her stories have appeared in
Esquire, Agni, Epoch, Prairie Schooner, and other magazines, and
she writes essays and book reviews regularly for such publications
as *The Harvard Review, Ploughshares,* and *Hungry Mind Review.*
She also edited the anthology *Twenty Under Thirty,* which was
published by Scribner in 1986 and which will be reissued, with a
new introduction, in 1996. She has worked as a management con-
sultant, a freelance editor, and a teacher at Emerson College, Tufts
University, and now Colby College. She received an NEA Fellowship and was a Bunting Institute Fellow at Radcliffe College. She
lives in Waterville, Maine, with the painter Garry Mitchell.

Coconuts for the Saint was published by Faber and Faber in
November 1994. Set in Puerto Rico, the novel focuses on three
teenaged sisters who are identical triplets; on their baker father,
Sandrofo Cordero Lucero; and on the woman to whom he has
proposed. In reviewing the book for *Ploughshares,* Ann Harleman
wrote: "Bright, wistful, and brash, Debra Spark's first novel, *Coconuts for the Saint,* snares the reader instantly. On the surface it is a
mystery story: Who is Sandrofo Cordero Lucero, and what is he
hiding? Beneath lies another mystery, *the* mystery, the one we all

live out. 'This is the world,' says one of the novel's several narrators, 'the one we're so desperate not to leave. Our attachment seemed beautiful, but an endless puzzle. Why? Why do we want to stay here?'...Spark's language greets us from the first page with lavish gifts for the ear and eye—indeed, for all the senses. Her maximalist prose seems made of color and light, like Puerto Rico itself...the gathering desires of Spark's characters envelop us like a gorgeous fever."

The novel was inspired in part by Spark's grandfather, who exported bakery ovens to Puerto Rico and lived there for a time, and by her desire to explore the relationships of sisters, which she feels has been under-examined in fiction. Spark herself has a twin sister, Laura. A younger sister, Cynthia, died of breast cancer in 1992. Spark credits two major sources of support for the final shaping of *Coconuts for the Saint:* Fiona McCrae, her editor at Faber, who has since moved on to Graywolf Press, and her writers' group, which includes Elizabeth Searle, Jessica Treadway, and Joan Wickersham.

MICHELLE MCDONALD

After the novel, in its original form, had been rejected by several publishers, McCrae read the manuscript and suggested restructuring it. "She made a perfectly obvious observation that I hadn't been able to see before," Spark says. "It involved flipping the book over, as if it were a pineapple upside-down cake, removing the mold, and seeing if it would still hold together. After that, it was clear what I had to do, and I raced back to rewrite it."

As for the writers' group, which meets about once a month, Spark says: "It's a group I trust completely. We're all so sympathetic to each other as people, as well as to one another's work. We make great critics for each other, not only technically, but also on an emotional level. After we meet, I don't go home to recover from criticism or weigh advice, but to get to work. They read the entire novel, all the way through, and I took every single suggestion they made."

Spark is now at work on a new book, comprised of two related novellas. The first is about a woman living in Boston named

Bertie, who has breast cancer and is struggling with a troubled friendship. The second section is from Bertie's mother's point of view and takes place in Barbados.

The Zacharis First Book Award was inaugurated in 1991. The past winners are: David Wong Louie for *The Pangs of Love;* Allison Joseph for *What Keeps Us Here;* Jessica Treadway for *Absent Without Leave;* and Tony Hoagland for *Sweet Ruin.* The award is nominated by the advisory editors of *Ploughshares,* with founding editor DeWitt Henry acting as the final judge. There is no formal application process; all writers who have been published in *Ploughshares* are eligible, and should simply direct two copies of their first book to our office.

STAFF DEPARTURES DeWitt Henry, who co-founded *Ploughshares* with Peter O'Malley, has stepped down as executive director to devote more time to his writing and teaching. He almost single-handedly ran *Ploughshares* for the journal's first fifteen years, and more recently has been in charge of its organizational development. He will, however, remain involved with *Ploughshares* as a board member, joining an expanded board of trustees that now includes Frank Bidart, Jacqueline Liebergott, James Alan McPherson, Carol Houck Smith, Charles J. Beard, S. James Coppersmith, Elaine Markson, John Skoyles, and Marillyn Zacharis.

Jessica Dineen, our former associate editor, has moved on to become the managing editor of *New England Review.* Jessica worked at *Ploughshares* for a total of six years over the past decade, beginning when she was eighteen years old.

We fondly thank DeWitt and Jessica for their many years of tireless dedication and service.

NOTE TO OUR SUBSCRIBERS Please note that on occasion we exchange mailing lists with other literary magazines and organizations. If you would like your name excluded from these exchanges, simply send us a letter stating so. Also, please inform us of any address changes with as much advance notice as possible. The post office usually will not forward third-class mail.

CONTRIBUTORS' NOTES

Winter 1995–96

LEE K. ABBOTT is the author of five collections of stories, most recently *Living After Midnight* (Putnam). He is Director of the M.F.A. program in creative writing at Ohio State University in Columbus.

NIN ANDREWS is the author of *The Book of Orgasms*. She is currently writing *The Book of Lies* and studying the art of levitation.

JENNIFER ASHTON is a graduate student in English at Johns Hopkins University. Her poems have appeared in *The Paris Review, The New Republic, Chicago Review,* and *Poetry Northwest.*

JUDITH BERKE's first book, *White Morning,* was published by Wesleyan University Press in 1989. She is also the author of a chapbook, *Acting Problems.* The poems in this issue are from a manuscript in progress entitled *The Sky Inside.*

GINA BERRIAULT's new collection, *Women in Their Beds: New and Selected Stories,* will be published by Counterpoint Press in the spring of 1996. Her books include *The Infinite Passion of Expectation* and *The Lights of Earth.* She has been awarded grants by the Guggenheim and Ingram Merrill foundations and the National Endowment for the Arts.

TERESA CADER is the author of *Guests* (1991), which won the Norma Farber First Book Award from the Poetry Society of America and the Ohio State University Press/*The Journal* Award in Poetry. Poems from her new collection, *The Paper Wasp,* have appeared in *TriQuarterly, Poetry, Agni, Harvard Magazine, Radcliffe Quarterly,* and *The Black Warrior Review.*

ROBERT COHEN's second novel, *The Here and Now,* has just been published by Scribner. He is also the author of *The Organ Builder.* He teaches creative writing at Harvard University.

LAURA CONKLIN holds degrees in literature from Mt. Holyoke College and Pembroke College, Cambridge University. She currently teaches English and creative writing at the Catlin Gabel School in Portland, Oregon.

WYN COOPER's book of poems, *The Country of Here Below,* was published in 1987. His poem "Fun," from that collection, was turned into Sheryl Crow's hit song "All I Wanna Do." He has recent poems in *Agni, Harvard Magazine, Self,* and the anthology *Ecstatic Occasions, Expedient Forms.* He lives in Vermont.

JANET DESAULNIERS's fiction has appeared in *The New Yorker, TriQuarterly, The North American Review,* and twice before in *Ploughshares,* among other publications. A collection of her short stories is forthcoming from Alfred A. Knopf. She lives in Evanston, Illinois, and is currently Writer-in-Residence at Carthage College.

KATHY FAGAN, author of *The Raft* (E.P. Dutton, 1985), a National Poetry Series selection, co-edits *The Journal* and teaches in the M.F.A. program at Ohio State University. Her current manuscript, from which the poems in this issue are taken, is entitled *MOVING & ST RAGE.*

JAMES FINNEGAN lives in West Hartford, Connecticut, where he works as an underwriter in the field of banking insurance. His poems have appeared in *Chelsea, Poetry East, Ploughshares, The Virginia Quarterly Review,* and many other literary magazines. In 1995, he was part of a four-member team representing Connecticut in the National Poetry Slam held in Ann Arbor, Michigan.

LOUISE GLÜCK's most recent book, *The Wild Iris,* received the Pulitzer Prize for Poetry in 1993. She lives in Vermont and teaches at Williams College.

JORIE GRAHAM's *The Dream of the Unified Field: Selected Poems 1974–1994* was published this fall by The Ecco Press. An anthology of poems, *Earth Took of Earth,* will be released by Ecco in the spring of 1996.

DAVID GREENBERG was born in Minneapolis, Minnesota. He graduated from Yale and from the Writing Seminars at Johns Hopkins University. He works at a neighborhood development group in New York.

LINDA GREGERSON is the author of *Fire in the Conservatory* (Dragon Gate) and *The Reformation of the Subject: Spenser, Milton, and the English Protestant Epic* (Cambridge Univ.). She teaches Renaissance literature at the University of Michigan.

ALLEN GROSSMAN's most recent books are *The Ether Dome: Poems New and Selected* and *The Philosopher's Window,* both from New Directions, and *The Sighted Singer,* from Johns Hopkins University Press. He teaches in the English department of Johns Hopkins University.

BETH GYLYS is currently a Ph.D. student in creative writing and literature at the University of Cincinnati. She received a master's degree in writing from Syracuse University. She has work published or forthcoming in *The Paris Review, Poetry East,* and *South Coast Poetry Journal.*

DANIEL HALPERN is the author of eight books of poetry, most recently *Selected Poems,* from Knopf. He is editor of The Ecco Press, and divides his time between Princeton, New Jersey, and New York City.

EDWARD HARDY's novel, *Geyser Life,* is forthcoming from Bridge Works. His short fiction has appeared in *Gentlemen's Quarterly, The Massachusetts Review,* and *Ascent,* among other magazines. Another story will soon be out in *Witness.* He lives in Ithaca, New York.

EDWARD HIRSCH has published four books of poems: *For the Sleepwalkers* (1981), *Wild Gratitude* (1986), *The Night Parade* (1989), and *Earthly Measures* (1994). He teaches at the University of Houston.

PATRICIA HOOPER received the Norma Farber First Book Award from the Poetry Society of America for *Other Lives*. She is also the author of *The Flowering Trees* (State St., 1995) and two children's books. Her poems have appeared in *Poetry, The American Scholar, The Hudson Review, The New Criterion,* and *The American Poetry Review.*

GRAY JACOBIK is an associate professor at Eastern Connecticut State University, where she teaches courses in twentieth-century poetry and the poetry of women. New poems appear in *Prairie Schooner, American Literary Review, Crazy Quilt,* and *Confrontation.*

NICHOLAS KAHN and **RICHARD SELESNICK** have been collaborating for seven years on painting, sculpture, photography, and writing that portray the fictional world of the Royal Excavation Corps in 1930's England. They are currently building a chapel of one hundred twenty heads that will be shown in April 1996 at Monique Knowton Gallery in SoHo, New York. Their work is in numerous collections, including the National Portrait Gallery in Washington, D.C. Kahn was born in New York City and now lives in Truro, Massachusetts. Selesnick, born in London, divides his time between Truro and Palisades, New York. The cover painting is a detail of *The Scotswoman of Eigg,* a 55″ x 55″ octagonal work painted in flashe on plaster in 1993. It is reproduced by courtesy of Gallery Camino Real in Boca Raton, Florida.

DAVID LEHMAN is the series editor of *The Best American Poetry.* He teaches at Columbia University and is on the core faculty of the Bennington Writing Seminars. The poems in this issue are from the title sequence of his new book of poems, *Valentine Place* (Scribner, 1996).

PHILIP LEVINE's *The Bread of Time: Toward an Autobiography* and *The Simple Truth,* which won the Pulitzer Prize in Poetry, were published by Knopf in 1994. He is presently teaching at New York University.

TIMOTHY LIU's books of poems are *Vox Angelica* (Alice James) and *Burnt Offerings* (Copper Canyon). He lives in Mt. Vernon, Iowa.

SUSAN MITCHELL's most recent book, *Rapture,* won the first Kingsley Tufts Award and was a National Book Award finalist. She has received grants from the Guggenheim and Lannan foundations and is a professor in the English department at Florida Atlantic University.

JOYCE CAROL OATES is the author most recently of the novel *Zombie* (Dutton, 1995). Her story in this issue, "Easy Lay," is from a forthcoming collection, *Man Crazy,* which will be published by Dutton in the fall of 1997. She is a co-editor, with Raymond Smith, of *The Ontario Review.*

JACQUELINE OSHEROW is the author of *Conversations with Survivors* (1994) and *Looking for Angels in New York* (1988), both from the University of Georgia Press. She is currently at work on a third collection, *With a Moon in Transit,* whose title poem was included in *The Best American Poetry 1995.* She is an associate professor of English and creative writing at the University of Utah.

STEPHEN SANDY's recent collections of poems are *Man in the Open Air* and *Thanksgiving Over the Water,* both from Knopf. His work appears in *The Best American Poetry 1995* and in recent or forthcoming issues of *The Atlantic, The Paris Review, Partisan Review, The Southern Review, The New Yorker, The Yale Review,* and *Western Humanities Review.* Johns Hopkins published his translation of Seneca's *Hercules Oetaeus* in its *Roman Drama* (1995).

LISA SAPINKOPF co-translated and edited *Clay and Star: Contemporary Bulgarian Poets* (Milkweed, 1992). Her translations from several languages have appeared in over fifty journals, including *The American Poetry Review, Poetry, The Paris Review,* and *Partisan Review.*

CHARLES SIMIC's first volume of poetry was published in 1967 and fifteen others have followed. His most recent books are *A Wedding in Hell,* a collection of poems from Harcourt Brace, and *The Unemployed Fortune Teller,* a collection of essays and memoirs from the University of Michigan Press. He won the Pulitzer Prize for Poetry in 1990.

GREG SIMON lives and works in Portland, Oregon. He co-translated, with Steven F. White, Federíco García Lorca's *Poet in New York,* which was published by Farrar, Straus & Giroux in 1988.

RONALD WALLACE's nine books include *The Makings of Happiness* and *Time's Fancy* (Univ. of Pittsburgh). He directs the creative writing program at the University of Wisconsin–Madison and edits the University of Wisconsin Press Poetry Series. He divides his time between Madison and a forty-acre farm in Bear Valley, Wisconsin.

MICHAEL WATERS teaches at Salisbury State University on the Eastern Shore of Maryland. His recent books include *Bountiful* (1992), *The Burden Lifters* (1989), and *Anniversary of the Air* (1985), all from Carnegie Mellon Press. New poems have appeared in *Poetry, The American Poetry Review,* and *The Georgia Review.*

HEATHER WHITE lives in Ithaca, New York, where she is working on a dissertation about sentences in modernist poetry. She also writes for *Rogue,* an online journal of cultural criticism.

MICHAEL WHITE's book, *The Island,* appeared in 1992 from Copper Canyon Press. Recent poems have appeared in *The Best American Poetry 1994, The Paris Review, Western Humanities Review,* and elsewhere. He teaches at the University of North Carolina at Wilmington.

CHARLES WRIGHT lives in Charlottesville, Virginia, and teaches at the University of Virginia. He had two books published in 1995: *Chickamauga,* poems, and *Quarter Notes,* improvisations and interviews. He was Mark Strand's student for one incandescent semester at the University of Iowa in the spring of 1962.

OKSANA ZABUZHKO, who was born in 1961, is one of the leading Ukrainian poets of her generation. She has published three volumes of poetry and a book-length essay, *Two Cultures,* as well as works of criticism and aesthetic philosophy, and translated the *Selected Poems of Sylvia Plath* into Ukrainian. Her work has appeared in *Partisan Review, Harvard Review, Agni, The Massachusetts Review, The Poetry Miscellany, Crosscurrents,* and other journals. She spent 1994 at Harvard University on a Fulbright grant.

∾

SUBMISSION POLICIES *Ploughshares* is published three times a year: usually mixed issues of poetry and fiction in the Winter and Spring and a fiction issue in the Fall, with each guest-edited by a different writer. We welcome unsolicited manuscripts from August 1 to March 31 (postmark dates). All submissions sent from April to July are returned unread. In the past, guest editors often announced specific themes for issues, but we have revised our editorial policies and no longer restrict submissions to thematic topics. Submit your work at anytime during our reading period; if a manuscript is not timely for one issue, it will be considered for another. Send one prose piece and/or one to three poems at a time (mail genres separately). Poems should be individually typed either single- or double-spaced on one side of the page. Prose should be typed double-spaced on one side and be no longer than twenty-five pages. Although we look primarily for short stories, we occasionally publish personal essays/memoirs. Novel excerpts are acceptable if self-contained. Unsolicited book reviews and criticism are not considered. Please do not send multiple submissions of the same genre, and do not send another manuscript until you hear about the first. Additional submissions will be returned unread. Mail your manuscript in a page-sized manila envelope, your full name and address written on the outside, to the "Fiction Editor," "Poetry Editor," or "Nonfiction Editor." (Unsolicited work sent directly to a guest editor's home or office will be discarded.) All manuscripts and correspondence regarding submissions should be accompanied by a self-addressed, stamped envelope (S.A.S.E.) for a response. Expect three to five months for a decision. Do not query us until five months have passed, and if you do, please write to us, including an S.A.S.E. and indicating the postmark date of submission, instead of calling. Simultaneous submissions are amenable as long as they are indicated as such and we are notified immediately upon acceptance elsewhere. We cannot accommodate revisions, changes of return address, or forgotten S.A.S.E.'s after the fact. We do not reprint previously published work. Translations are welcome if permission has been granted. We cannot be responsible for delay, loss, or damage.

INDEX TO VOLUME XXI

Ploughshares · A Journal of New Writing · 1995

Last Name, First Name, Title, Volume/Issue/Page

BOOKSHELF

Ploughshares Donors

With great gratitude, we would like to acknowledge the following
readers who generously made donations to *Ploughshares* during
our 1995 fundraising campaign.

Anonymous (6)
Harold Adams
Yolande and
    Marvin Adelson
Clarissa Armstrong
Samuel Atlee
Greg Barron
Robert C. Bartleson
Kim Batchelor
Jesse Berger
M. Kuno Bernheim
Tony Bill
Melanie Bishop
Michael Bodnar
G. Frederick Braun
Mary Anne K. Brush
Scott Buck
Linda Butler
T. Edward Bynum
Rafael Campo, M.D.
Edward H. Cardoza, Jr.
Sue D. Carlson
Margaret Carr
James Carroll and
    Alexandra Marshall
Julie Chagi
Craig Challender
B. N. Chiñas
Helen Stevens Chinitz
Deborah Clark
Don Colberg
    Willow Creek Books
Katya Coon
Jane Cooper
Michael T. Corrigan
Lydia Cortes
Bernard Cosgrove
Madeline DeFrees
Janet Desaulniers
Patricia Dewey
Betty Dietz
Suzanne Dion
David Dresser
Andre Dubus
Barbara P. Erdle
Greg Fontana
J. J. Foote
Charles C. Foster
Cynthia Fowler

Robert Friend III
Mari M. Fukuyama
Laura Furman
George Garrett
Iris Gersh
Sarah Getty
Celia Gilbert
Elizabeth Gilbert
Norton Girault
Michele Glazer
Joanne Goodrich
Leonne Gould
Ann Graham
James Haug
Caroline Hemphill
Kathy Herold
Marcie Hershman
Ted Higgs
Marion Hoppin
J. Perry Howland
Meredith Hutchins
Grace Sims Irvin
Jean Isabel
Anne Ward Jamieson
Karen Janicki
D. Gordon Johnston, M.D.
Bruce Kauffman
Lilian Kemp
X. J. Kennedy
Rebecca D. Knack
Joseph Kostolefsky
Maxine Kumin
William Lamb
Victor Lee
Anne Lewis
Martin Lipsitt
    Lipsitt Design Unit
H. R. Lohr
John Macchione
Cynthia Macdonald
David Madden
Joseph Maggio
Ayaz Mahmud
Anthony Majahad
Gigi Marino
Gail Mazur
David McAuliffe
    Angles Gallery
Michael McCarty

Mac McCloud
Jill McCorkle
Fiona McCrae
    Graywolf Press
Desmond McLean
Robert H. McNeely
Margaret Michaels
Judith H. Montgomery
Jean Musser
Nebraska Tech.
    Community College
    Library/Resource Center
Nina Nyhart
Stuart E. O'Brien
Shaun O'Connell
Fionna Perkins
John Pertell
Margaret Petruska
John Powel
Joan Powell
Mollie Pryor
James and Linda Roman
Ken Rosen
Tammy J. Senk
Sheldon Silver and
    Judith Mathews
Barbara Snider
Gary Soto
Dorothy Swedelius Spater
Donald A. Sperling
Dr. Robert M. Stanzler
Paul Stein
Helen Strickland
Eleanor Ross Taylor
Esther P. Thomas
Cathleen Tillson
Sue Tribus
Ray Valdez
Helen Vendler
Peter Virgilio
Dick and Marion Vittitow
    Path Setters
Bob Weidel
Jehanne B. Williamson
Sarah S. Wilson
Bert Wright and
    Chris Wooster
    Waterstone's Booksellers

MFA in Writing
at Vermont College

Intensive 11-Day Residencies

July and January on the beautiful Vermont
campus, catered by the
New England Culinary Institute.
Workshops, classes, readings,
conferences, followed by

Non-Resident 6-Month Writing Projects

in poetry and fiction individually designed
during residency.
In-depth criticism of manuscripts.
Sustained dialogue with faculty.

Post-Graduate Writing Semester

for those who have already finished
a Graduate degree
with a concentration in creative writing.

For More Information

Roger Weingarten
MFA Writing Program, Box 889
Vermont College of Norwich University
Montpelier, VT 05602
802–828–8840

Vermont College admits students regardless of race,
creed, sex or ethnic origin.

Scholarships, minority scholarships and
financial aid available.

Low-residency B.A. & M.A. programs
also available.

POETRY FACULTY

Robin Behn
Mark Cox
Deborah Digges
Nancy Eimers
Richard Jackson
Sydney Lea
Jack Myers
William Olsen
David Rivard
Mary Ruefle
Betsy Sholl
Leslie Ullman
Roger Weingarten
David Wojahn

FICTION FACULTY

Carol Anshaw
Tony Ardizzone
Phyllis Barber
Francois Camoin
Abby Frucht
Douglas Glover
Diane Lefer
Ellen Lesser
Bret Lott
Sena Jeter Naslund
Christopher Noel
Pamela Painter
Sharon Sheehe Stark
Gladys Swan
W.D. Wetherell

Graywolf Press

PUBLISHING ORIGINALS FOR 21 YEARS

Little a novel by DAVID TREUER
"Mr. Treuer's accomplishment is a wonder. Out of the landscapes of a Minnesota reservation David Treuer has forged a strong intricate narrative complete with the intimate voices of fully realized characters." *Toni Morrison* "A splendid debut that promises great things to come." *Kirkus Reviews*
OCT. 1995 CLOTH (1–55597–231–4) $22.95

Yolk stories by JOSIP NOVAKOVICH
"The stories in *Yolk* send the reader through the core of the former Yugoslavia in a way that broadcast media never will." *Library Journal* "An exhilarating hybrid compound of wry understatement, dazzling aphoristic wit, infusions of peasant superstition, and a deadpan, down-to-earth Central European variant of Latin American magical realism." *Kirkus Reviews*
OCT. 1995 PAPER (1–55597–229–2) $12.95

Fables and Distances *New and Collected Essays* by JOHN HAINES
"John Haines is a master writer, as we have known for years. His negotiations with language, in both poetry and prose, have been brilliant. Now this book, in effect his collected essays, reveals more: a range of intelligence and affection such that I cannot imagine any reader being unmoved by them. It is a great and splendid book." *Hayden Carruth*
FEB. 1996 CLOTH (1–55597–227–6) $24.95

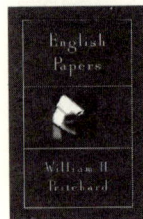

English Papers *A Teaching Life* a memoir by WILLIAM H. PRITCHARD
"Quietly fierce, resoundingly literate. . . . The decline of the American university has been frequently detailed but rarely with the kind of elegiac grace that characterizes this remembrance of things past. . . . His intelligence and thoughtfulness are a welcome antidote to the spew and babble that have become all too characteristic of today's culture wars." *Kirkus Reviews*
OCT. 1995 CLOTH (1–55597–234–9) $22.95

Cortège poems by CARL PHILLIPS
"These are some of the most sensitive homoerotic poems to be found in contemporary literature." *Library Journal* "Wry humor, elegy, and eros meet and mingle (rubbing wings, not elbows) in the matrix of Phillips's meditations. His is a unique and subtly disquieting voice." *Rachel Hadas*
SEPT. 1995 PAPER (1–55597–230–6) $12.95

So It Goes poems by EAMON GRENNAN
Grennan is a poet of immediacy and surprise, a craftsman of the first order. His supple, expressive verse finds sensuality and delight in the smallest gestures of the world. "Eamon Grennan's writing brings us over and over again to the discovery of what is naturally so and had passed unrecognized." *W. S. Merwin*
NOV. 1995 PAPER (1–55597–232–2) $14.00

GRAYWOLF PRESS
2402 UNIVERSITY AVENUE SUITE 203
SAINT PAUL, MINNESOTA 55114 [612] 641–0077

Graywolf Press

THE REDISCOVERY SERIES

*The **Graywolf Rediscovery Series** aims to give new life in paperback to previously out-of-print literary favorites. We are pleased to bring these books back to a wider readership and are grateful to all those who have brought the titles to our attention.*

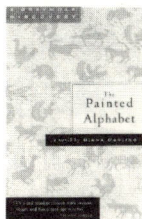

Places in the World a Woman Could Walk   stories by Janet Kauffman
"Deeply felt and bitingly precise. The author's dual professions of farmer and poet give the stories two gifts: an intimate, gritty sense of life on the land and a skill with language that amounts to alchemy." *Anne Tyler* "Kauffman takes us through these stories with an intensity that leaves us reeling." *MS.*
JAN. 1996 PAPER (1–55597–233–0) $12.00

Dream House   a memoir by Charlotte Nekola
"Nekola's balanced and exquisite vision of domestic life in 1950s America evokes both the halcyon memories of 'Leave It to Beaver' and the dark anxieties of David Lynch's 'Blue Velvet.'" *Los Angeles Times*
PAPER (1–55597–225–X) $12.00

All the World's Mornings   a novel by Pascal Quignard
This is the first U.S. publication of a French number-one best-seller and inspiration for the Alain Corbeau film, *Tout les matins du monde*, starring Gerard Depardieu.
PAPER (1–55597–203–9) $9.00

The Men in My Life   recollections by James D. Houston
"No one should get the idea that this is another celebration of the New Age male. Indeed, *The Men in My Life* is more of a revelation." *San Francisco Chronicle*
PAPER (1–55597–206–3) $12.00

The Painted Alphabet   a novel by Diana Darling
"A dazzling little gem of a novel. . . . [Darling] presents this odd mixture of the modern and the magical with such ease and conviction that it feels instantly timeless." *New Yorker*
PAPER (1–55597–214–4) $12.00

Still Life with Insects	*Beyond the Mountain*	*The Estate of Poetry*	*Leah, New Hampshire*
a novel by Brian Kiteley	a novel by Elizabeth Arthur	criticism by Edwin Muir	stories by Thomas Williams
PAPER	PAPER	PAPER	PAPER
(1–55597–189–X)	(1–55597–171–7)	(1–55597–182–2)	(1–55597–191–1)
$8.00	$11.00	$11.00	$12.50

GRAYWOLF PRESS

2402 UNIVERSITY AVENUE   SUITE 203   SAINT PAUL, MINNESOTA 55114   [612] 641–0077

FACULTY:
Toi Derricotte
Cornelius Eady

GUEST POETS:
Elizabeth Alexander
Michael Weaver

CAVE CANEM
A WORKSHOP/RETREAT FOR AFRICAN-AMERICAN POETS

Sunday, June 9th to
Saturday, June 15th, 1996

CAVE CANEM was created to offer a comfortable setting for African-American poets to write and share their poems in daily workshops and readings. The faculty will choose 20-24 participants on the basis of their manuscripts.

Fee: To keep the cost to participants low, there is no tuition. Faculty and guest poets are donating their time. Room and board will be $325 for the six-day conference.

Location: Mt. St. Alphonsus Retreat Center is a castle-like building on more than 400 acres overlooking the Hudson River, 90 miles north of New York City. Each student will have a private room.

Applications: Submissions must be received by February 29, 1996. Send your manuscript with 6-8 poems and a cover letter to:

> **CAVE CANEM**
> Eady/Derricotte
> Mt. St. Alphonsus
> Route 9W, P.O. Box 219
> Esopus, New York 12429

Participants will be notified of acceptance by March 25th. Manuscripts will not be returned.

BENNINGTON WRITING SEMINARS

MFA in Writing and Literature

Two-year low-residency program

FICTION
NONFICTION
POETRY

For more information contact:
Writing Seminars,
Box PL,
Bennington College
Bennington, Vermont 05201
802-442-5401, ext. 160

FACULTY:

FICTION:
Douglas Bauer
Susan Dodd
Maria Flook
Lynn Freed
Amy Hempel
Alice Mattison
Jill McCorkle
Askold Melnyczuk

NONFICTION:
Sven Birkerts
Susan Cheever
Bob Shacochis

POETRY:
Kate Daniels
David Lehman
Liam Rector
Stephen Sandy
Jason Shinder
Anne Winters

RECENT ASSOCIATE FACULTY:
Lucie Brock-Broido
Robert Creeley, Bruce Duffy
Donald Hall, Barry Hannah
Jane Hirshfield, Edward Hoagland
Lewis Hyde, Jane Kenyon
Bret Lott, E. Ethelbert Miller
Sue Miller, Robert Pinsky
Katha Pollitt, Tree Swenson

Be an Expatriate Writer for Two Weeks.

Join an international group of selected fiction writers for an intensive working seminar in the tranquillity of a Dutch Renaissance castle. Guided by six distinguished instructors, this seminar is designed to be intimate and productive. The team taught workshop is an editorial roundtable where writers are advised on strategies for analyzing structure and developing and sustaining character-in-action. Designated writing sessions and individual conferences enable new or revised work and redefined writing objectives. The seminar concentrates on the craft and technique of fiction while also considering the pragmatics of the literary market. The dynamics of the seminar are carefully planned to include both published writers and those in the early stages of promising careers. The seminar is sponsored by Emerson College and inspired by the literary traditions of the journal *Ploughshares*, an Emerson College publication. Four academic credits are offered and all applications received by April 1 are considered for a $500 fellowship. DIRECTOR: Alexandra Marshall. FACULTY: James Carroll, Pamela Painter, Thomas E. Kennedy, Alexandra Johnson, Askold Melnyczuk. WRITER-IN-RESIDENCE: Robie Macauley. VISITING WRITER: John Updike.

Seventh Annual

Ploughshares International Fiction Writing Seminar

*Kasteel Well
The Netherlands
August 20-31, 1996
Emerson College
European Center*

For a brochure and application to the seminar, mail or fax this form to
David Griffin • Program Coordinator • Emerson College
100 Beacon Street • Boston, MA 02116 USA
Tel. 617-824-8495 • Fax 617-824-8618

Name

Address

wc&f

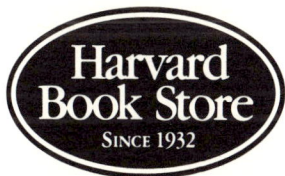

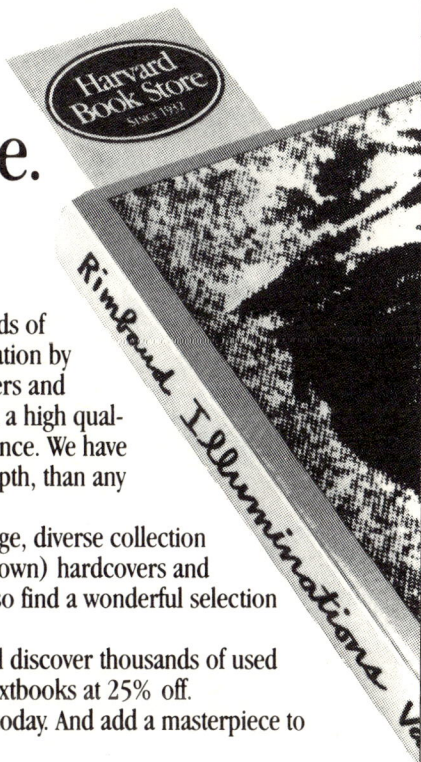

the modern writer as witness

Contributors

John Balaban
Alan Cheuse
Richard Currey
Jim Daniels
Mark Doty
Stuart Dybek
Bia Lowe
James A. McPherson
Peter Najarian
Joyce Carol Oates
Mary Oliver
Alicia Ostriker
Linda Pastan
David Shields
Joan Silber

"Witness *is one of several excellent new literary and intellectual journals of the past few years that confirms our sense of the variety and scope of the imaginative life in the United States. Its focus upon thematic subjects is particularly valuable.*"

Joyce Carol Oates

Call for Manuscripts:

Witness invites the submission of memoirs, essays, fiction, poetry and artwork for a special 1996 issue on **Working in America**. *Deadline: August 1, 1996.*

■ Writings from *Witness* have been selected for inclusion in *Best American Essays, Best American Poetry, Prize Stories: The O. Henry Awards,* and *The Pushcart Prizes.*

the Cream City

REVIEW

> This journal is fast becoming a leader in the literary world.
> • *1994 Poets Market*

■ RECENT CONTRIBUTORS:

Tony Ardizzone	Amiri Baraka
Michelle Boisseau	Michael Bugeja
David Citino	Stephen Dixon
Rachel Hadas	John Haines
Donald Hall	Ursula K. Le Guin
Audre Lorde	Mary Oliver
Marge Piercy	Alberto Ríos
Eve Shelnutt	Lewis Turco
Mona Van Duyn	Carolyne Wright

■ Name _____

■ Address _____

■ City/State _____ Zip Code _____

☐ **TWO YEAR SUBSCRIPTION** • 4 Issues $21.00
☐ **ONE YEAR SUBSCRIPTION** • 2 Issues $12.00
☐ **CURRENT ISSUE** • 1 Issue $7.00
☐ **SAMPLE BACK ISSUE** • 1 Issue $5.00

Please enclose check or money order payable to:
The Cream City Review, UWM English Dept., P.O. Box 413, Milwaukee, WI 53201

THE NATIONAL POETRY SERIES

5 WINNERS TO BE CHOSEN

$1,000 AWARDS + BOOK PUBLICATION BY

Graywolf Press • W.W. Norton
Penguin Books • Sun & Moon Press
University of Illinois Press

The National Poetry Series was established in 1978 to recognize and promote excellence in contemporary poetry by ensuring the publication of five books of poetry each year through a series of participating publishers. Five distinguished poets will each select one winning manuscript for publication from entries to the Open Competition. Each winner will also receive a $1,000 Award.

Recent Judges: Charles Simic, W.S. Merwin, Sharon Olds, Margaret Atwood, James Merrill, Seamus Heaney, Louise Glück, Heather McHugh, and Robert Hass.

Entry Period: January 1 - February 15, 1996.

Entry Requirements: Previously unpublished book-length manuscripts accompanied by a $25.00 entrance fee. You must be an American citizen to participate. Due to the large volume of submissions, manuscripts cannot be returned.

FOR A COPY OF OUR COMPLETE GUIDELINES, PLEASE SEND A SASE TO:

THE NATIONAL POETRY SERIES
P. O. BOX G, HOPEWELL, N. J. 08525